ADRENALINE

Laurel Glen Series Book One

B. L. Scott

Adrenaline, LLC

This is a work of fiction. All names, characters, and incidents are the product of the author's imagination. Any resemblance to actual occurrences or persons, living or dead, is coincidental. Historical events and personages are fictionalized.

Adrenaline

ISBN: 978-1-953831-00-2 (Print)
ISBN: 978-1-953831-01-9 (E-book)

Cover Design: Meredith Simmons

Published by Adrenaline, LLC

Follow the Author: blscottauthor.com

Dedicated to

My sister, mentor, and best friend—
Merry

»Prologue«

Abu Dhabi, United Arab Emirates

It was all that bitch's fault. She'd driven him to this. He'd slaved for more than eight damned years at her company and knew *he* was the reason that she'd hit the big time. It was *his* experience, *his* ideas, *his* talent. She'd amassed a great fortune. What did he get? Nothing, zilch, nada...

She'd fired him—so he'd had to reinvent himself.

The UAE operation had started out strictly as a contract for training. In a few short months, it had morphed into something much larger. Sure, the operation wasn't without risk, but that meant he had a fat account in the Caymans.

It was the money that brought him to this dark narrow alley behind a warehouse near the Mina Zayed Port. In the cryptic message from Rashid he'd received at the hotel, he'd been told the door he should use would be along here somewhere. He usually met Rashid in a street café or in a carpet shop near the Iranian Souk, not at a rear entrance of a warehouse off the beaten track, in the middle of the night.

He felt that crawling sensation along his spine that told him something wasn't right. He had what Rashid wanted rolled in the document carrier under one arm. What else did this crazy man need now?

The last meeting with him hadn't been pleasant. Had he underestimated the fanatic? This whole deal was beginning to give him the creeps. Was he in league with terrorists?

A thin line of light defined the door. This must be it. As he reached out for the knob, someone behind him murmured "Hansen?" and at the same time he heard the whoosh of a heavy object swinging through the air. He didn't see it coming, only heard it, sensed it. His training kicked in automatically. He ducked to the right, spinning around.

That's when he caught a glimpse of a bala-clava-clad figure and the blackjack crashing toward him. When it slammed into his temple, his knees buckled, and he fell to the pavement. His last thought was, *"I'm getting too old for this shit."*

»Chapter One«

Four Weeks Earlier

As she accelerated out of the high-speed turn onto the back straight, Lindsey Kelly pressed the Ferrari F430 Spider to full throttle, cracking off four rapid up-shifts with the car's Formula One style paddle shifter. All her worries melted away as the speedometer inched up over 120 miles per hour. Her total concentration was centered on the exact moment she would need to brake before the hairpin turn at the end of the straightaway.

Speed made Lindsey feel truly alive and free. All her senses were involved while she raced along the track. The sleek red automobile was designed for just this type of high-performance driving and here at Laurel Glen, it could be put to the test. The roar of the engine reached a higher pitch with every foot of pavement streaking beneath the nineteen-inch alloy wheels and sticky Pirelli rubber. She felt the vibration in her hands and heard the sound change as the monster within reached five thousand revolutions per minute. It was a full dose of the wailing 483 horsepower V8 diva that was sitting just behind her right shoulder and the staggered quad exhaust pipes provided the chorus.

She felt the wind pull the tendrils of her hair that escaped from her helmet. The incredible shape, design, and speed of this work of art, her "baby," always thrilled her. Lindsey slipped her toe onto the brake pedal. With a strong downforce she slowed swiftly from 150 and maneuvered into the apex of turn one.

She once again began to accelerate down the chute into turn five, but something didn't sound quite right. There was a bit of a hesitation, a change in the engine noise. She couldn't take the chance of damaging her most prized procession, so she glided to a stop beside a corner station and turned off the motor.

The red Ferrari was the only car left on the track for this Twilight Testing session, and the immediate silence caught Gavin Blake's attention. One mechanic and an EMT always stayed on duty until the last car was out of the gate and the track facility could be locked up for the night at eight. Usually this was easy overtime money, but the knowledge that the silence could mean trouble brought both men to their feet.

"I'll check it out and give you a call if you're needed," Gavin said, touching the radio clipped to his belt.

He jumped into the company pickup and drove around the track until he saw the beautiful vehicle drawn up alongside the pavement. A long, lanky form was just unfolding from the driver's seat as he approached. The figure straightened and pulled off the helmet, allowing long brunette curls to fall around the driver's shoulders. A woman. Most definitely a woman. But he'd known that before she'd removed the helmet. The one-piece driver's suit accentuated all of her most positive points. And that suit hugged one gorgeous ass. Gavin realized there might be more perks to working Twilight Testing than just the overtime. He was warming to his new job, new location, and what he hoped would be a new, simpler life.

When he rolled in behind the silent sports car, the alluring vision walked back toward the pickup. "Need some help?" Gavin asked, climbing from the truck. He sure would like to help—help this stunning woman into bed. With that lusty thought on his mind, he smiled warmly.

"I think so," she said. "The engine sounds like it's missing slightly. I didn't want to hurt anything, so I stopped. I'm not much of a wrench." She followed him to her car, and he was a little annoyed that she continued to chatter nervously like some of his former air-head type dates. "Antonio, at Italian Motors, does the service, and I do the driving. I'm at my happiest when I can take a few fast laps out here at Laurel Glen. It's really an adrenaline high!"

"Let's take a look." Gavin stepped behind the crimson sports car, marveling at the 32-valve V8 beneath the glass engine cover. This was decidedly sexy machinery. The styling was suggestive, like a beautiful woman—all curves and appeal, with engine detail inside that wouldn't fail to excite. God, this was one spectacular car. He felt a surge of envy.

Why was it you only truly wanted something when you could no longer have it? With a shake of his head, he opened the cover, flipped on his small flashlight, and peered in. "Could you start it up for me, uh..."

"It's Lindsey," she said. "Sure, I'll crank her up." She gave him a slightly crooked smile which could have seemed like a flaw in her perfection, but only served to charm him.

He listened intently to the irregular vibration of the powerful engine. "Well, for starters, it sounds like you need to replace the sparkplugs, and the valves seem to be sticking. Was the valve timing ever adjusted?"

"I'm sure Antonio did that."

Gavin's eyes widened in dismay by the poor state of the engine. This Italian exotic cried out for some professional care. The Antonio she mentioned might be a nice guy, but he obviously had no business working on this incredibly engineered masterpiece.

For the way her eyebrows drew together, he could tell he was wearing his emotions on his face. Gavin must have glared at her. Even with her perplexed frown, she was certainly beautiful. Intriguing dark blue eyes and long tawny brown hair. He turned back to the engine. She was probably some rich man's fluff and the guy had bought her this extremely expensive toy. What a waste.

He shook his head and wiped his hands on the shop rag from his back pocket. He pasted on a smile.

"It'll get you home like this, but this incredible machine needs some professional work. The plugs should be replaced with high-performance iridium spark plugs." He couldn't keep the irritation from his voice.

Lindsey's head turned up quickly to meet his gaze. "My mechanic was recommended to me, and he's done okay so far. What makes you think you're a better mechanic? You work on Ferraris every day?" She raked her eyes up and down his body. "You must be new since I've never seen you out here before. Anyway, Antonio has looked after my Spider since I bought her, and I've never had any problems. He's worked on Italian sports cars since he was sixteen."

Where? Under a tree? He thought but bristling at her dismissive comments and throwing caution to the wind, said, "Well, if you had half a brain, you'd take your car to Ferrari of Washington, and get it properly tuned. Or let your husband take your toy into the dealer."

He looked down quickly and cleared his throat. He knew he had stepped over a line. It wasn't like him to talk to anyone like that, let alone a customer. Damn, something about her put him on edge.

Lindsey turned a bright shade of red. She was obviously furious. With eyes burning from the depths of hell, she said, "I definitely have a *full* brain, and I don't *have* a husband and don't *want* a husband. Men!" And with that, Gavin watched her slam down the motor cover, get back into the car, speed on around the track, and exit the main gate.

"Shit. That went well," he said.

✿

She slowed as she turned out of the track onto Route 310 and took some deep, calming breaths. She couldn't imagine what they were thinking up here at Laurel Glen hiring such disagreeable employees. Who did that smart-ass think he was?

She felt a rueful smile pull at the edges of her mouth. She didn't know *who* he was, but she'd definitely noticed *what* he was the minute he'd stepped out of the truck. The man was one hundred percent, unadulterated, prime male. His blue chambray shirt stretched tight across mile-wide shoulders, and his jeans molded to his long legs. When he leaned over the engine, she had a ridiculous impulse to stroke the nicely displayed butt to see if it were as firm as it looked.

Dear Lord, she'd wanted to fondle some strange man's butt! She was losing it. The turmoil at work must be affecting her mind. She wasn't the kind of woman who did that sort of thing, or even thought about it. Experience had taught her to run away when she met a handsome man with a devastating smile.

Had his smile been devastating? It must have been part of the package, but she mostly remembered his physique. Shit! She was obsessing over some damned mechanic's build. A mechanic who probably had grease under his fingernails and a wife and three kids waiting for him back home. It was her unexpected reaction to the man that had partially prompted her irritation. It had been years since she'd, well, *noticed* was probably the best description. And all parts of her body had damn well noticed.

Mary was always yammering at her about getting out more, about finding some nice man, and for the first time Lindsey thought her friend might be right. Celibacy must be rotting her brain. Not that she'd been totally celibate. There'd been, uh, gad, she couldn't even remember his name. Must not have been very memorable. And now she was fantasizing about some hot mechanic. Yeah, brain rot for sure.

Of course, anything was better than thinking about the reason she'd made the trip to the track in the first place. The high-speed, adrenaline fix usually cleared her mind, and it had worked while she sped around the circuit. But as the darkened countryside slipped by on her way back to her northern Virginia home near Upperville, the evil genie that was Brad Hansen sat on her shoulder and whispered threats about his lawsuit in her ear.

What in the world was she going to do to save the company she'd worked so hard to build? The problems scrolled through her mind as if caught in a do-loop with no solution in sight. She was a woman who was seldom filled with self-doubt, and now she was riddled with it. Had it just been luck and timing that had made her successful, or were her ideas unique? Since the lawsuit, she'd begun to question her own ability.

She'd grown her small security training and logistics business into a multimillion-dollar company with multiple government contracts by dint of hard work and inspiration. And now that bastard Brad Hansen was trying to take it all away from her.

There had been a time when she'd trusted Brad. He'd been her first major hire. As Director of Training, his impeccable credentials had helped them win bigger contracts, and on a personal level, she'd warmed to his charm and Nordic good looks. But he was too perfect—suave and smooth, to the point of slick. When she wouldn't go along with his risky expansion ideas, he'd become so difficult, she'd had to let him go. Now he was trying to force her into bankruptcy—first by the breach of contract suit, which she'd won, and now the appeal. Would there ever be a resolution to this never-ending lawsuit.

Lord, she absolutely did not want to think about this. She could feel her muscles tightening and the persistent dull throb of a headache returning to her left temple. She was better off fantasizing about a firm, jeans-clad butt, but the press of her business difficulties kept even that tantalizing memory at bay.

Finally, she turned onto her small lane, and she was home. A refuge from her stormy thoughts. She loved her cottage adjacent to the Trenton's sprawling horse farm. It was log and stone, not large, but just right for her and her silly cat.

Over time she had transformed the mid-nineteenth century tenant house into a warm and inviting home surrounded by three acres of English cottage garden. In keeping with the local custom of naming houses, she'd called hers Sticks-and-Stones. She hoped the name would prove prophetic.

The smell of the damp garden earth and blooming wisteria on the arbor met her when she stepped out of the car. She let herself into the quiet cottage, and Mosby appeared, rubbing against her legs. His accusatory "meow" conveyed, "so where have you been." Mosby was an unexceptional gray tabby of uncertain parentage, but she treasured his company.

"I'm not so late, Mose," she said, picking him up for the required ear scratching. She dutifully opened a small can of chicken tidbits cat food and plopped it into a bowl before she poured herself a glass of Malbec. The normal pattern of her evenings folded around her as she nestled into her wingback. With Mosby purring loudly in her lap, she browsed through the mail she'd retrieved from the box by the road.

Thank God, there was nothing that looked like an official envelope hiding between all the catalogs and travel brochures. Brad's attorneys had started mailing copies of everything to her home address, as if she were ignoring all the missives that arrived at her office. Lindsey suspected it was a subtle form of harassment. If so, it was working. But tonight, there were no manila envelopes here to disturb her sleep.

She took another sip of the ruby red Malbec, the earthy, full-bodied taste sliding across her tongue. The wine, the comfort of the room, and Mosby's buzz-saw purr vibrating on her legs all helped her relax. She'd won the lawsuit once. There was no reason to think Brad's appeal would be successful. But that damned evil genie still sat on her shoulder telling her this wasn't over.

»Chapter Two«

The hum of the air compressor and the rattle of the impact wrench acted as a counterpoint to the grumbling and shuffling of men who hadn't yet had quite enough coffee to get their inner motors started. At least Gavin felt a little muzzy headed. Sleep had been elusive last night, and ever since his law school days he hadn't been much of a morning person. Consequently, he flinched when a hand knocked his shoulder.

Jeff Carper's freckled face grinned up at him. "Thanks for filling in for me yesterday evening," he said. "I know overtime isn't your usual idea of fun, but you really pulled my fat out of the fire."

"Glad to help." The corners of Gavin's eyes crinkled, and he smiled. "How'd Timmy's game go? Did the team make the playoffs?"

Jeff bobbed his head up and down. "Yeah, yeah. They won three to two. I was mighty proud of my son. He hit in the winning run, and Marcie was one tickled mama."

Gavin shook Jeff's hand. "Congratulations on the win."

Jeff's smile widened. "So, how'd it go last night? Did we have many cars?"

"Just three and the two Miatas went home early," Gavin said, returning Carper's smile. There was something about the man's Howdy Doody face that could brighten the worst morning.

"Did the babe in the red Ferrari show up? She's up here a lot for the Twilight Testing."

"Hey, yeah, red Ferrari," Silvio from Grounds interjected as he walked by. "But old married guys like you, Jeff, aren't supposed to notice the driver is a babe."

"A guy'd have to be dead not to notice," Jeff called after Silvio's retreating figure. Jeff turned to Gavin. "Marcie don't mind if I do a little looking, but if I did anything else, my balls would be on the chopping block." For some reason, the man looked quite happy about the prospect.

"Yeah, there was a gal in a F430 here last night," Gavin said. "Quite a looker." Jeff was right. A man would have to be dead not to notice. But Gavin wasn't pleased her image had followed him home and kept him awake for most of the night. When he did get to sleep, he'd awakened this morning with his sheets making a tent that was big enough to house a Bedouin family. "She had a slight mechanical problem but doesn't seem to know a damned thing about taking care of her expensive plaything. Is there any chance the guy who paid for her pretty little toy comes up here, too, and we can give him a heads-up about her maintenance problem?"

"No guy," Jeff said with a quick shake of his head. "Ms. Kelly bought that Ferrari Spider for herself. She knows what she's doing on the track and has the line down pat. And...there's the way she fills out her one-piece driver's suit." Jeff wiggled his eyebrows up and down in a comical manner.

Gavin was beginning to realize Lindsey was the whole package. Beautiful, rich, and not a half-bad driver. He paused to think. "So, she's a trust fund chick?"

"Nah, she's one of those *Beltway Bandits*. Makes oodles of money from government contracts."

Gavin had to pause to integrate this information into his pre-conceived notions about Lindsey. Her full name was evidently Lindsey Kelly, and she had to be smart as hell in addition to her other, more conspicuous, attributes. No one bought a car that cost a quarter of a million unless they had a *very* successful business. His fingers itched for a keyboard, but he'd have to wait until this evening to do a computer search on Ms. Lindsey Kelly and her *Beltway Bandit* company.

He realized Jeff was giving him a speculative look. "Ya interested? I mean, are you interested in getting to know Ms. Kelly better in a, well, more personal way? I forgot to mention that she's really nice. She's never treated anyone here like we're a bunch of grease monkeys."

Gavin barked a laugh. "Well, I may have fucked that up for the rest of you, then. Last night she was not real pleased with me."

"What'd you do to piss her off?"

"I strongly suggested that having her car serviced by some guy who sounds like a shade tree mechanic may not have been her smartest move. The valve timing sounded off, and she had the wrong spark plugs for such an exquisite piece of equipment. Anyone competent should have caught that long ago. I also didn't endear myself when I suggested she have her husband take care of things."

Jeff's big grin got bigger. "Oh, yeah, that'd do it. There is no husband."

"So I was informed."

"But rumor has it that there used to be one. Evidently a complete shit. He happily spent her money on other babes, though why someone would do that with such a hot wife waiting at home is beyond me. But I guess it takes all kinds."

"And Ms. Kelly may not have your Marcie's ball chopping tendencies."

"Ya got that right."

And then they both had to get to work, but the idea of Lindsey Kelly and computer searches shadowed Gavin throughout the day. Maybe if he made her less mysterious, she wouldn't metaphorically follow him into bed tonight. The problem was that if he removed the "metaphorical" part, the idea was very appealing. But who was he fooling? Ms. Lindsey Kelly belonged to a world he no longer inhabited, and she didn't look like the type who enjoyed slumming.

Lindsey got to her office in Roslyn well before most of the staff. As always, the heavy glass door emblazoned with the *Security Training and Logistics Solutions* logo filled her with pride. She'd made this happen, had built something substantial from a dream and hard work. She pushed through the door and was met by the tantalizing smell of fresh coffee. Mary Walker, her long-time friend and now the CFO of the company, handed Lindsey the coffee mug, hazelnut scented steam already working on her niggling headache.

"How many times have I told you this isn't necessary?"

"About a million," Mary said. "And as soon as you come through that door and you look like you've had a good night's sleep, I may start to believe you."

Lindsey sipped the coffee and leaned against the desk. "Good God, you're the CFO, not my assistant anymore. Making coffee is not in your job description."

"Old habits die hard." Mary laughed. "You look like hell. What's going on?"

Lindsey released a long breath. "The judge's ruling was overturned on appeal. I got the word from the attorney on my drive in."

Mary went to Lindsey and hugged her around the shoulders. "Bummer. Don't let it get you down. We'll win in the end."

Lindsey shook her head. "You're unbelievable and a great friend. You always look on the bright side."

Mary sipped her traditional cup of Earl Grey and smiled slowly. "So, how was your fast-lap therapy at Laurel Glen, last night?" Her eyebrows went up, and her nearly jet-black eyes widened, questioningly. "The way you stormed out of here yesterday, I wasn't sure you'd make it to the track before putting the Ferrari into light-speed. You really can't afford any more tickets, you know. You're pushing the points."

"Yeah, the drive up—no speeding tickets. Yay!" Lindsey did a small happy wiggle and smiled. The accumulation of speeding tickets was the downside of having a car that idled at fifty. "At the track, it was going great until I had to deal with the hunky, smartass mechanic on duty. Why is it the eye-candy always has an attitude?" Lindsey unconsciously assumed her power position, putting her hip out, shoulders back and one hand on her hip. "The guy really ticked me off."

"Mm, so he really got to you?" Mary said, with a broad grin. "Wanna tell me more?"

Lindsey drank more of her coffee. "He got on my case about the maintenance on the Spider. He obviously thinks he's God's gift to women and super-wrench all rolled into one."

"Well, maybe he knew what he was talking about."

"Hmm, maybe, but I haven't seen this guy at the track before. Jeff is usually the Twilight Testing mechanic. I don't know who this Gavin is."

"Gavin is it?" Mary interjected her smile widening.

"Yeah, but somehow he didn't seem to fit as a mechanic," Lindsey mused staring into space.

"Why's that?"

"Darned if I know," Lindsey ran her hands through her hair. "There was just something about him that didn't seem right." Mechanics weren't supposed to be really built, with wavy dark hair, and flashing deep brown eyes you could get lost in. But she'd never say that to Mary. "He had too much confidence," she said instead. "Cocky even. He should have been climbing out from behind the wheel of a Porsche instead of a track maintenance truck."

Mary laughed and waggled her finger at Lindsey. "I can see this guy really affected you and not *all* in a negative way."

"What in the hell does that finger wiggle mean?"

"You're preening like a love-sick teenager," Mary said with a chuckle. "Gavin could be just the guy to, uh, light your fire, I guess."

"He's a mechanic."

"So?" Mary quipped, "He's someone you'll run into up at Laurel Glen every time you go there for your speed-therapy. Who knows? I'm sure hunky mechanics know how to, you know." She moved her pelvic area back and forth in a suggestive manner.

"Oh, good Lord!" Lindsey rolled her eyes.

"If you're going to ignore really good-looking guys, then at least tell me your speed-therapy worked."

"Okay, it did take my mind off the lawsuit and Brad Hansen, but by the time I drove ten miles from the track the problems started swirling around in my head again. Will this ever be over?"

✳

Lindsey was going over the Profit and Loss statement for the first quarter when Michael Walden's call was put through to her office. He'd already called her in her car. Now what did he want?"

"We have some problems," Michael said.

Lindsey felt her gut give a quick spasm. Michael was the king of understatement. If he said "problem" there was probably another catastrophe.

"What now?"

"It looks like Brad's lawyers' gamble to go to the Fourth Circuit Court of Appeals paid off, and they didn't waste any time. I just got their demands from a courier asking for thirty-three million in damages."

"You've got to be kidding!" How had she landed in this mess? It seemed this new development was all her doing, but it didn't make sense to her. The judges' panel at the circuit court said her letter dismissing Brad was a breach of contract. But, how? He had been the one who had talked a good game but hadn't delivered. The accountants had gone over all his projected revenue from the expansion into the Middle East market and documented that the projections were way off. Brad's assumptions were completely faulty. It was just his pipe dream.

The phone's crackle in her ear brought her back.

"I couldn't agree more, but..."

"Wait, Michael. I thought you said when the

judge dismissed the case citing breaches on both sides that there was very little chance Brad Hansen would file an appeal, much less win it. How did that weasel manage this?"

Walden cleared his throat. "I think we can still salvage this. Our team needs to bring in some high-powered expert witnesses to show he wouldn't have made the millions in profit-sharing bonuses he expected from the satellite office in Dubai."

"You're telling me it will cost even more money?" She knew her voice had jumped an octave.

"Sorry for the bad news, Lindsey. I'll get Tim Mathews right on it. He should be able to get a list of experts together." Lindsey could hear muffled talking in the background. Michael cleared his throat again. "We'll get back to you on that, but maybe you could suggest some professionals in the security industry who wouldn't mind testifying on your behalf."

Lindsey hung up before she could tell him that's what she thought she'd hired him to do. How could this be happening? She'd thought her only worries were how to pay for the already exorbitant attorney's fees that had accumulated for the first court appearance. God, she'd been deluding herself. Now the nightmare was continuing. The lovely hazelnut coffee she'd so enjoyed turned to acid in her stomach.

She wadded up the page she was working on and threw it toward the door. "That incompetent boob."

Mary stuck her head full of dark curly hair around the corner of the doorframe, her dark eyes sparkling. "Hey, who are you talking about? I think I'm pretty efficient." Mary's vibrant demeanor never failed to cheer Lindsey.

"Oh, not you, Mary. It's Walden. He assured me the chances of Brad's winning the appeal were negligible. It looks like we'll have to fight like hell to get of paying damages."

"Whoa, that's not good." Mary let out a long breath.

"Walden is going to email the court documents with the official letter from Brad's attorney, but he gave me the gist of it. Since now he can claim damages, Brad's asking for thirty-three million. I might as well fold my tent. The whole company isn't worth that." She leaned forward with her elbows on her knees and cradled her head in her hands.

Mary put her hand on Lindsey's shoulder and gave it a little squeeze. "We'll work it out, one way or another."

She shook her head and looked up miserably at Mary. "Right now, I don't see how."

"Lindsey, you didn't bring STLS this far by accident. What's happened to your confidence? That bastard, Hansen, took us *all* in. I don't think he ever intended to build the Dubai branch. That phony only wanted to steal your company."

"Well, he's doing a pretty good job of it."

"Buck up! You're a fighter, and I'm pretty scrappy, too. This company is still strong, and we have some very good allies in the industry. We'll fight this. We'll figure it out, together."

"Thanks, I needed to hear that. I'm just not sure where to start to make a winning battle plan."

※

Gavin always felt like a voyeur whenever he did a Google search. It had become way too easy to peek through the windows into anyone's life. And Lindsey was no exception. Information went on for pages.

Damn, this was impressive. In a Washington Post article when the world was finally breathing easy again after 9-11, her wedding to William Haines, announced by her parents, Colonel John Michael Kelly and the late Helen Ayres Kelly, listed her many accomplishments. Graduated magna cum laude from the University of Virginia and went on for an MBA at William and Mary. According to the article she was employed by Triple Shield, a large defense contractor, and her husband, Bill, was working at the United States Department of State.

Hmm, her mother was dead. He wondered what had happened. Lindsey was young to have already lost her mother.

Gavin clicked on a Washington Business Journal reference about five years old. *Triple Shield and STLS Awarded WPS Contract.* God, what were all these acronyms? Scanning the article Gavin read that Security Training and Logistics Solutions, Lindsey

Kelly, President and CEO, had teamed with Triple Shield to land a large portion of the State Department's Worldwide Protective Services contract. Ronald Young, president of Triple Shield, stated, "This is a formidable team. Triple Shield's expertise lies in the tactical hands-on training while STLS has developed the classroom training and provides the personnel logistics."

Although it was past midnight, Gavin couldn't quit reading. The name Lindsey Kelly kept jumping out of the screen as if highlighted in yellow. Had he stumbled on this site by accident, he would have found the subject mesmerizing.

There was a whole section on personal security specialists. The article quoted Lindsey. "The personal security specialist candidates undergo a rigorous screening process and those who make the cut move on to in-class training in counterterrorist operations. Once trained STLS arranges all the details for the tactical training venue and the personnel logistics for deployment."

Gavin was still a little hazy on exactly what a *personal security specialist* did and what constituted *personnel logistics*. He followed a slightly different thread and found an article by a military affairs analyst with the Cato Institute that explained what he called the *shadow force*, aka private contractors in Iraq and other high-threat areas. Shadow force sounded ominous.

Gavin had no idea this was going on in his government. It all sounded too much like cloak and dagger to him. Was Lindsey training people to be espionage agents? He was fascinated. Lindsey's business activities were nothing short of spy thriller material.

The article went on to say that the State Department's reliance on private security contractors had dramatically increased in recent years. The press reported that the amount of money paid to these contractors had soared to nearly thirty-five billion dollars a year. Damn, this was undeniably a lucrative business.

He couldn't believe he was able to learn so much about a person by simply googling, but more information would have to wait for another day. With a yawn, he powered down his laptop. He was unraveling the pieces of the mystery of Lindsey Kelly, but he felt the bare facts didn't serve to really explain the woman he'd met.

The internet information swirled in his head and kept him tossing as the clock moved into the wee hours. He must have finally dozed off. Suddenly, he jerked awake with the clear memory of hiding in the brush on top of a hill spying on someone with binoculars. And Lindsey Kelly lay prone beside him.

»Chapter Three«

Lindsey's need for speed and the Ferrari Club's next event coincided the following weekend. She had reluctantly followed the hotshot mechanic's advice and taken her baby in to the Ferrari dealership for a complete tune-up. Now the spark plugs were new, and the valves were humming. The mechanics at the dealership had even replaced a recalled exhaust manifold. Her Spider was as good as new.

She sat in line for tech inspection. Laurel Glen required a mandatory check for each vehicle. Both the club and the track were adamant about safety, and neither wanted a potential hazard out on the circuit. The mechanics made sure the hoses and belts were in good repair and that there were no fluid leaks. They also examined the wheels, brakes, roll bars, and the brake lights. Loose items in the cockpit or the trunk had to be either secured or removed.

She inched forward in the line and wondered if she might see ole brown eyes with the tight jeans and smiled to herself. Then she rounded the corner, pulled into the open-sided tech shed, and saw him. Gavin punched Jeff's shoulder and was laughing, his eyes all crinkled up at the corners. He had his sleeves rolled up and the morning sun slanting in through the eaves glinted off the sprinkling of dark hairs on his arms. What was it about a man's arms that were so compelling? He had a strong athletic body, but it was a lean strength and the happy light in his eyes made him look as if he didn't have a care in the world. There was a slight breeze and it gave his hair a sexy tousled look.

Gavin looked up from his clipboard, and he must have recognized her, as he grinned and winked. She actually felt a blush rising. How had he so immediately disarmed her? The part of her that hadn't been warm in a long time tightened and became very warm indeed.

"Hi, Ms. Kelly," Jeff said, opening the driver side door with a bow and a flourish. "Please step out of your carriage. This won't take a minute."

"That engine has a healthy hum," Gavin commented, wiping his hands on a shop rag.

She wanted to tell him that she was still pissed off with him, but that Antonio was history, and she'd taken his advice about the dealership tune-up. Instead, she just stood there dumbly and smiled up at him, looking coyly from under the hair over her eyes. Coyly? God, coyly? What was wrong with her? "Yeah, thanks for the advice," she finally said.

His hands with their long slender fingers stroked over the rear of the car before lifting the engine cover. Clean fingernails, she noticed, and she was wishing he were stroking her rear with that loving gesture. Her brain wasn't functioning properly. How did he have such an effect on her? God, she was getting all moist inside. It must be pheromones. She felt like a lustful firefly blinking on the lawn.

"The belts and hoses are fine. Hit the brakes, Jeff."

Then Gavin gave each wheel a shake to make sure there was no excessive play in the steering linkage. Lindsay had seen it done a hundred times. Why was she suddenly so enthralled by his flexing arm muscles?

"Everything checks out, Ms. Kelly. You're good to go." Gavin straightened, giving her a quick smile.

"Thanks," she mumbled, hoping he hadn't sensed her starry-eyed demeanor.

"Hey, Lindsey, ready for the drivers' meeting?" Tim Nelson, the president of the club, hailed her with a wave. A nice guy, she thought, but were most male Ferrari owners short, bald, and stout? Of course, she still had her mind on the mechanic from tech inspection. He would look perfect sitting in a fast sports car.

"Yeah, hi Tim, I'm about ready to head to the classroom. I think there are still a few cars in tech, but mine passed already. What a day, eh?" Gad, she was babbling. She needed to calm down and just enjoy the present.

Tim put one hand on Lindsey's shoulder and pointed to the track café with the other. "Let's grab some coffee."

Minutes later, with paper coffee cup in hand, Lindsey walked into the meeting room and noticed Jake Ash. He was the opposite of the Tim Nelson version of a Ferrari driver—medium height with an attractive well-built tanned physique. He was surrounded by a group of other drivers. Jake was the best driver in the club and was part owner of Ferrari of Washington. He had started the group years earlier to help market the Ferraris, but it was apparent he enjoyed the camaraderie and competition. Lindsey eased to one side of the cluster and heard them discussing the upcoming meet at Lime Rock.

Jake looked up and must have noticed Lindsey's approach. He smiled and said, "Lindsey, we were just talking about you. Are you going to make it up to Connecticut next month?"

The customary patter of gearheads gave Lindsey an oddly comforted feeling. Most of these drivers headed powerful and stress-filled companies during the week but traveled to road-racing circuits near and far to relax and unwind by driving at high-speed. What they all had in common today was escapism and a love of beautiful automobiles. She could see the layers of constant tension sloughing off her friends as they laughed and compared notes on the latest gadgets for their cars. Laurel Glen was a diversion from their everyday lives, and it was obvious they were all enjoying their time together.

"No, I'm not going to make it to the Rock this time." She made a pouty face. She hated to spoil the familiar friendly atmosphere by mentioning anything to do with work, but added, "I'm attending a security conference in DC that weekend."

"Boo," Jake bellowed, smiling warmly. "Lime Rock, DC, Lime Rock, DC?" He said in a singsong voice, his hands making an either-or gesture. "Connecticut is beautiful this time of year. You really ought to reconsider." A chorus of "yeah, Lindsey" came from the others in the group.

"I'll get ahead of you in the points standing," Jake jabbed good-naturedly.

"I'll just have to beat your socks off today then!" Lindsey said playfully chucking his shoulder and walking away.

This was her other world. Seemingly carefree and all jokes and laughs. But at the same time, her mind was reeling with concerns about the future of her business, and that creepy Brad Hansen. Hovering on the fringe of all worries, those crinkling gorgeous brown eyes of a certain sexy mechanic pulled at her attention.

"Earth to Lindsey." Henley Gant gave Lindsey a hip bump. "You're a thousand miles off."

Lindsey smiled at the only other woman driving today. She liked Henley, but she didn't share her background. Henley came from old money. Lots of old money. Her biggest decision of the day was what to wear to the event or activity she was attending. Today she sported a retro Dunlop driver's suit probably tailored specifically to her slightly hefty frame. When she smiled, the small gap between her front teeth did nothing to soften her somewhat masculine jaw-line.

Maybe she thought it made her look like Lauren Hutton. Unfortunately, she didn't quite pull that off, but Lindsey wasn't being fair. Henley probably had her own set of worries and problems that Lindsey was dismissing. She should get to know her better. Wealth didn't necessarily mean happiness.

"Oh, Henley, I was just calculating how to get ahead of Mr. Jake Ash, aka speed demon, on the back straight," Lindsey said with a fiendish smile while rubbing her hands together. She was striving for an airiness she didn't really feel.

"I was hoping you were planning to come up for the Vintage Races in a couple of weeks. I'm in charge of organizing the picnic for the Ferrari corral."

"Sounds like fun, Henley. What can I bring?"

"I'm having the barbecue catered, so just bring yourself. We have about forty coming, so far."

"I'll be there."

The morning sessions went smoothly. It was a glorious day—sunny, not too hot, with a light breeze. Lindsey was out for her third run of the day with the other four-liters and above. Even at low revs when she was braking in the turns, the engine emitted a wicked growl, but when she stabbed the throttle the sound changed to that of a scream from an orgasmic banshee. Lindsey had quite a competitive streak, and she always held her own against most of the racing field.

Jake was one guy she hadn't surpassed, and now she was right on the tail of his Ferrari F430

Challenge. Lindsey was on her final lap, driving on the edge, and she was sure she could take Jake on the straight this time. She pulled nearly alongside his yellow Challenge then realized, too late, she wouldn't be able to get back on the line before turn one. She applied the brakes more forcefully than necessary, swerved to the outside, missing the line of the apex completely, began a skid, and flew off turn one into the gravel.

Everything went into slow motion. The gasoline smell of the super revved engine filled Lindsey's nostrils. There was an almost deafening cacophony of pings from the gravel against the bodywork of the Ferrari. This model had the strongest braking power from the ceramic discs, but there was simply no traction off the hard surface of the track. The gravel was supposed to slow her. It wasn't working.

"Shit, shit, shit." She gripped the steering wheel with the prancing horse staring her right in the eye and tried to regain some control. The car began to slow, but it was just going too fast for the length of the runoff. With a bump and harsh rubbing sound the car glanced off the tire wall and came to rest next to the berm, the engine ticking.

The corner workers ran with fire extinguishers in hand and reached the side of the crumpled car in moments. Lindsey was aware of their presence as they calmly went about their procedures to ascertain if Lindsey were injured while remaining on alert in the event of a fire.

Lindsey was dazed, and her hands shook on the steering wheel. She sat mutely while the corner worker thoroughly checked her physical condition. Her neck, arms and each leg in turn.

"Paul, it looks like Ms. Kelly isn't injured, but let's get the unit down here to check her out," one of the workers radioed to the EMTs. "Call in the tow truck, too."

Against the corner workers' advice, Lindsey climbed out of her damaged masterpiece. The passenger side was crushed in from the nose to door. Lindsey was demoralized and miserable. What else could go wrong?

She still felt wobbly and shaken, but she signed the release denying medical treatment. No bones were broken, just her spirit. Just then the rollback truck pulled up and she heard a familiar voice say, "Well, at least the valves aren't sticking." When Lindsey turned, Gavin was standing there, a charming smile lighting his suntanned face.

Lindsey had to smile, too.

"Yeah, it's been expertly tuned at the dealership, on the advice of some brash mechanic, and is now running perfectly," she said mockingly, "except it's a little crumpled on one side."

"We'll slide that baby right onto the rollback, and I'll bet someone will be able to make her hum again." He worked to maneuver the red wreck onto the truck, then turning toward Lindsey said, "Hey, good news—looks like there's no damage to the frame."

"It will still probably cost a fortune to make it right again," she said glumly. "If I'd been paying attention..." her voice trailed off. Running her hands through her hair abstractedly, she murmured, "It couldn't have happened at a worse time."

His eyes studied her.

"Don't be so hard on yourself," he said with a smile. "Up at the shop we can probably even bend the aluminum bodywork out around that front wheel-well, so you could drive it home. Or I know Betsy, in the office, would be happy to get a rental over here for you to drive."

His attitude seemed to have changed toward her. "Do you think it could be repaired enough for me to drive her home?"

"Sure. Jeff is a wonder with cars." Gavin's gaze turned serious, and looking a bit chagrined he said with sincerity, "Say, Lindsey, maybe we could start over. I was a little hard on you the first time we met. I guess I was out of line. I'm sorry. Want a ride up to the shop where Jeff can take a look?"

Gavin's genuine concern sent a jolt through Lindsey. Had she misjudged him when they first met? Could he be for real? His deep brown eyes and crooked smile drew her in. She wanted to trust this man, but her past experience told her to hold back.

With all the light-heartedness she could muster she said, "Great," and climbed into the truck beside him.

"It's not too bad, Ms. Kelly," Jeff Carper said,

sliding from under her Ferrari. "Mechanically, it seems fine, and the bodywork will be an easy fix, but expensive." Jeff's eyes were turned down at the corners like a sad clown. His normally cheery face was a mask of gloom, obviously hating to impart the bad news.

"Wonderful." Lindsey groaned.

"The paint job will be the worst part. These babies have a lot of coats of *very* special lacquer."

"Can you fix it enough, so I can make it home tonight?"

"Sure," Jeff said, brightening. "I can bend out the fender and use a little duct tape to keep that loose piece from flapping, but you'll still be taking a chance. If you make any sharp turns, you might damage the tire."

"I'll take it easy. I've simply got to go home." Lindsey sighed dispiritedly, her shoulders hunched forward.

"You really need someone to follow you, but I can't leave until the club day is finished."

"I'll be fine."

"Really, no. I'd hate to see you stuck on the side of the road," Jeff cautioned.

"Just get me road worthy, Jeff, and I'll take my chances. It's only about thirty minutes over the mountain."

"Gavin is off duty in twenty minutes, and he lives in Berryville not far from you. Maybe he could make sure you get home safely," Jeff offered.

Lindsey's breath caught. "No. That really

won't be necessary."

"C'mon, Ms. Kelly, you're one of our best customers. We don't want anything to happen to you." He grinned.

With that intro, as if on cue, Gavin appeared, entering stage right. Was this a set up?

"Hey, what's the story on the 'baby'?" Gavin asked Jeff, in a concerned manner, a frown crease materializing between his brows.

How did he know she called the car her baby? Had the two mechanics been discussing her? Her pulse quickened, and she noticed her voice got a little breathless when she said, "Jeff thinks he can fix it enough, so I can drive her home."

"I told Ms. Kelly she would have to be real, careful and I also told her someone should follow her home," Jeff said with emphasis and another one of his clownish grins.

Was this obvious, or what. God, Lindsey felt she was being maneuvered.

"I'll be fine," she said again, but without much conviction.

"I'm headed to Warrenton on an errand, so wouldn't mind following you to Upperville. It's right on my way."

How did Gavin know she lived near Upperville? They *had* been talking.

"Okay," Lindsey finally said exhaling noisily. She was just ready to be home.

Gavin stayed close behind the powerful

sports car thinking only of the dazzling driver within. Lindsey *was* a little arrogant, but he attributed that to her amazing success. Or maybe he was looking for arrogance. Was it his preconceived notion of how a "rich bitch" would act? Gavin tried to analyze his reaction to Lindsey. He'd dated a plethora of beautiful women when he was with Carter, Clooney & Davis. He always wondered if they were dating him because of his innate "magnetic" personality or whether it was solely the power and money that attracted them. Did they only see him as a way to a life of leisure and a country club membership? God, he was getting too cynical.

He followed the sleek crimson machine east over the Blue Ridge. As they approached Upperville, Lindsey turned left off of Route 50. In under a mile, she turned again—this time into a narrow gravel lane lined with Cleveland Pear trees and blackboard fencing. Fly-blanket clad horses occupied the paddocks on either side. Was all this Lindsey's? She must be super successful.

When he rounded the curve, a cottage came into view. Off to one side was a wisteria-laden arbor that was just catching the red rays of the early evening sun. The light filtered through the tangled vines casting irregular shadows on the flagstones beneath. Lindsey stopped under an ivy-covered carport and eased out of her wounded vehicle. She looked small and defeated. Where was the fiery, defiant babe he had seen at the track last week? Lindsey looked not only down, but distracted and self-absorbed. Not in a conceited way, instead, more as if she was overwhelmed. Her face was a study in misery.

"Well, you made it," Gavin said getting out of his silver Volkswagen Jetta. Trying to cheer her, he continued, "Would you like to join me for a bite to eat at the pub in Upperville?"

"I don't think I'd be very good company tonight."

"I could pick up a couple of the pub's famous organic burgers and a bottle of wine and we could toast the sunset sitting under your arbor. You look like you could use a little wine therapy." Damn, did he just come on to her? "Everybody's got to eat." God, now he was speaking in clichés.

Lindsey gave a tired smile. "That actually sounds terrific. I'll take you up on it, but I've got the wine. Come inside a minute, and I'll call Pete at Hunter's Head and order the burgers. That way you won't have to wait long."

He ducked through the oak plank front door of the cottage and was immediately enveloped in the warmth and charm of the old place. The ceilings were low and beamed. The floors were timeworn random-width heart pine with a beautiful patina. Lindsey had chosen antique oriental rugs in faded jewel tones and what looked like significant early American and English historic furniture. Interesting oils of landscapes and farm animals hung on the off-white walls.

He admired her choices of furnishings, much

like those he'd had in his former life. He remembered how excited he'd been when he'd gotten his first big bonus at Carter, Clooney & Davis. He'd plunged into home ownership with enthusiasm. The narrow, three-story, brick row house on a tree-lined street off Wisconsin Avenue in Georgetown had been a real find. It'd needed a little work, but the repairs and painting had been a labor of love for him. The historic home had called out for equally historic décor. He'd started frequenting antique shops and auctions to find the perfect period pieces. Surprisingly, it'd filled him with a sense of joy to create his own "sanctuary."

But he had left that world behind. Hadn't he?

An aged gray tabby rubbed up against his leg and meowed loudly.

"Don't mind Mosby, he's a glutton for affection," Lindsey said, picking up the scruffy cat and scratching just behind his ear. "I'm usually rewarded with a vibrating purr when I hit just the right spot."

"What a wonderful home. It looks like you've lived here for a hundred years."

Her eyes widened. "Oh, the cottage does date back to the mid-eighteen hundreds, but I've only been here for six years."

"Is it a family home?"

"No, it was formerly the tenant house for a large estate. The 360 acres were divided several years ago into three parcels. Mine's the smallest, but it has the advantage of being surrounded by the rest of the original holding with the bonus that all of it has been put in scenic easement, so can't be sub-divided again."

He suddenly felt like he was asking too many questions. Invading her privacy. He turned toward the fireplace and made a pretense of examining the pastoral oil hanging above the handsomely carved mantel.

Lindsey walked back into the hallway and called the pub, then turned back to Gavin. "Pete says the order will be ready in twenty minutes."

"I'll go on up there now, so you can unwind," he mumbled, feeling unexpectedly uncertain. Where was the self-confident attorney he'd been only months ago? "I need to get some gas anyway."

"See you in about a half hour, then."

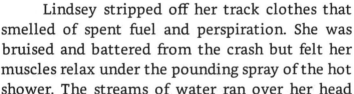

Lindsey stripped off her track clothes that smelled of spent fuel and perspiration. She was bruised and battered from the crash but felt her muscles relax under the pounding spray of the hot shower. The streams of water ran over her head rinsing out the shampoo and the warm rivulets caressed her sore body. She could stay here for an hour, but she turned off the shower and stepping onto the thick terry cloth mat, vigorously rubbed her body with the Turkish towel until her skin was glowing under the effort.

After slipping into a pair of jeans, she rummaged in her closet. She didn't want to look like she was dressed for a date. She was striving for a casual, unstudied look. The navy vee-necked pullover? No, too much cleavage. Her fingers brushed over the slightly worn looking Indianapolis Formula One T-shirt. Just right. She would dry her hair, using the large round brush. Shouldn't look like she set it. Now a bit of mascara and lip-gloss.

Mary was whispering in her ear now. "Preening like a lovesick teenager?"

Lindsey made her way into the neat kitchen, all wood and granite. She loved her remodeled kitchen with the long row of east facing windows that let in the wonderful morning light. The room was in shadow now. Serene. Calming her bruised psyche.

She grabbed a couple of wineglasses, a bottle of Merlot, and what she called her jumping jack wine bottle opener. Juggling everything, she made her way to the side arbor. She knew she should probably be getting out plates, napkins, and the mustard and catsup for the burgers, but she felt deliciously relaxed from her warm shower and, strangely, from the comforting thought of Gavin returning soon with dinner. She opened the wine to let it breath, rested her head against the wall behind the chair, and looked out at the silhouette of the undulating hills of the Blue Ridge pasted on the horizon.

As her thoughts drifted back to Gavin, she felt a fluttering in her stomach. Stop it, you fool. Why are you reacting this way? She was getting somewhat annoyed with herself. Was she forever going to be attracted to handsome men with charming smiles who would betray her trust? She would have to tread carefully here. But for this evening she would try to lighten up and enjoy the moment. Some women in this day and age had a different lover every night.

She heard the car door close, and Gavin rounded the corner of the house, arms laden with white plastic containers and brown paper sacks filled with plastic ware and all the condiments they would need.

Gavin was conscious of how he must look—and smell, for that matter. After working all day at the track, he knew he was permeated with the odor of gasoline and burnt rubber. He'd taken a moment at the gas station to wash his hands and face in the men's room and run a comb through his damp hair. But for what? He must be certifiably mad to think he would be attractive to this smart, complex, successful woman who seemed to have everything and also have it all under control. He wasn't sure he wanted to get involved in her complicated life. Hadn't he made the decision to go for simple and *un*complicated? She was probably pretty high maintenance. He didn't want the kind of responsibility he'd once had. Would he ever feel guilt-free from his past mistakes?

He came around the side of the house from the driveway and noticed her sitting at an old wooden table in what could only be described as a garden room. The spot was a tranquil oasis, and all thoughts of the past flew away. She smiled up at him and said, "Shall I pour some wine? Hope you like Merlot. It's one of my favorites."

"Mine, too." She not only looked good enough to eat, scrubbed and glowing, but smelled of lavender.

Putting the containers on the table he moved to the chair beside her and accepted the glass of the ruby red liquid.

"Mm, it tastes like a French merlot—earthy and complex," he said inhaling deeply and reaching for the bottle.

"I like the simple Napa Valley merlots, some of the time, but the old-world reds are more satisfying to me," Lindsey replied, looking at him quizzically. "All blackberry infected. God, I sound like Robert Parker, wine critic." She laughed nervously. "My dad taught me to love the wines of Europe when I traveled with him for his work. He said there were really no good or bad wines, only ones you liked or didn't." She took another sip and let it rest on her tongue before swallowing. "Luckily, I don't like Ripple as that's *truly* a bad wine. Does anybody like Ripple?"

Gavin put a mock hurt look on his face. "I love Ripple!" And they both laughed.

The awkwardness he'd felt at first melted away. They talked of nothing much while they ate their burgers and sipped the wine. Discussing different wine regions and wines seemed natural, and they found they had similar tastes on that subject.

She told him of her teen years living with her parents in exotic places, since her father, Jack, was posted all over the world with first the army and then the State Department.

"He is a straight arrow, someone I can always count on, though a little gruff at times." She grinned, looking away as if remembering. "After West Point, he was a career Army guy, Delta Force. He always said"—her voice lowered to sound more manly—"'when I say jump, ask how high on the way up.' I always felt a little like a private in the rear ranks. A lot of structure, but I have fond memories of a wonderful childhood."

"You're lucky. That's rare." Gavin assured her.

"Then after getting out of the service, he decided to double dip. He went into the State Department and was an RSO for twelve years."

When Gavin looked at her questioningly, she added, "Regional Security Officer." "That's when we really started moving around."

"Where all did you live?" he asked.

"Most of the time Europe—Germany, Italy, but he also had one posting to the embassy in Tanzania." A shadow passed over her face, but she went on with determination. "Africa is a place I'd like to see again." There was a wistful look in her eyes.

Gavin made few comments, listening intently to this interesting, multifaceted woman. He was beginning to see an inner strength, but still sensed a certain caution. His "rich bitch" opinion of her was melting away.

The warm velvety wine was gone, and the night was darkening. The tree frogs had started their songs of love, and thunder rumbled to the northwest. Gavin knew he should leave. After all, he'd said he was on his way to Warrenton. Did she know he was lying? Somehow, he didn't ever want to lie again to this seemingly vulnerable woman. Maybe it was just her sadness over wrecking her beautiful Ferrari, but Gavin sensed something deeper was bothering her. Should he ask? How to phrase it? No, he would leave before he got more involved.

Lindsey stared into the distance and stifled a yawn. Gavin could see the fatigue in her face. He stood casually and gave her his most captivating smile.

"Well, I'd better get on down to Warrenton. I need to pick up some lawnmower parts at Tractor Supply."

She looked amused. "Since its Sunday, it might be closed by now."

Looking at his watch he shrugged. "Damn, time flies when you're having fun!" He chuckled. "Guess I'll head home then."

She rose to stand a foot from him. "Goodnight then, and thanks for making sure I got home safely." She looked up into his face. Maybe it was wishful thinking on his part, but was it a hint of delight dancing in her sparkling blue eyes?

"The pub dinner under your relaxing arbor

was just right." God, she looked delicious in the old T-shirt and jeans. When she brushed past him to stand at the edge of the brick patio, the tension knotted deep in his belly. He definitely needed to leave. His heart was beating faster, and, oh damn, pumping blood to all parts of his body. Whoa, he really had to get out of there. He went to his car in the drive as Lindsey followed him to the front of the house.

"See, you around the track after you get your 'baby' fixed." He waved from his car and gave a beep-beep on his horn, then sped away into the night.

Lindsey cleared up the debris from their dinner and carried the empty wineglasses and bottle back into the house. Gavin was an enigma who intrigued her. She'd caught him checking her out several times during dinner, like maybe he was interested, but that was crazy.

The truly strange part was that she was interested, too. He was definitely not your average mechanic. God, he knew more about the wines of the world than most wine connoisseurs. And though he didn't say so, it sounded like he had been to most of the vineyard regions. How many mechanics knew about the "terroir" imparting a unique quality to the wine? Did he actually say, "Giving the grape a sense of place?" Or that "1986 was a particularly good year for Margaux?" No, certainly not your run of the mill mechanic.

When he stood to leave, oozing masculinity,

she'd risen, and he'd been so close she could feel his body heat. Her knees had nearly buckled. Damn the man. Was she responding once again to another handsome male who would break her heart? What was she? Some love starved ninny? Between the accident at the track and this magical evening with the mystery man, this was a day she wouldn't soon forget. She may need to find out more about the secret past of Gavin Blake.

»Chapter Four«

Joe Johnson walked into Brad's office and handed him the large brown official-looking envelope.

Brad ripped it open. "Yes!" Brad Hansen stood behind his desk shaking the official letter in the air in jubilation. "I can't believe the Fourth Circuit Court of Appeals turned this thing around." He was gleeful and astonished. "This will give us another run at Lindsey's company." A crooked grin was pasted on his face. "Your idea to sue Lindsey was exceptional. Can you believe it, Joe?" And Brad waved the letter again.

"It's definitely an opportunity. If we can steal her company, we can exploit STLS's contacts and client list to have all the customers we'll need for the training facility we'll be building in the Middle East." Joe's demeanor was calm, but with an underlying excitement. Their scheme was coming together.

"When she's on her knees, a takeover will be easy." Brad chuckled.

Brad and Joe Johnson, his attorney and business partner, had talked *ad nauseam* about the possibility of using STLS as a platform for their mercenary training. Rashid had said his client would pay dearly for the information and expertise in building and managing a training camp. But with Lindsey's company, Rashid's group would be only the first of many. The possibilities for high yields in the volatile world of twenty-first century security training would be endless.

"Arms dealers used to be the ones raking it in, but now, with cheap arms everywhere, I think we've figured out a better money maker. It's brilliant, Brad."

"Yeah, now the hot button is *training intelligence* and training foreign nationals in counterterrorist techniques." He was determined to get back at Lindsey and show her his ideas were valid, but he was also looking for an incredible bottom line.

"How long will this new phase of the legal action take?" Brad asked.

Joe smirked. "A matter of a few months, and in the meantime, the added burden of the mounting defense attorney's fees will only weaken Ms. Kelly's company more. Plus, she'll have the looming damages claim hanging over her head."

Brad's head snapped around. "That's new."

"Yeah, the letter I just sent her attorney included our claim for damages. I thought thirty-three million had a nice ring to it." He looked at Brad with a smug smile.

"Geez, that should do it. I don't see her lying down for this. She'll fight it. She's a feisty bitch."

"The on-going defense costs alone will make STLS hemorrhage. Her cash-flow will all be flowing in the wrong direction—out." Joe chuckled.

"Don't sound so gleeful," Brad said with an

ironic smile. Then shifting gears, he continued, "I think we should go ahead and set up the camps." He exuded a certain swaggering confidence in his statement. "That way we'll be ready when STLS fails and we take over."

"I'm not sure, Brad." Joe frowned. "We could be out a lot of time and money if it doesn't all go our way. Those portable camps would put us back several million just to set up the housing and training facility, and that's if we use those sea container Conex units."

"What's a few million on loan when we can reap billions in the long run?"

"Let's keep that idea on the back burner for now. I'll keep working on the lawsuit. You keep me posted on the training setup out of your temporary office in Abu Dhabi."

After Joe left, Brad got on his computer to check his flight schedule to Dubai, his preferred airport in the UAE. Dubai had a lot more flights per day than Abu Dhabi, and, to be honest, he loved flying on Emirates. First class, of course.

His next task—to prepare himself to meet, as soon as was humanly possible, with Rashid Abdul-Azim. What an unpredictable prick. Brad hoped showing Rashid some of the copied classified lesson plans Lindsey had compiled for the WPS contract would impress him and keep him quiet.

Ultimately, though, the entire scheme depended on Lindsey's company folding under the legal pressures, then he'd be able to acquire STLS for next to nothing. He couldn't wait to get his hands on all her confidential training records. With or without Rashid, he'd make way more money than Lindsey. He'd show her. Yes, he'd waited a long time to turn his special ops experience into some *real* money.

For now, he had to stay focused. He had to keep Rashid from exploding. He'd have to steer clear of the camp location topic. Rashid was volatile on that subject. Brad remembered Rashid had first talked of a site for the training area in Yemen. He'd yelled over and over, "It must be in Yemen!"

Then he had unexpectedly changed his mind, making the original camp location in Yemen, *Brad's* idea. Rashid had ranted about that country being too dangerous. Brad could hear him shouting at him, "What were you thinking? With the Houthi rebels still fighting the pro-government forces, and the continued bombing from Saudi Arabia, it would be *impossible* to operate out of Yemen." In the end, Rashid had vaguely hinted the favored site would be in Oman close to the Yemeni border.

Brad started pacing. He was abnormally antsy. He sat abruptly in his desk chair, ran his fingers through his hair, and rested his head on his hand. He couldn't let it go. His thoughts always came back to Lindsey. She'd used him. That malicious bitch had never paid him what he was worth to her organization. Just when he was poised to reap millions in bonuses and more importantly payments from the new Arab contracts he was working on, she'd let him go.

He'd once thought her appealing, so intelligent and all wrapped in gorgeous good looks. She'd trusted him for a time. He would figure out a way to use that to his advantage.

The alarm beeped with its normal persistent regularity as the first rays of sun filtered through the maples into Lindsey's large, east-facing windows. That was Mosby's cue to start with the mournful meowing of a starving cat. Lindsey loved the mornings on the farm. She rolled out of her four-poster, wrapped her hot pink robe around her trim form and padded down the wooden stairs into the kitchen. First things first. Feed the gray tabby making the racket.

"Okay, Mosby. I'm working on it." She opened the can of shredded tuna and eggs. Placing the small dish in front of the now purring cat, she began her normal morning ritual. After making the coffee, she retraced her steps to her bedroom where she donned her running shorts and T-shirt, laced her Adidas Adizero Tempos, let herself out of the kitchen door and started a slow jog up the long lane. When she got to the road, she was already feeling warm. She stretched her hamstrings and quads and began the one and a half-mile run down to the entrance of the Trenton Farm.

Running away from her property, she allowed herself to think of the many issues that were

bothering her. They streamed through her mind—
how to get the Ferrari fixed? What to drive in the
meantime? When to schedule a meeting with her
contact at State Department's Diplomatic Security Service in Dunn Loring for endless discussions
on curriculum changes? When will the government
client finally issue the delivery orders for the new
contracts so STLS can get paid?

She picked up her pace and shifted to her
legal worries—how to find expert witnesses to refute Brad's allegations? Should she hire another attorney?

At the stone pillars on either side of the entrance to Trenton Farm, she slowed and made the
turn to head home. She refused to allow a single
worrisome thought. Lindsey's entire focus was on
positive or happy considerations. This was her rule.
Worries on the way out, happy thoughts on the return.

When she crossed Cromwell Run, she noticed
the big sycamore trees with their huge leaves fluttering in the light breeze. She observed how the
sun sifted down and made sparkly patterns on the
swiftly running stream. She laughed at the blue-
birds who sat on the top rail of the four-board fence
and flew as she neared, only to land on the fence
again a hundred feet farther along. It was as if they
were keeping her company on her run.

She thought of how lucky she was that George
Trenton had divided his property and, since she
knew him from his ownership of Laurel Glen, was

able to purchase her beloved cottage before it even came on the market. Yes, George Trenton, had been a wonderful mentor. He was a jovial man with a thick shock of white hair and a tanned, well-worn face. His eyes sparkled as if was up to mischief. Yes, she felt privileged to know him.

He had taken a special interest in the young Ferrari owner six years before and had personally coached her on the proper line at Laurel Glen, plus he'd added some valuable racing tips from his glory days as a Formula V and Formula Atlantic champion. He'd also taught her a lot about business, primarily how to team with larger companies to be able to utilize the entire government contracts market. She wouldn't be where she was today without his sage advice.

Then her reflections of the previous evening abruptly changed her stream of thought. Gavin. The easy conversation. The casual laughter. The way Gavin looked in his jeans, the slight odor of the track, but also a clean smell of soap. Had he washed his hands at the pub? His deep brown eyes and that marvelous smile. It was happening again. She was so drawn to him. She was following the same pattern.

She broke her "positive thoughts" rule and focused on her ex-husband, Bill Haines. Hadn't *he* been the same kind of handsome devil with a smile that was so charming and sincere? He'd rocked her world. She'd been devastated when she'd caught him fondling the naked breasts of her best friend's cousin on that boating trip. Just six months into the marriage. She'd believed in him and trusted that they would be together "until death us do part." Then because she hadn't confronted him about the cousin episode, he thought he'd gotten away with it. Only a few short weeks later she'd come home early from her job at Triple Shield and heard his familiar laughter from the bedroom, then a lighter chuckle echoing his. She knew then and was gripped with a pain as searing as if hot coals were beneath her feet.

No, she couldn't let this happen again.

Lindsey arrived at her lane and slowed to a walk to cool down. The Trenton's horses in the fields bordering her lane came to the fence and nickered softly. They greeted her most mornings, and it filled her with a simple joy.

"Hey, Sue-bear, you old furry girl." At least she could trust in these beautiful horses.

Mosby was waiting just inside the kitchen door and as usual wanted that scratch behind his ears. She poured a cup of her favorite brew and eased across the house to sit under the wisteria arbor to cool down from her three-mile run. Her thoughts wandered back to Gavin. Maybe he was the man he seemed to be, but something wasn't right about him. She needed to be cautious. She was no longer a lighthearted, dreamy-eyed girl.

Yes, she would be very cautious.

❖

Gavin woke early feeling lighthearted. The memory of his pleasant evening with Lindsey still lingered. Was he imagining it, or did he still smell her lavender scent?

Since he'd worked the weekend, he was off today and was meeting Tom Duncan for lunch. God, it'd be good to see Tom again. They'd been friends ever since they had roomed together their last year at Penn. Tom was the reason he'd even tried for Harvard Law. He was still surprised they'd both been accepted.

Wasn't it that crazy bastard, Yarborough, who'd been the ultra-liberal professor who'd inspired them to become public defenders? He'd have to ask Tom about him. Those were heady days when they thought they could save the "poor and huddled masses" from the clutches of a big and impersonal legal system. Damn, how idealistic they had been.

He wondered if Tom would make another pitch to get him to join his Leesburg firm. Tom had tried to talk him out of leaving law when he'd quit Carter, Clooney & Davis last year. He'd just tell Tom again that he was doing just fine without the hassle.

Gavin left his small rental bungalow and drove his Jetta east along Route 7 toward Leesburg. He loved his VW with its advanced German engineering and sleek lines. It reminded him of his old Porsche, but when he decided to simplify, the Boxster had to go. The VW was less conspicuous and fit his new life-style. Forty-two miles per gallon, but still plenty of torque, and a five-speed transmission, reminiscent of his more exotic car.

Thirty minutes later he pulled into the parking lot behind Lightfoot Grill in the historic district. It was across from the Courthouse and close to Tom's office. He walked through the back door and Tom hailed him from a corner table. He stood when Gavin approached, a warm smile lighting his face.

"How've you been?" Tom grabbed Gavin's outstretched hand, shaking it and putting his other hand on Gavin's shoulder.

"It's been too long." They sat across from each other. "Six months?"

"Yeah, at least that long."

The conversation ceased when the waiter slid the menus in front of them and began reciting the daily specials. Then he asked, with a smile, "What can I get you to drink, while you're deciding?"

"Just water for me."

"I'll have iced tea," Tom replied.

They each opened their menus as the waiter drifted off and the silence lengthened. Tom reached one finger inside of his collar, loosening the noose of his tie. "So, how's it going?" He awkwardly looked at Gavin. "Do you like the new job?"

Gavin put down the menu and stared straight into the eyes of his old friend. "It's fine, and I like the other mechanics in the shop." To clear the air Gavin went on. "It's what I chose, Tom, and I'm making the best of it. You know how I love anything to do with cars and engines. The life is simple, and it keeps me from making any other major errors in judgment."

"C'mon, Gavin. You're not still letting that Boyle business get to you, are you? It wasn't your fault. Anyone in your position would have done the same thing. As a public defender, it was your job to give him the best defense you could. We were young, right out of law school, and idealistic, believing that the poor were getting a raw deal. Remember how we used to call each other and compare cases. At the end of nearly every conversation we'd say, 'Don't forget. If you're poor, you're guilty until proven innocent.' Your Richmond days are a lifetime away."

"Yeah, a lifetime away," he said looking down and picking at the edges of the menu.

He looked back up at Tom. "Even though it was over ten years ago, and I was with the Richmond office for only two years, I took it seriously. It was my duty as a public defender to represent Martin Boyle. My mistake was believing in the son-of-a-bitch. We were taught to be skeptical, but I fell for the 'downtrodden, dreadful childhood, father who beat him, wrong place at the wrong time' story he fed me. The consequences of my error were catastrophic."

His voice had risen, fighting a sudden surge of emotion that took him back to what had happened thirteen months before. A few heads turned their way, and Gavin coughed into his napkin and looked down. The pain was still raw. He'd never forget that he had freed a predator.

"Gavin, you have to quit blaming yourself. Don't hide your talent. You became one hell of a corporate defense attorney in the ten years after you left the Public Defender Offices in Richmond." Their drinks came and they both grew quiet again.

Finally, Tom broke the silence. "How can being a grease monkey be a challenge to you after your successes in the courtroom?"

"It's just one day at a time for me right now." Gavin was beginning to get pissed. He'd chosen his new path. Now he'd have to stick with it.

"Sure." Tom sounded disappointed and looked down at his hands. Maybe Tom was simply trying to help and give him encouragement. Gavin calmed and looked at his old friend.

Smiling and lowering his tone he went on. "Okay, to be fair, I have to admit I miss the adrenaline rush I used to get as the jury was filing in to deliver the verdict. We won some big ones for our clients." He looked into the distance through the window. Across the street the branches of the big oak on the Courthouse grounds swayed in the summer wind. "That's history now, Tom. I'm living the simple life."

"I can't believe it, Gavin. You were always much better in the courtroom than I was. I'm the one who's more cut out to be a country lawyer. The Carter, Clooney & Davis firm in DC was too demanding for me, but you were a star, and once we learned Carla was pregnant with our baby girl, I knew I wanted to spend time with my family. I'm glad I left two years ago. Now Carla is expecting again." He grinned broadly.

"Oh, Tom, that's great. Congratulations! Here

I was blabbing on about my problems, and I didn't even think to ask about your family."

"It's going to be a boy this time. Carla and I are so happy."

They ordered. Their lunches came, and the conversation drifted to what Tom's parents were doing now on their small farm in Pennsylvania, and if Gavin's brother, James, had chosen a hospital for his residency. The uncomfortable moments from the beginning were forgotten.

"Hey, ride out on your Harley some evening and have a beer and burger with me. You'll love my less-than-charming abode. A real bachelor's pad." He chuckled.

"Carla is taking Kara to visit 'Grandma' in a couple of weeks. How 'bout a week from Saturday."

"That will be good. There's a big vintage car race that weekend, but I should be home from the track by 5:30 since I'm on the early shift. Any time after that will be fine."

They stood. "If I get finished with the lawn early, I'll swing by the track and look you up."

"Yeah, I get it. Any excuse for a longer ride in the country on your bike is better than none." They laughed again.

"See you soon." And with a wave they were headed in opposite directions on the sidewalk moving into the warm afternoon.

»Chapter Five«

"Okay, Steve, I'll drop the keys by on my way into Roslyn today. You can come by and load it any time. I'm just waiting on Enterprise to arrive with my rental." Lindsey talked with the phone braced between her chin and shoulder while she stepped into her shoes and put on her last earring. "How long do you think it will take?"

She grimaced. "Alright. Call me as soon as you can give me an estimate on the cost and the length of time to finish all the repairs." She disconnected and raced down the stairs as the white Honda Accord on the transport vehicle pulled into her drive. She had already called Mary at the office to tell her about the accident and that she'd be in late today.

Lindsey watched as the car was off-loaded. The operation took under ten minutes. Then the delivery man walked over to Lindsey in a few short strides. "Lindsey Kelly?"

Smiling at the Enterprise employee, she said, "Yes, I'm Lindsey, and thanks for being so prompt. Do I need to sign any paperwork?"

Producing a clipboard, the courier said, "Just a few forms to sign and we'll all be on our way." Leaning the clipboard against the hood of the car, Lindsey signed the documents.

"That should do it. Thanks, Ms. Kelly. Hope you enjoy the ride."

"This will keep me moving while my car is repaired. Thanks for the delivery."

Lindsey went back to the house to lock up and turn on the entry lights. She liked to return home to the warmth of the welcoming glow. And tonight, she would be later than usual since she was getting a slow start.

Since it was after nine, the traffic was lighter than normal. At least part of the trip into town was through rolling countryside. It reminded her so much of Tuscany. She and her parents would often escape the embassy compound for the hill country near Sienna. They'd stayed in a small *pensione* that served the most marvelous handmade veal ravioli and her parents would take her on long walks in the hills cheerfully greeting the locals as they went through the villages. She remembered the *pensione* was named Villa Le Barone. The tall ochre-colored building had been surrounded by large gardens and several terraces that offered what the brochure said were "beautiful views allowing one to think, relax and forget the stress of daily life."

She'd been lucky in so many ways to have lived and traveled in such a variety of countries. In her teens, she'd taken it for granted. It was a wonderful life, but there were days when she longed to be a regular teenager and go to high school stateside. Hang out at the mall. See a movie without subtitles. Be a cheerleader for the varsity football team. But the only "football" she'd watched then was soccer.

She swung by the Ferrari dealership in Herndon to drop the key and was sitting behind her desk before eleven. She had a staff meeting at one to discuss the new Iraq immersion curriculum STLS would be submitting to the State Department and at three thirty, a meeting with Michael Walden and his team from the Walden Group.

She wasn't looking forward to seeing the leprechaun-like attorney. Michael seemed perfectly capable of vetting government contracts, but she probably needed a corporate defense lawyer who was current with employment law for the Hansen suit. She was fooling herself when she thought she could have avoided this lawsuit. If she'd just handled the Brad problem differently. It seemed Brad Hansen, Mr. Charming, had planned all along to sue Lindsey over something—anything—to be able to drive her out of business. But she was confused about his motive. Surely, he wasn't that vindictive.

Mary pulled her out of her reverie when she walked in carrying the draft curriculum for her one o'clock. "I was in Hank's office and said I'd bring these over for your early perusal. He's really been working hard to develop exactly what the client wants. The State rep has been pushing certain changes, and this draft incorporates those new techniques."

"Thanks, Mary. I'm so pleased with Hank Atkins' performance as the new Director of Training. He probably doesn't have the government contacts Brad had, but he sure is a lot easier to be around. And a hard worker to boot."

"Yes, we lucked out on that hire."

Lindsey nodded. "I'll scan through the curriculum paperwork before the meeting. I'd like you to attend since we will need to assess the man-hours and pricing for each course. You have the most experience with pricing. And Geena should attend, too. She will be spearheading the scheduling and logistics."

"Yay, I'd be happy for her to take that off my plate," Mary, nearly shouting, pumped her fist in the air. "I've been wearing too many hats for quite a while. We're still handling the same type of projects we've done from the beginning, only now it's just a heck of a lot more of everything."

Sitting down at her desk Lindsey said, "If you have a minute, I'd like to discuss Geena Morales with you."

"Sure, I have some time." Mary took a seat in one of Lindsey's Martha Washington chairs and set her notebook on the desk. "It's an hour before the staff meeting."

Lindsey continued, "When we hired Geena, we knew she was over qualified for the Executive Assistant position. With a business degree from Penn State, and her brief stint with the Justice Department managing several of their overseas projects, I think she's ready to take on more responsibility."

"I agree. I think she took the job to get her foot in the door."

"What do you think of having her work with Hank, getting out in the field more and coordinating the schedule with Triple Shield's Assistant Director of Training?"

"I think she's ready, and I'd like to see her spread her wings. She's been good at most everything we've thrown at her."

"Great. That's settled. But you said it, Mary. You're still trying to supervise many teams when your main concern should be the accounting department and guiding the company's financial decisions. You're the CFO, my best advisor and a true friend, so, let's move toward getting you some free time."

Lindsey looked at her good friend and colleague and remembered the time when they had started the company together. Both young and right out of grad school. Full of ideas. Mary had said she would be the assistant since Lindsey had all the brains. But it turned out Mary had had a knack for getting the contract pricing exactly right. Low enough to win the contract, but high enough to make a nice profit. They both had worked tirelessly to make the company a success, but sometimes, Lindsey thought, Mary was more dedicated than she was.

Turning back to her friend, she said with laughter in her voice, "I sometimes think you live in an office drawer. You arrive before everyone and are frequently still here when the last of the staff leaves. You know I couldn't do this business without you."

"Stop! We'll have to get a wheel-barrow for my head soon, it's getting so big."

"Okay, think about what duties you'd like to turn over to Geena and we'll talk again tomorrow."

Leaning forward and resting her warm brown hands on the desk, Mary shook her head. "You're the visionary for STLS. This company wouldn't be where it is today without all your hard work and strategic decisions. Remember, it was your idea to team with Triple Shield and their consortium of companies that pulled us into the big league. It's been a win-win situation that you made happen."

"Now who's going overboard? At least it's obvious we're the founding members of the mutual admiration society."

Mary chuckled, her bright white teeth sparkling. "Okay, okay, but to help the bottom line, we just need to remember Triple Shield is our customer as much as the government. STLS needs to continue to be indispensable."

Standing and gathering her notebook Mary added, "Oh, I meant to mention... Hank said something odd when I was in the IT office."

"What's that?"

"He said he had what looked like a security breach in the curriculum files." Mary frowned. "I'm no computer whiz, but how can anyone hack into our computers with all our firewalls and other bells and whistles we were convinced were absolutely necessary to keep our data safe? And, more importantly, why?"

"It doesn't make sense. We already have the task order for the training. Now we're in the process of tweaking the lesson plans to accommodate the new counterterrorism techniques developed by State."

"The folks at the State Department would work with any of our competitors and reveal the same information, if one of them had gotten the contract. All the major training contractors have security clearance to see this material, so, you're right, it doesn't make much sense."

"Maybe Hank is mistaken about the breach." Lindsey glowered creating a furrow between her eyebrows. With all this worry, she'd probably need Botox soon.

"Hi, Michael," Lindsey said with her hand outstretched. Michael gave her an anemic handshake, and he and his two associates followed her into the conference room where Mary and Geena were waiting. "I think you know STLS's Chief Financial Officer, Ms. Walker, and my Executive Assistant, Geena Morales."

"Yes, and these are my two colleagues, Tim Mathews and Dave Evans."

Kelly had to stifle a laugh when she looked at the two associates trailing behind Michael. They were nearly the same height and on the rotund side. Each was wearing a navy-blue, three-piece suit, bow tie and matching black wing tip shoes. They reminded her of Tweedledee and Tweedledum from

Alice in Wonderland. All they were missing was the beanie. She would never be able to shake the image.

She turned from them raising her eyebrows at Mary and sat at her desk.

After a few more pleasantries, Michael mumbled, "I think we have a strategy Ms. Kelly."

"Umm."

"Well, we called the contact at the State Department that you suggested, and he gave us the name of the firm that has represented the government on a few issues. We would like to bring in attorneys from that firm. They are principally involved in government contracts, employment law, and corporate defense. As you know the Walden Group specializes in government contracts, but not the litigation side. We primarily advise clients on the legality of their contracts with the government and help with formatting successful quotes to the government. We..."

"Please, Mr. Walden, I'm well aware of the Walden Group's area of expertise. That's why we hired you as our government contracts' attorney. But shall we move on to the solutions for our present problem, namely Brad Hansen?" Lindsey tried to keep the irritation from her voice. The man's dithering made her crazy.

"Oh, eh, yes. Let's do. Well, uh, we'd like to propose using someone from Carter, Clooney & Davis. They have excellent contacts with the government and have an entire department devoted to expert witnesses in contracting and employment law, as well as on-staff economists to analyze and refute Mr. Hansen's damages claims."

"Do you have an estimate of the costs involved?" Mary asked.

"Well, eh, not the total costs, yet, but their normal expert witness fee is $550 an hour, and each expert will need to read all the transcripts, motions, rebuttals, and the like to familiarize himself with the case."

"Tim started to work on a preliminary expert witness list, but we haven't contacted Carter, Clooney & Davis yet, Ms. Kelly," Tweedledum interjected. "We wanted to pass it by you for the approval."

"It certainly is a lot of money. Are there any alternatives?" Lindsey asked.

"I really think this is our best s-so-solution," Michael stammered.

What was it about this guy that so got on Lindsey's nerves? She knew she was pushing him, which only made him more befuddled. She had to try to be nicer to the insipid fool.

"Alright, then, Michael, please go ahead and contact Carter, Clooney & Davis to get an estimate of their costs to represent STLS and provide expert witnesses for our defense."

"Thank you, Ms. Kelly. We'll get back to you by the end of the week." He smiled broadly with an air of relief. With a wave of his hand he and his entourage, as well as Geena, filed out of the office.

Mary closed the door behind them and sat

back down with Lindsey. "I guess we have no choice, but just visualizing all the paper that's been generated in this case, figuring the time to read it all, times the cost per hour, times the number of expert witnesses, plus the attorney fees...well, it doesn't look good." Mary's shoulders slumped forward, and she rubbed her brow like a headache was coming on. "We might have a cash flow problem once we exceed our open line of credit."

Lindsey pushed above her eyes with both hands to try to relieve the tension. "What else can we do? I wish we had someone who knew his way around in the corporate defense field who could advise us. It would be nice, too, if he were independent of the Walden Group. Michael Walden is fine with contracts, but on this problem, he doesn't fill me with confidence. Tweedledee and Tweedledum are dolts, too."

Mary's eyes crinkled at the edges and she laughed, "What? The two nerds with Michael? Ha, now that you mention it, they did resemble the Disney version of Lewis Carroll's characters, and it's pretty obvious what your opinion of Michael is."

"Okay, I know I don't display much tolerance for the nincompoop, but he has really dropped the ball this time."

"I think we should move forward on our projects, invoice as quickly as we can for our services, and hope like hell we can keep our heads above water."

"Spoken like a true CFO!"

"We should also hope for fast readers in the expert witness pool."

It was raining on the way home and the traffic on the Dulles toll road was horrible. The red tail lights in front of Lindsey looked like the canvas of an impressionist painter. The downpour continued, slowing traffic even further. Finally, on route fifty, she drove through Middleburg, stopped at the Salamander Market, picked up some prepared Tilapia and curried rice for her dinner, and pulled into her drive by seven fifteen.

It was clearing from the west. The interior of the car was permeated with the aroma of the curried rice and the distinctive odor of grilled fish. Opening the small car's door, she stepped out into the warm moist air and felt as though she had stepped through a portal in time.

In the scent of the spicy rice and fish she smelled the sea. She heard the _ndombolo_ music beating in the background? She was suddenly standing on a street in Dar es Salaam waiting for the _daladala_, the consistently over-crowded local bus. Masses of sweaty bodies pressed in from all sides. Then she was sitting at a wobbly metal table in an old metal deck chair under shade trees in the late afternoon heat. The odor of garbage mingled with the aroma of charcoal smoked goat, seaweed, and diesel exhaust.

She was in Dar es Salaam with her parents during a summer break before she went to the boarding school in Bern, Switzerland for her last two years in high school. Her dad, Jack, had just turned to her and was smiling, sipping a Krest bitter lemon. They were discussing their plans for tomorrow. He was heading to Mombasa for two days. Her mother, Helen, was talking of her visit to the embassy the next day to meet with her friend in the attachés' office. Lindsey's idea for the next day was to go with friends to the south coast of Dar by the small fishing village of *Mjimwema*. It had the most beautiful unspoiled white sandy beaches and cool ocean breezes. She was looking forward to a relaxed day in the sun with her friends from the local international school.

It was the last time they'd all been together. The bombing of the US Embassy in Dar es Salaam the next day took them all by surprise. Her mother had been one of the few American casualties.

Lindsey blinked and realized she was standing by her rental car in the driveway of her snug, safe home in the Virginia countryside. Dar was long ago and far away, but it still seemed like yesterday.

Lindsey couldn't seem to settle into the evening routine. It was strange for her to be so disconcerted. Mosby's usually calming presence wasn't working tonight. She ate her dinner without tasting a bite. Before going up for a long, hot soaking bath she decided to check her email. Only a message from Mary. "Keep the goal in sight," was all she had written.

Since she was right there at the computer, on a whim Lindsey googled Gavin Blake. She felt a little sneaky and excited at the same time to be investigating another person. If Gavin was just a mechanic who worked at Laurel Glen, then he probably wouldn't pop up in the Google search.

Bingo! Over a dozen listings. There was a Gavin Blake that was with the law firm of Carter, Clooney & Davis. Heavens, that was just too bizarre. Six thumbnail photos of five men and a woman all looking very lawyerly ran down the side of the article. The heading said, "Six Attorneys join Carter, Clooney & Davis." One was definitely Gavin, but with longer hair. Confusion engulfed her. If Gavin was a lawyer, what was he doing working as a mechanic?

She looked at the date of the item and found it was from 2008. Once on the internet, always on the internet. It was the profile of the new attorneys with the firm. Lindsey clicked on the thumbnail of Gavin. The photo enlarged, and the profile was beside it on the page. Yes, it was definitely *her* Gavin, only looking much younger.

She scanned down the entry and couldn't believe this was the same guy she'd met at the track, although it did explain his polished persona and upscale interests. *This* Gavin graduated from Penn and went on to Harvard Law. *No slouch in the brains department.* He did his stint in public service with the Richmond Public Defender Offices, then in 2008 was hired by the Carter firm.

She clicked on the other entries, but they were all the same announcement. There was no new information on the inexplicable Gavin Blake since then. He'd just disappeared into the halls of the huge corporate firm. Why had he quit being a lawyer? Whatever it was, it wasn't for publication. Not a word on the internet.

In their evening together, he'd never even hinted he was anything but a mechanic. What was he hiding? Could she trust a guy who wasn't straight with her? She powered down the computer, locked all the doors, turned out the lights, and went upstairs.

Lindsey lay back in the deep tub, but the longed-for relaxation didn't come. She continued to think of her struggling business. Actually, the business was still strong; it was just the pressure of the ever-present lawsuit. The legal fees were a terrible drain on the company's operating capital. Maybe they could increase the line of credit to cover the additional cost.

She was usually so sure of her direction, but now she wasn't even sure she wanted to be the head of a defense contracting company. What had happened to her confidence and her vision of saving the world from terrorism? She'd naively thought that by making the targets more alert to threats, lives would be saved. That had been her reason for starting STLS. If her mother had only been more aware of the terrorists watching the embassy, would she still be alive today?

Gavin kept thinking about his conversation with Tom and his defense of Martin Boyle. He should have seen through Martin's *poor me* story and studied the evidence more closely. It was one thing to help defend an innocent man who was too poor to hire a high-powered defense attorney and another thing to get someone off for a crime they had really committed.

He felt sick inside and not a bit sleepy, but he got ready for bed and thought he'd read awhile to get his mind off everything. He had to get some sleep since he needed to be at work early, as usual. The book he picked up was a good thriller by Clancy, and he began to relax and get into the story and the dialog.

He heard the small girl screaming and could see her tiny body beneath the man. He was slapping her and thrusting, thrusting into her. There was blood. She was so little. She seemed to be reaching out to Gavin. Her high-pitched *help me* echoed in his mind. She was still screaming when he woke with a start. The bedside light was still on, and his book open over his chin. His heart pounded in his chest, and he was breathing heavily. Sweat poured from his brow.

He hadn't had that damned dream in several months. It must have been the lunch with Tom that triggered it. When would he ever be able to let it go? How could he make it right?

»Chapter Six«

After his one troubled night, the rest of Gavin's week was turning out to be routine. He punched in at eight o'clock and usually left the shop around five. He had one challenging mechanical project, overhauling the motor on the road grading machine, but generally he just changed oil and tires on the track machinery, and maintained the go-karts for the kart track part of the business.

The only highlight of this week was that he would be managing the Twilight Testing sessions on Thursday for Jeff. Would Lindsey Kelly be there? He couldn't see how she would have the Ferrari fixed by then, but he found himself hoping he'd see her.

Good Lord! Here he was thinking of her again. What did that mean? He had to admit to himself he *was* attracted to the woman. She was competent, gorgeous, and somehow also vulnerable. She made him laugh, and he didn't think he imagined it, but the look she'd given him as he was leaving her place Sunday evening...well, she seemed genuinely interested in him.

Maybe he should call her. *Dumb idea.* He was a nobody, and she was the head of a thriving corporation. Run into her while roaming the streets of Upperville? *Also, dumb.* "Oh, hi, Lindsey. Amazing to see you. I was just hiking along route fifty." What were her haunts? He might frequent Hunter's Head for a few nights in hopes she would come in.

God, he must have it bad. He was thinking like some teenage boy, hanging out at the local Dairy Queen hoping to see the head cheerleader come in for an ice cream. Lying in wait at the pub was probably stupid, too, but he thought he might give it a try. There was one thing about this job he didn't like. He had too much time to think.

"When you're finished with that engine check, come see me, Blake." Jeff said.

That brought Gavin back to the present. Five minutes later, wiping his hand on a shop rag, he walked into the cool office area. "What's up?"

Jeff was on the computer ordering parts for the school cars. "I'd rather be working on a car, but here I am on this damn computer and up to my eyeballs in invoices and paperwork," he grumbled. "All this inventory control and work order stuff for management is getting me down."

"Jeff, you're never down. What can I do to help?"

"Thought you'd never ask." Jeff grinned. "You are so calm and collected, Gavin, and seem pretty smart, too. I know you're kinda new, but how'd you like to take over the inventory control and work orders for the shop? The rest of the guys like you, so you'd be able to show them the new system without making them mad. Do you know how to work one of these damn computers?"

Gavin was beginning to wonder if *damn* was a new brand of computer. "Well, sure, I know how to run a computer, but I, I uh, don't know." Gavin looked down. "I really like working on the motors the most, but I guess I could give it a try."

"I'd still do all the ordering, but it would help me out so much, 'cause I have to admit, I'm not too good with a computer. I really don't get how to work the spreadsheet program." He sighed. "I've had to stay late a lot, so now Marcie's on me to get home at a decent hour." He looked miserable.

Gavin felt he was being boxed into a corner, but he figured he could probably set up the inventory system with one arm tied behind his back. He'd had to build a program for billable hours in law school. Surely this couldn't be too different. To Jeff he said, "I like computers. How 'bout I try it for a few weeks. Maybe I can figure out an easier way for all of us to track parts and jobs. Then, I could go back to the cars."

"It's a deal," Jeff said with a broad smile. Gavin could see the relief in his face. He looked like the old clownish Jeff again.

"See ya tomorrow and have a good evening," Eddie said while he packed up his tools in the next bay and locked them into his red tool chest.

"You, too." Gavin picked up his lunch bag and headed to his car. Laurel Glen was working out alright. Simple was good, he thought. Or was he trying to convince himself?

At home, he lifted weights for thirty minutes, then showered and changed into slacks and a polo for his short ride over to Upperville. He really was going to *loiter* at the pub. He must be demented.

He sat at the bar and ordered a Newcastle Brown. Umm, cold and tasty. Why did the British serve their ale room temperature when it was so wonderful ice cold?

"Good to see you again. How were the burgers?" Pete was the perfect barkeeper. Never forgot a face. Of course, Gavin had shot the breeze with him while he was packing up their dinners on Sunday. But still, to remember what he'd ordered. That kind of detail was definitely good for business.

"Done to perfection." He smiled at the recent memory of the beautiful evening. Watching the sun set behind the Blue Ridge, sharing stories with a remarkable woman—now, that was perfection.

Pete's slightly British-accented voice broke into his reverie. "Will you be meeting Ms. Kelly here for dinner tonight, then?" The cadence was more Irish than English.

"Oh, uh, no. I'm here because I'm addicted to your rare pub burgers, so thought I'd have another one tonight." And again, tomorrow and the next night, if necessary. He chuckled. This was a damn, stupid idea, but he was committed now. "Just cooling down with a pint first."

"Well, I only thought you might be meeting Ms. Kelly since she came in about fifteen minutes ago and is in the next room. She stops in a couple of times a week, and mostly eats by herself working on her computer, but I thought..." Pete cocked one eye up. He looked amused and smiled genially. He went back to polishing glasses.

Gavin's face reddened. He had been caught out. Should he slink out after one beer or bluff it out? Should he *accidentally* bump into her in the other room and strike up a conversation? Nothing ventured, nothing gained. He might as well confess the truth. He picked up his glass and moved into the dining room.

Lindsey was studying her laptop screen, her left hand resting on the stem of her wineglass.

"Is it a merlot tonight?" Gavin said. He ambled toward her table, striving for casual.

Lindsey raised her eyes to Gavin's, and there was a momentary flash of annoyance until she recognized who had spoken. Her face was transformed by the warmest quirky smile and she looked at him with her head cocked to one side. "What brings you to this neck of the woods? On your way to Warrenton?" Her eyes danced mischievously.

"I guess I could say I was checking out the scene. Then the conversation would drift to 'what's your sign?' But, no, to be honest, I was hoping I might stumble into you here. I was actually contemplating eating here every night until you came in." There, he had said it. Would she stand up and run screaming from the room or invite him to sit down.

Lindsey laughed. "You're a funny guy. Would you like to join me? I've ordered the Shrimp Caesar.

The chef at *Sticks and Stones* didn't feel like cooking tonight." Did she really need to explain? She had wanted to see him again, but God, what did she look like after a harrowing day at work and an hour and a half in stop and go traffic? Probably worn out. But the crooked smile on his face and the merriment in his eyes said he didn't notice at all. "After my long commute, I like to check my email for any fires that need putting out before I power off for the evening."

"I can imagine running your own company is fairly stressful."

"Like Harry Truman said, 'the buck stops here,' so, yeah, I do sometimes feel the burden of success or failure riding on my shoulders."

Gavin ordered the Organic Ayrshire Burger, with another Newcastle Brown. "What's your business like? I mean what exactly do you do?"

"Simply put, we do logistics and training for the government. I also like to think our training helps keep Americans safer when they travel to high-threat areas all over the world. That's my idealism seeping in."

"Sounds impressive." Gavin cleared his throat. "I have to come clean. I did google 'Lindsey Kelly' and know that you own a company called STLS, but honestly, I couldn't completely understand what exactly you do for your clients. Are you a spy?" He was grinning from ear to ear. He must be kidding. So, she laughed.

"No, not a spy, just crazy." In all truthfulness, she'd probably trained a few spooks, but she didn't think this was the time to mention that. "Yes, a little crazy to be in government contracting. It's great because you know the government will always pay. The dicey part is when."

Changing the subject a bit, and leaning back in his chair, Gavin said, "I think I got promoted at work today, so we should celebrate."

Lindsey noticed he seemed totally relaxed —comfortable with himself—like the first evening they'd been together. Had that really only been a few days ago?

She smiled up at him. "Congratulations!" They clinked glasses. "Aren't you sure if it's a promotion or not?"

In answer to her question he said, "I guess you have figured out that I'm a rookie mechanic at the track, but now Jeff, our delightful mutual friend, has asked me to sort out the new computerized inventory and job order system for the shop. Computerizing vehicle maintenance is something management is pushing, and Jeff just doesn't have enough computer background to be comfortable with the new program."

"Will you still work some of the evening and weekend events?" Did she sound desperate to see him?

"Oh, I expect I'll still do that, but working at a desk most of the day will be more like penance instead of a promotion. The responsibility was one of the reasons I left my former job."

More like a life-altering career switch, Lindsey thought. He had admitted to googling her, but she wasn't ready to disclose her own computer search of Gavin Blake, Mr. Harvard Law. "What did you do before Laurel Glen?" She felt a little deceitful knowing what she did, and a blush started up her neck.

"Uh, I had some legal training, so I worked for a law firm in the city."

That was an understatement. "I can commiserate with the agonizing decision to work and live in a city versus to live and work in bucolic surroundings. There are advantages and disadvantages to both. I guess I'm on the fence. Even though I work in a high-rise office building right across the Potomac River from the Kennedy Center, I don't think I could ever *live* in the city for long. The hour-long or more commute is a bummer, but it's an acceptable trade-off for spending evenings listening to the cicadas and tree frogs singing and waking to the birds chirping in the big oak outside my window."

"You really *are* a country gal."

"I suppose. Did you live in DC when you were working there?"

Gavin cringed, and a look of pain crossed his face before he said, "Yes, I had a small place in Georgetown. It had a narrow garden space behind it, so I had a tiny slice of nature where I could relax. There was a family of squirrels that live in the old maple. I sold the house when I took the job at Laurel Glen this spring." There was something grimly final about his last sentence. Then his expression lightened, and he said, "How 'bout you? Did you ever live in town?" He took another sip of his ale and sat forward, listening attentively.

"When I first started my business, I had a miniature efficiency in Rosslyn. It was convenient to the office, but it made me feel claustrophobic. No balcony or garden. The windows looked out at the building next door. A place like yours might have made city living bearable."

"Yeah, the garden was special, almost magical. Very private." Gavin had a sad look around his eyes again. He seemed suddenly older. She suspected there was something in his past life as a lawyer that haunted him.

"I lived in a lot of big cities when I was a kid, but our family would get out into the country every chance we could." She smiled to herself remembering the rolling hills along the Rhine, fields of sunflowers in Tuscany, and even the beautiful high fields of Sky Meadows Park only five miles from Upperville. When she and her parents could breathe in the fresh country air or absorb the serenity of the natural setting while hiking the hills, they would pull into an invincible unit and block out the everyday problems of the world.

"I think of the countryside as a refuge where I go to forget the complications of work, and it's a place to reenergize."

"What kind of complications could you possibly have at work just now?"

She looked directly into Gavin's lovely deep

brown eyes. He seemed genuinely concerned, and she got the feeling she could confide in him. All sense of light banter left her, and Lindsey said, "It's not very socially acceptable to bring up business problems at a friendly dinner, but with your somewhat legal background maybe you could listen to my situation and point me in the right direction for help."

A slight crease appeared between those marvelous eyes, and he sat forward in his chair, resting his arms on the table. "I'm a good listener. Go ahead." Gavin's pub burger came, but he ignored it. His gaze was fixed on Lindsey.

"I got involved with a man, ooh, strictly in a business sense," she corrected, a little flustered for the mixed connotation, "uh, was associated with a business colleague who wanted to take my company in a different direction—away from its current path." She sighed, wondering how best to explain. "That was the sugarcoated short version. To be blunt, this scoundrel is trying to steal my company!" Lindsey stretched her neck to the right to ease the tension and exhaled slowly.

Gavin's eyes widened, and his eyebrows went up. "Yes, that does sound like a major complication."

"Let me back up. His name is Brad Hansen. He was the Director of Training and had been working for STLS, well, working for me, for nearly nine years. About eight months ago he walked into my office and said he had a new idea for the company. He thought we should go global. His new vision for the business included a training center in Dubai, where we would be able to conduct the same type of training we do here in the States at a fraction of the cost in the Middle East."

She took another deep breath. Gavin seemed to be engrossed. "Even though most of our students are eventually deployed to the high-threat areas centered in that region, the cost of building the facility on foreign soil, and then transporting and housing the instructors and students in Dubai was exorbitant. We found out the cost of living in Dubai or Abu Dhabi is equivalent to New York City. The accountants poured over his proposal, analyzing the project from every direction, and the numbers just weren't there." Lindsey paused, frowning.

"It was as if Hansen had *cost* figures for a remote third world country and *income* figures for Dubai. He had an agenda for business in a parallel world. First, he tried persuasion, then he was adamant, before becoming downright abusive. The long and short of it was, I had to fire him."

Gavin's eyes widened. "Whoa, that would get his attention. He sounds like a nutjob, so what did he do?"

"Within three months he sued the company and, of course, me personally for breach of contract. He wanted damages equal to the bonuses he said he would have received from his wildly successful plan. Is this getting too long?" She was hesitant. This was probably too much. She hardly knew Gavin.

"No, go on. I'm interested and want to help if I can."

"Okay. The federal judge dismissed the case stating that both sides had breached the employment contract for whatever reasons and told both parties to pay their own legal fees and go home. It was a lot of money, but I thought it was over. Then the son-of-a-bitch, oh sorry, I'm getting worked up again. Anyway, Hansen's lawyers appealed the decision to the Fourth Circuit in Richmond. Unbelievably, the appellate panel remanded the suit back to the original judge, it was Buckley, for damages. I just got the notice today." She sighed again, but it felt good to tell the story. Maybe someone else could make sense of it.

"Yes, I've heard of Judge Buckley. He has an excellent reputation for reasonable and fair decisions. Go on."

"I simply can't understand what I did that could be seen as a breach. He was out of line, so I let him go. Maybe it was something I wrote in his termination letter. Also, I have this incompetent lawyer who leaves me cold. I have no confidence in his less than savvy ability to get me out of this thing without jeopardizing my company. Hansen wants millions!" She was getting too emotional. She took another deep breath and a sip of her wine. More calmly, Lindsey went on, shaking her head, "And I can't for the life of me comprehend his motive for trying to bring my company down."

"At first glance, it sounds like Hansen thinks

he can win the lottery here at your expense. He must think the cost is worth the potential reward. Also, his lawyer may have been hired on a contingency basis. Hansen won't pay him unless he gets a settlement. Then the lawyer will get a hefty percentage. But there may be another motive."

Gavin's usual languid demeanor was gone, and he leaned over the table, an intense look emanated from his eyes. He took one of Lindsey's hands. "May I ask a few questions?"

The pub was emptying. Most patrons didn't stay too late on a weeknight. Lindsey looked around the nearly vacant restaurant. "Would you think me too forward, if I asked you back to my place? We'll be able to speak more freely."

"That's probably best." Gavin paid the bill at the bar, said goodnight to Pete, and followed Lindsey to the parking area. "What're you driving?"

"It's the white Honda over there," she said pointing to the back corner of the lot. "I'll be right behind you."

Gavin was wired. He hadn't felt this alive in months. He loved a problem to solve. Lindsey was the first part of the equation, but the challenge of the lawsuit was also exhilarating. This Brad Hansen character was probably simply a vindictive bastard, but there could be something else. He'd worked with many a defense contractor when he was with Carter, Clooney & Davis, mostly companies challenging government contract awards, but by plain proximity to these movers and shakers, he knew it was a sensitive and secretive industry. Each company thought their proprietary information was sacrosanct.

This was another piece in the Lindsey puzzle. Now he knew what'd been bothering her. That distractedness he'd noticed. Such intense worry and stress probably caused her to lose focus. It may have been a factor in her ultimately wrecking her beautiful Ferrari. The mind had such an effect on the body. Oh, and what an incredible body it was. Okay, now who was getting distracted?

They were pulling up her lane. He parked his VW in the circular drive and got out.

"Come on in. I'll quickly feed Mosby, and then we can start to work."

She was suddenly all business. No wonder. This was the survival of her company at stake.

He followed her through to the kitchen where she quickly opened the cat food, and leaning down by the refrigerator, said, "Here you go, Mosby." He couldn't help noticing how nicely her butt fit into the slacks she was wearing. *Hold that thought, Gav,* he said to himself. *Later.*

"Would you like some coffee?" she said, moving to the Krupp's. "I think I need a double shot, coffee that is."

"Yes, I'd love some." He studied the pictures on the refrigerator, zeroing in on one photo of two people at an old metal table and chairs somewhere in the tropics. The table was in the shade of a huge tree, a kind that was unfamiliar to him. They were laughing heartily as they looked directly at each other, not at the camera. "Are these your parents?" he said, immediately realizing his mistake. He felt he was surely touching another nerve, since he knew her mother was no longer living.

"Yes. It was the last time we were all together. My mother was killed the next day in the bombing of the US Embassy in Dar es Salaam, Tanzania."

"God, I'm sorry. That must have been awful."

"It's still awful, but I'm handling it better. I don't burst into tears at the mention of it anymore. Although it has been a long time, it seems like the recent past."

Damn, he could kick himself for dredging up this history. She looked stricken. "Umm, the coffee smells great."

Lindsey poured two cups and set them on the table. "Do you need cream or sugar?"

"Black's fine." They sat at the breakfast table across from each other. "Shall we get back to business? Let's start with a few questions."

Gavin took notes on a pad Lindsey had given him, while she explained the intricacies of her business. She answered Gavin's questions about training locations, the structure of the business, and questions about the curriculum. Lindsey answered everything calmly with professionalism and expertise. Gavin was beginning to see the incredible mind inside this attractive woman's head. It was no accident that she had become so successful.

"I don't quite understand. You're saying that you don't do the hands-on training?"

"No, a company called Triple Shield uses an old army base in Southern Virginia, or sometimes Laurel Glen, when space is available, to conduct all the firearms and driver training. They also use a large gymnasium for the personal protection training. I think it's in Herndon or Fairfax. We provide the surveillance detection module, medical training, and all the classroom curriculum with Power Point presentations for the firearms and driver training. STLS also implements the logistical plans for housing and transportation before and after the students are deployed to the foreign postings. We started out just doing surveillance detection, but just kind of grew into the other areas. It's a team in the true sense of the word. Sort of a symbiotic relationship. Each company needs the other."

"Now, I'm even more confused. In Brad's scheme for this Dubai branch, would you have been taking over a hundred percent of the training? You know, like the driver training and firearms, too?"

"Yes. It seemed strange, but Hansen's plan included building a two-mile training circuit out in the desert, as well as an entire training camp with indoor firing ranges, gym complex, shoot house, immersion village for realistic urban combat exercises, living quarters, and a cafeteria. Possibly even a Mock Embassy."

"What would happen to your work with Triple Shield?"

"Brad said we would keep that here, then get other contracts to support the overseas facility, but everybody in the industry knows those contracts can be illusive. There are no guarantees in this business."

"Did he indicate what clients he had in mind?"

"There he got really mysterious and just said he had his contacts. He got blustery whenever the board pressed him, and he'd say things like, 'I've got my sources. That's why you pay me the big bucks, Lindsey.'" She shook her head. "What a jerk."

"Could he be thinking of foreign clients?"

"I don't think the United States Department of State would approve of an American company training foreign nationals unless the contract went through our government. In fact, I think it's illegal."

"Maybe you've hit on something there," Gavin said excitedly. "What if Hansen were thinking of training mercenaries and his clients were Middle Eastern countries? He'd definitely want to keep that to himself."

"How could he get by with that? I guess he could teach a foreign defense force how to drive and shoot, as long as he didn't give away any of the government's proprietary information." Lindsey shook her head slowly, and the lines deepened between her eyes. "But, no, I think that would still be illegal."

Gavin's enthusiasm was mounting. "There was a piece in the Washington Post recently, about a big-shot defense contractor who sold his company here in the States for millions and was going to build a facility and train an army for Bahrain or maybe it was China or somewhere. Brad might have thought he could do that."

"God, I don't know. That kind of scheme seems like a long shot." She sighed. "Thinking about what Brad might be plotting is giving me a headache." Lindsey rose and went over to the cabinet above the coffee maker, got out the bottle of Advil, and shook out two tablets. She gulped down the pills with some water and said, "This should help. I need to stop thinking about this tonight. Would you like more coffee or does a nightcap under the trellis sound better?" The hint of a smile lingered at the corners of her luscious mouth.

Gavin thought going anywhere with this intelligent, intriguing woman was fine with him. The trellis would be a good start. He smiled and stood up, stretching his shoulders back. Pushing the chair in he said, "A small after dinner drink would be a nice end to the evening. You'll probably sleep better, too, if you can stop thinking about this scoundrel."

Gavin was going back over in his mind all that Lindsey had revealed to him. He almost felt honored. It was rare to find a person so open and trusting. This worry she was carrying made her seem defenseless, and he suddenly wanted to protect her. In this mind frame he blurted out. "One day I'd like to meet this Brad character, so I can punch him out." He cleared his throat. "Oops, sounds like I'm vying for the Male Chauvinist of the Year award. I'm sure you can take care of yourself." Lindsey's smile broadened. "I just meant, I can tell I wouldn't like this guy if I met him."

She looked amused. "I like a manly man." She bent both of her arms up at the elbow and made muscles pop in her upper arm. Then she laughed again and asked, "Would you rather have a Hennessy or a B & B?"

"A touch of the brandy will be perfect."

Lindsey poured Gavin's Hennessy into what looked like a Waterford crystal brandy snifter. *This woman is a class act,* he thought. Then he followed her to the side patio.

They both sat on the same side of the table with their heads resting against the logs of the house. The silhouette of the mountains looked like a cutout. There was still enough light beneath the arbor, though the sun had set forty-five minutes earlier. It was cool for late May and had been less humid the last couple of days.

Gavin hated to break the comfortable silence. Maybe he should wait for her to speak first. He really liked this woman and didn't want to goof this up. "I see what you mean about the tree frogs. A very relaxing tune." He heard a slight titter.

"You're a nice man, Gavin, but an enigma." She sipped down the amber liquid and set her glass on the table. "How can you be a mechanic who knows what's wrong with my Ferrari engine by just listening for a moment, and also a guy who knows all about the wine regions of the world and the reputations of federal judges? Yes, quite a mystery man." She turned and looked up at him expectantly.

Against his better judgment, he leaned forward and brushed his lips across hers. Lindsey responded by leaning into him. His second kiss was more urgent, and he felt himself losing control. She tasted of the sweeter Brandy and Benedictine, and her lips were soft and alluring. His hands swept over her back, and he pulled her against him.

He kissed the top of her head, and she nuzzled into the crook of his shoulder beneath his chin. She felt so right, and he had a surge of emotion. He wanted to protect this woman from everything evil.

He pulled back from her, tilting her chin up with his hand, and looked at her. Really looked at her. This was a woman he could love. He spoke softly. "I think you know I'm beginning to care for you, but I don't want to rush you." He ran his hand through his hair breathing deeply to slow his racing pulse. "There is so much I need to tell you about who I am. It's just too much to start into now. I'm not trying to be mysterious or keep anything from you. I'll need time to explain, really explain. I hope you'll give me a chance."

She started to speak, and he put his finger over her mouth. "No more questions for now." He stood up and drew her to her feet. Holding her hand, he led her to the edge of the arbor. The night was cooling, and the sky was nearly black. He moved behind her and wrapped his arms around her and gathered her to him.

"Let's watch the stars twinkle on. I used to do that as a kid. Look, there're two." He pointed high above the western hills. "It always makes me realize how small I am in the whole scheme of things." They stood in companionable silence for a time. He knew in his gut that everything was changing. He had been frozen inside since the incident thirteen months ago—now something was thawing in him. He would wrestle with the painful memories later.

»Chapter Seven«

She woke to a gray sky and a light drizzle, but nothing could dampen Lindsey's spirit. She was on auto pilot for her routine morning run to the Trenton Farm entrance gate. The usual two rattletrap trucks with "Farm Use" tags and the one ancient red Honda Civic rumbled by on the run out. With so few vehicles passing by, it was like having a private road for running. Her heart was soaring, and there was a spring in her step. She couldn't stop thinking of Gavin. She'd been ready to lead him upstairs to her bedroom the evening before, but he was right, they needed to know each other better. His amazing restraint had been admirable.

Lindsey was remarkably attracted to him, and it wasn't just his dark good looks, deep brown eyes she could get lost in, or the hard, muscular body. She had felt every ripple in his chest and arms when he'd gathered her against him last night. No, it wasn't only the physical attraction. It was much more. He was funny, spontaneous, sincere, and had an extraordinary mind. There was a certain chemistry between them—something electric.

She smiled when she thought back to when she'd looked up to find him standing by her table in the pub. And he'd actually all but admitted his plan to "lie in wait" until she showed up one night. Was that flattering or was it...something else?

She slowed her pace for the return journey

and began analyzing her feelings. Of course, the euphoria would wear off soon. In the meantime, she would relish the happy sensation. For a long time, she'd kept her emotions buttoned down. After Bill's betrayal and the divorce, she'd drawn into herself and concentrated on work and on making her company bigger and better. Was she ready now to break out of the workaholic mold and start experiencing life with someone else? A relationship?

The doubts were slipping in again. Did Gavin really care for her? What was it in his past that made him change his lifestyle so abruptly? Maybe he was putting the brakes on their budding romance because he was one of those guys who couldn't commit. Lord, she didn't really know this man. Was he really a secret mole for Brad Hansen? If so, he was an amazing actor. But, still. When she got home, she would make a list of things to find out about Gavin before this would go any further.

Gad, how anal could she be? A list? It wasn't like she could go to a store with a list of attributes and pick out the perfect man. An interesting concept though. She snorted. A list. Ha.

The mist was lifting, and the drizzle had stopped by the time she jogged down her lane. Suebear, the Trenton Farm's oldest horse, trotted close to the fence and greeted her with a string of nickering. The old girl had to be thirty if she was a day. She was wearing her summer fly blanket and fly mask as usual. Lindsey had thought the poor creatures were being blindfolded until the farm manager told her that they could see through the masks. It was a delight to have the view from her property out over the fields with all the wonderful hunter jumpers and equestrian event horses, but she really didn't understand the horse business. She just knew she could admire the beautiful horseflesh and she didn't have to muck out the stalls. The best of both worlds.

She slipped out of her running shoes and clothes by the washing machine, grabbed a cup of coffee, and was starting up stairs to get a quick shower when the phone rang. She looked at the caller ID. Gavin! What could he want at six-thirty in the morning?

"Hello?"

"Lindsey, hi, it's Gavin. Hope I'm not calling too early."

"No, it's fine. I just got back from my run. What's up?"

"I've been thinking about your case for part of the night, okay, most of the night, and I'd like to get together to talk with you some more this evening, if possible, about this guy, Brad. I have some ideas about his motive. Right now, I need to get to work, but wanted to check to see if I could stop in for an hour sometime after six?"

Lindsey hesitated just a moment. Maybe this relationship was moving along too fast. She felt like a yo-yo. Her emotions were tight as the string and her feelings seemed to be bouncing up and down. She took a deep breath and said, "Sure. I should be home by six-thirty. I'll make a big salad, and we can grill some shrimp. Nothing fancy. Then we can work on the case again."

"Great. I'll bring a baguette, some cheese, and a wine. See you then. Sorry I have to rush off." And the line went dead.

Lindsey stood there and looked at the receiver. Was this a lightning romance, or was it strictly business? Now she was not only questioning Brad's motives for the lawsuit, but also Gavin's motives for seeing her.

"We've been working with you for over eight months, and still no training camp." Rashid Abdul-Azeem's sneering face conveyed menace. Brad was startled by his intensity, but he couldn't show weakness. These Arab types got what they wanted with scare tactics, and they were all volatile assholes. Rashid could explode any minute like one of those roadside bombs. Brad mustered all the courage he could to keep his voice steady.

"I've brought the new prototype in counterterrorist maneuvers," he said rapidly, "along with the curriculum for teaching it to your recruits, and I also have all the blueprints finalized for the training center. It will include that mock urban area you wanted, and we have those additional layouts you requested."

"Yez." He drew out the word. "But *when* will you build the training camp, and *when* will I see the layouts?" Rashid voice had raised to a bellow.

Brad had come to Abu Dhabi to calm Rashid,

and he was anything but calm. Brad spoke in a low voice. "Let's take a look at the training center." Brad spread the site plan out on the table in the office of the carpet warehouse. The Mina Warehouse was in an industrial area off Twentieth Street close to the Iranian Souk. He had a car and driver waiting for him since this was not a part of town frequented by tourists. In fact, it made Brad edgy to be alone with Rashid in this isolated part of the city. He tried to focus on what Rashid was shouting now.

"You and that idiot lawyer of yours are just stringing us along. What about the woman who owns the company you were supposed to control by now? She's only a woman, and all women are whores." Rashid's derision was so thick, it was like a dense foul-smelling fog in the air.

Brad was at a loss. This guy was out of control. It crossed Brad's mind for the fiftieth time that he might be dealing with terrorists. Why was he fooling himself? Legitimate businessmen didn't pay their contacts in cash deposited in a numbered account in the Cayman Islands. Now Rashid was pacing and throwing his hands up in large gestures. His eyes looked wild. God, he must be on something.

"I'll have the front company, her company, in a matter of weeks now, and we can start construction. The lawsuit to cripple her company is proceeding as anticipated. It's really only a matter of weeks," he repeated. "Soon." He tried to use a soothing voice and exude confidence. This guy was crazy.

"Why don't you simply get rid of her?" he hissed.

"Relax, Rashid, the camp will happen."

"You just don't get it. It's not just the training for our agents so they can counter the new anti-terrorist techniques. We need a lot more intelligence from you and from this 'woman' and her company." Rashid spoke with such vehemence when he said *woman*. These Arabs must hate women. On the contrary, Brad thought that women could be manipulated into doing what men, obviously the smarter sex, wanted, but he also thought women were useful in a softer and more sensual way. The thought of sensual women made his mind drift off to the alluring Ms. Lindsey Kelly. What a babe.

Rashid was shouting again. "We want to start an offensive, a jihad, against the infidels! My *Mudabbir* is counting on me. Me! My name, Abdul-Azim, means 'Servant of the Mighty.' Now I must prove myself. You must build the training camp. Now!"

How much longer could he take this abuse? Rashid was getting scary. Brad had to remain in command of the situation. He smiled deprecatingly and spoke in a quiet voice again. "Azim, we'll work this out very soon. Once we have control of STLS, we'll be able to begin a sham training center near Dubai, while we're building the operational training camp in Oman. You'll see. It won't be long."

Rashid slammed his hand down onto the table with a bang. "You ass. Don't placate me. I need results, or you can forget about any more money

being transferred to your account in the Caymans."
Rashid's smirk coupled with the manic look in his
eyes had transformed him into a demented looking
fanatic.

Brad was beginning to think he might be in
over his head. He'd call Joe Johnson tomorrow. His
lawyer would know what to do.

"Just calm down Rashid. I'll be back to you tomorrow about the revised timeline."

Gavin was working in the shop office on the
inventory program. Why had he ever agreed to set
this up? Surely it wouldn't take him too long. He
just didn't have his heart in it. His brain was filled
with all the *what ifs* on the Brad Hansen business.
Obviously, Brad was doing something that wasn't
quite Kosher. How could he be using Lindsey's
company to somehow get money—big money? He
wouldn't be going to this much trouble and expense
for peanuts. He kept mulling over his theories.

"How's the programming coming?" Jeff asked
with a wide grin. That brought Gavin back to the
task at hand. Did Jeff know this was like torture?
Gavin might prefer bamboo slivers driven under his
fingernails.

"Fine. I should have the entire inventory entered and the work order program up and running
by next week."

"That's terrific, Gavin. I couldn't have figured
this mess out in a million years."

"Oh, you might have been able to get it together in a hundred years." They both laughed.

Jeff cleared his throat. "Remember, tonight is the Thursday Twilight Testing. You can still do it, can't you?"

"Damn, Jeff, I forgot and made an appointment for tonight. Is there anyone else that could take your place?"

Jeff's normally cheery face set in a frown. "Well, no. It'd be pretty hard to get a replacement this late in the day."

"Let me try. I'll ask Eddie. Would that be alright?"

"I guess. But Gavin could see he wasn't pleased.

Gavin caught Eddie at lunch and asked him to sub for him at the Twilight Testing.

"Gee, Gav, I just can't do it tonight. I gotta take Momma and the twins to get new sneakers for soccer. Momma, ya know, my wife, Kate, likes for all these family things to be done together. I'm a real family man these days. I used to play around with other gals or go drinking with my buddies, but once I found the Lord, I knew that wasn't right. I go home every night on time now. It's made me and Momma much happier."

Gavin thought this was TMI, but he just said, "Well, maybe next time."

Gavin asked Jimmy next. He was also tied up. Bordering on panic, he approached Benny. "How does some incredible overtime sound to you?" Hopefully, this was the right spin on the situation.

"What'cha need Gavin?" Benny's eyes were flat, and he looked at him blankly.

"I was hoping you would be available to close up for the Twilight Testing session this evening." Gavin was crossing his fingers.

"Well, sure. I'm not doing nothing tonight. I only done it one other time. It were last year. Can you show me agin what I need to do?" Gavin was cringing inside as good old boy, Benny, slaughtered the King's English, but Gavin knew he was a super mechanic. Who cared? At least he was communicating.

"It's not too hard, and I'll be here the first half hour." So, Gavin went through all the procedures. Benny would be alright.

Gavin had everything organized for Benny. He made sure all the participants had signed the release and reviewed all the emergency procedures with Benny and the EMT who was on duty. The evening event was well underway, and Gavin was driving beneath the front gate sign at Laurel Glen by five forty. He ran by his bungalow, showered, changed, and was out of the door by five after six. He would make it to Lindsey's on time if he didn't get behind a hay truck. Recently, they had been out in force on the small country lanes. It must be time for the first cutting. Musing on farming techniques? Gavin smiled to himself. He might become a country boy, yet. He was nearing the turn for the road that went through Millwood when he remembered what he'd promised.

"Damn! The wine and baguette."

He turned around in the next drive and sped back to the Food Saver in Berryville. Not exactly gourmet, but it would have to do. Gavin parked in the "Mothers with Infants" spot, ran into the store, decided no basket, picked up an Argentine Malbec, not a half-bad wine as he recalled, grabbed a loaf of the Artisan bread in the deli along with a small round of Camembert, checked out quickly in the express lane, and was back in the car in seven minutes. Hell, now he would be late.

»Chapter Eight«

Gavin stood on the flagstone steps clutching a bottle of wine in one hand and a paper bag with the French bread and cheese in the other. He awkwardly transferred the wine to the bag hand and knocked. The door opened almost immediately, and Lindsey stood in the doorframe, her hair shining in the pale light. He felt something tight uncoil within him.

"Sorry, I'm late. It's a long story." He smiled and shrugged his shoulders.

"Not to worry. I ran late, too. I got here about thirty minutes ago, changed, and just got back downstairs to start the prep for the salad." She led him through to the kitchen.

"I'll help chop, or I can start the grill instead, if you want."

"Why not open that bottle of wine and I'll get out the glasses. Surely the wine will inspire us to excellence in the culinary arts." Lindsey chuckled.

Gavin was surprised Lindsey was in such a playful mood. He cut the foil from around the top of the bottle and twisted the opener into the cork. Without her prompting he warmed the Camembert in the microwave a minute while he sliced the French bread. Pouring the wine and placing his handiwork on the center island, he motioned to his offering. "Voila! Instant hors d'oeuvres."

"Ooh, what talent!"

"At your service, my lady." Gavin made a

grand gesture with his hand and bowed.

They stood on either side of the granite kitchen island, and Lindsey used the cheese knife to lather the warm Camembert on to a piece of the baguette.

"Mmm, this is yummy," Lindsey commented while she licked the drip of warmed cheese from her finger. "Maybe a salad will be enough after this delicious cheese."

"Fine with me." Gavin ran a hand through his hair. Watching Lindsey lick the cheese from her fingertip and gazing into her sparkling blue eyes had his temperature rising. All he wanted for dinner was her. Lindsey smoothed the cheese on another hunk of bread, then looked up directly into Gavin's eyes and smiled. Did she have any idea the effect she was having on him? It was enough to drive a man wild. With a start he realized she was speaking to him.

"The office was relatively uneventful today. No new developments from the Brad Hansen quarter."

"Oh, yeah, Brad. I've been thinking about that scoundrel." The atmosphere was still light between them. "I didn't mean to sound secretive or short this morning, Lindsey, I was only in a rush to get to the shop on time and didn't have a moment to explain. I think I've been behind all day. Sorry again for being late."

"Well, I've been in suspense about your take on Brad's motive. What have you figured out?" Lindsey sat on one of the barstools at the kitchen island.

"It's fairly obvious; Brad is up to no good. Since I had to be in the shop office all day working on the inventory program, I had time to look up a few things on the internet over my lunch hour."

"Detective work?" Lindsey was still teasing.

"Yes, on the infamous Mr. Brad Hansen. There's quite a bit about his career when he was with the Navy SEALs, then with two other defense contractors before being hired by STLS, but nothing current. It's like he disappeared from the security industry when you fired him a year ago."

"Well, I can attest to the fact that he hasn't disappeared. He may not be working, but he is alive and kicking, and a royal pain in my rear end."

Lindsey sipped her wine. Gavin could see she was holding it on her tongue before she swallowed. He got a glimpse of cleavage as she leaned low across the island to pick up the bottle. She studied the label intently, then gazed up at him. "This is so-o-o velvety and rich." She stretched out the word *so* for several beats. "What is it?" Lindsey ran her tongue slowly over her lips.

Gavin pulled out one of the other barstools tucked under the end of the island. He had to sit down before his knees gave way. This woman was driving him crazy. "It's one I like from Argentina."

"Great choice. I love a smooth Malbec." She set the bottle down between them and took the other stool. "Okay, back to business. Brad, the creep." She grimaced.

"Yeah. The way he dropped off the defense

contracting radar made me start wondering. With no visible means of support, what's he using for money?"

"Maybe he saved a lot of the exorbitant salary I paid him." Lindsey spread another slice of the bread with the silky cheese and made one for Gavin, too. She slid it toward him on a cocktail napkin. He bit into the crunchy bread, and the cheese slid across his tongue leaving a rich satisfying taste in his mouth. Smiling, Lindsey crossed one leg over the other, showing a lot of tanned muscular thigh in the process. She seemed oblivious to his discomfiture, or was she trying to seduce him on purpose?

"Not enough for all the travel he's been doing." Gavin was having a hard time concentrating on the conversation.

"How did you find out he'd been traveling?" Lindsey sat up straighter and rolled her shoulder to her neck, tilting her head in a quizzical look.

Gavin felt ridiculously proud of his information gathering skills. "I have a friend, who shall remain anonymous, in a government agency, that shall remain nameless, who has access to flight records and manifests. Either there is another Brad Hansen from the DC area with a business in Dubai, or *our* Brad Hansen is finding it necessary to fly to the United Arab Emirates about once every ten days. *And* he goes Business Class."

"Oh, yeah. That's expensive. About four or five thousand dollars for each trip expensive! And that's for the flights alone, and then he would have to pay for hotels, meals, and transportation." Lindsey sipped her wine, catching an errant drip with her tongue and pulling it into her mouth.

His mind wandered to Lindsey's lively tongue. He had to concentrate. "He definitely has a compelling interest in that part of the world, and my guess is that it is not totally above board." Gavin reached for another piece of the crusty bread.

Lindsey reached over and caught Gavin's wrist. "How can we find out?"

Her soft warm touch sent his heart racing. "What?"

"You know. How can we discover if Brad is doing something illegal or, at the very least, nefarious?" Her sly look told him she was teasing him again, but he was dead serious.

"I've been thinking about that. It would be expensive, but we could hire a couple of private investigators that would work as a team. One here in the Washington area and a partner working in Dubai."

"I can't imagine there's a PI firm with offices in both Washington and Dubai." Lindsey smirked. She drew a happy face with a drip of wine on the counter.

"There are two, actually." Lindsey looked up at Gavin, wide-eyed and mouth slightly agape. He knew he was the one grinning from ear to ear, now.

"How did you do this, and how much are you talking about"

"Two questions, two answers. Internet,

mostly, and probably a minimum of twenty thousand dollars, but it could be more, much more."

Lindsey's shoulders slumped, and her demeanor finally turned serious. "It might be worth it if we can figure out why he's in the Middle East and what that has to do with his lawsuit against me."

"My thoughts exactly. The motive behind the lawsuit must be connected to all these trips out of the country, and it must involve a great deal of money. Of course, he may get millions from you, if he wins, but that's not very likely. He may simply be trying to wear you down personally and at the same time weaken your company, since STLS is hemorrhaging money while you're fighting the legal battle. Right?"

"You definitely have my attention."

"What we need to determine is what his advantage is in taking over your business? I really think that's his main goal."

Lindsey was silent. She looked past him as if in thought. Then she spoke slowly, "As a front for something less than legal, in some way." She paused, those creases between her eyes deepening. "But to what purpose?"

"The motive has to be money and there's one way to find out."

"Okay, yes." She nodded. "I want to hire the private investigators." Lindsey sounded convinced.

"Alright, I'll take care of setting up a meeting tomorrow with Gary and Marisa at the Grant Agency."

With the decision to hire the investigators behind them, Gavin sensed Lindsey's mood change from worried to resolved. She smiled and blew out her breath, staring at the happy face she'd made with the wine on the granite counter.

"Penny for your thoughts," he said.

"I was thinking how relieved I am by being proactive. That sounds like such a dumb business term way to explain an emotion, but I'm a person that feels most comfortable with action. I'm excited that we have a plan."

The *we* wasn't lost on Gavin. "You know I'm excited, too. I'm happy to be able to help you. Here's to unraveling the mystery of Brad Hansen." He raised his wineglass to Lindsey's, and they clinked.

"Okay, Gavin. How do you know how to do all this stuff?" She laughed. "*Stuff* is a technical term, of course."

Gavin tried to explain in a few sentences. "I want to be completely truthful but revealing all this is hard for me. There are things in everyone's life that aren't for publication, and no one likes to examine every one of life's choices too closely."

He sighed deeply then took a long slow breath. "I'm an attorney who graduated from Harvard Law, practiced in the Richmond, Virginia's Public Defender Offices for two years, worked for Carter, Clooney & Davis, in Washington, DC, for about ten years, and quit the legal profession thirteen months ago to lead a simple life as a mechanic. Laurel Glen hired me about six months ago, during the off-season. That's why I'm a new face at the track this year."

He felt almost lightheaded and realized he'd told his entire tale without taking a breath. He looked up and saw that Lindsey was just staring at him as if he had grown a set of horns. Had he made a colossal blunder?

"Oh," was all she said. Then after a moment, "But why did you quit being a lawyer?"

"It's a long story."

"You said that earlier about being late. Is this a longer story?"

"Yes." He knew the look on his face was grim. So, she wisely let the topic be.

Lindsey sensed Gavin was uncomfortable, so she suggested they take the last of their wine to the arbor. Dinner was the furthest thing from her mind, but she looked up at Gavin and said, "Shall I grill the shrimp?"

"I'm fine for now."

The evening had cooled, and the patio area was a pleasant respite. The sun was just kissing the top of the Blue Ridge, and the shafts of light shimmering through the wisteria vines created an intricate pattern against the wall of the house. The blooms were no longer at their peak, but the cool shade of the vines was inviting.

They sat once again side-by-side, with their backs resting on the log structure. Gavin reached for Lindsey's hand and held it gently but didn't look at her.

"I like to help people. Once I was naïve, more idealistic, and I believed that I could save the poor and oppressed from being penalized unjustly. I can't believe I was ever so stupid." Gavin sighed. Lindsey could tell this was difficult for him. He gave the impression of a balloon slowly deflating. She reached up with one hand and tried to smooth the worry lines from around his eyes.

"Surely, you still have some faith that you can help, or you wouldn't be lending me a hand." Lindsey was then silent. She realized that nothing she could say would take away the hurt that was clearly in his face.

"The simplest way to explain it is to say, I believed in a guy I was sworn to defend. I got him acquitted, then he committed the same crime again, but even a more heinous act. It could have been prevented if I had not done such a bang-up job defending him originally."

"Wait, you're saying you were able to overturn a charge against a guy you were convinced was innocent, who later committed a related crime, and now *you* feel responsible? Gavin, you're not responsible for someone else's actions."

Gavin leaned forward, his elbows on his knees, and buried his head in his hands. "A little girl is dead because of me," he said so softly Lindsey almost didn't hear.

Lindsey was stunned into silence. She didn't know what to say, so she said nothing. She held

Gavin's hand, grasping it fiercely, hoping to give him strength. Then wrapped her arms around his shoulders and buried her head against his neck. Finally, she said quietly, "Thank you for telling me."

Gavin pulled away from her comforting hug and turned to her, a warm look in his eyes. He rubbed her check with his thumb. "Thank you for listening. I haven't been able to voice those feelings to anyone."

"You can't keep blaming yourself."

"How can I stop? One little girl is damaged for life, and another one is dead."

"But you weren't responsible for the first one."

"The mother of that child will never forgive me. He molested her child, and I got him off!" His voice was rising.

"But you didn't do it. You were just doing your job."

"God! Doing my job. Like one of Hitler's henchmen killing the Jews? I can't forgive myself," he yelled and beat his fist on the table.

Lindsey had sleepless nights worrying about her company. How much worse must it be feeling you're responsible for a child's death?

They were both quiet for a time, their heads apart, resting against the wall. Their emotions were laid bare, raw. Then she finally said, "You'll never be able to change the past. I'm not suggesting you'll ever forget, but its history. Move forward."

He pushed her away and looked straight into

her eyes. "I just don't want to ever make that kind of mistake again." From the pained look in his eyes, Lindsey could tell the defense of a man who had turned out to be a monster wasn't in the past for him at all. It was right there in his face. It was the present for him.

"C'mon, we all have regrets," Lindsey said in a gentle tone. "Get a grip."

Lindsey could see the anger flash in his eyes. He sucked in a quick irritated breath, "So, I'm supposed to forget it ever happened? I'm sick of hearing platitudes from my friends. My actions caused the death of an innocent little girl. And now I'm supposed to 'move forward,' 'can't change the past,' 'get a grip?' Well, that's easier said than done, to use another cliché."

"God, no. I didn't mean that." She took in a deep breath through her nose. "I'm just saying, oh, I don't know what I'm saying. I only want to somehow ease your pain."

Gavin looked stricken. She could see that he wanted the pain to go away but was unable to forget the part he played in this horrible incident. Lindsey felt she had gone too far, but he clasped her to him breathing unevenly. "You make me mad as hell, but you're an amazing woman and telling me the truth, too."

"I'm sorry, Gavin. I had no right." Lindsey said breathlessly.

"You said what I needed to hear. There's just so much pain and regret."

He held her for a long moment. His clean, spicy scent flowed over her. His firm body was pressed against hers, and she was unaccountably aroused. She felt so connected to him after they had both revealed their innermost nightmares to each other. Her hands began to move smoothly down his back, and she arched toward him. He stroked her shoulders and his hands began to explore her body. He kissed the top of her ear and his lips began to travel down her neck.

"You're melting me with your touch." She stopped and leaned back against the logs. Her body trembled. She could feel the warmth spread all over her skin, as her pulse quickened.

Gavin sucked in a deep breath. "I want you, Lindsey." He smoothed his hand over her hair and down her back. He drew her to her feet and held her in a tender embrace. He wasn't rushing her. Gavin just held her and spoke to her in a low tone.

"I usually take what I want," his voice was raspy, heated, "but in the past, it wasn't this important. I've never felt this deeply connected to a woman."

Lindsey leaned against his hard chest, and he held her closer. The warmth of his embrace couldn't completely dispel the fear of being hurt again. Could she trust this kindhearted, caring man?

Gavin continued to just hold her and caress her back. Lindsey could feel his arousal as he pressed her closer. He pulled back from her and gazed into her eyes. There was an unmistakable expression on his face of such longing. Lindsey tilted her head back. His kiss was urgent and deep, leaving little uncertainty about his intentions.

It had been months, no years, since she'd felt this rush, the overwhelming warm glow, this want. She pushed slightly away from him, took his hand and led him toward the stairs. All doubts were gone. She knew this was right.

They both began frantically shedding their shoes and clothes as they ascended the stairs, and by the time they reached her bedroom, passion was consuming reason. Lindsey unbuckled his belt and unzipped his jeans. He stepped out of them with a sense of urgency while he released the hooks on her bra and threw it aside.

Lindsey was shaking. How long had it been since she'd been in bed with a man?
Her brain was no longer functioning on an intelligent level. She wanted this man with all the animal lust of a lioness in heat.

Gavin eased her back onto the bed, throwing the quilt and a pillow haphazardly to the floor. He drew back from her enough to look at her. His voice had darkened and had a low gravelly quality when he murmured, "God, you're beautiful, Lindsey."

She was lost in this man, and she knew her heart was in her eyes. He kissed her gently at first, then with an intense passion. Lindsey responded to the heat with crazed delight. All her past frustrations and wild desire collided in a storm of emotion.

Her hands didn't seem to be under her control. She touched every part of his naked body. She ran her fingers through his luscious dark thick hair and continued down his muscular back to his firm buttocks. Oh, he felt so good.

"Mmmmm." Gavin was making her feel on fire from her head to her toes. His lips moved from her now swollen mouth down her neck to the nub of one of her breasts. He first rubbed over this with his thumb pulling it to attention. Licking his tongue around the nipple, he drew her into his mouth, suckling gently. She pressed toward him and a warm tingly flutter began in her stomach and began to move lower. Then his mouth was on hers again searing her lips, and the blood began to surge through her veins. He was at once tender, passionate, begging. Her pulse was pounding, and the wave of heat slipped down between her legs. She was slick with desire.

Lindsey moved under him and pulled him to her, kissing him with an ardor that surprised her. His hands were caressing every part of her body, and she was gasping with the pleasure. She wanted him, needed him inside her.

Gavin mumbled against her neck, "Condom?"

Lindsey's cloud of lust cleared enough to motion toward the bedside table. She fleetingly worried Gavin would think she was prepared because she frequently entertained this way. Then his mouth again found her breast, and she didn't care.

Gavin pulled open the top drawer, picked up

one of the three small foil packets she'd placed there earlier. He ripped it open with one hand and his teeth, rolled it quickly into place and to Lindsey's relief hardly missed a beat.

Lindsey was grasping Gavin and guiding him into her. Her body had never been so responsive. She moved against him and the pure pleasure of it sent electrical impulses coursing from her brain down through her body. She ran her hands over his sweat-soaked back and wrapped her legs around his hips. The present lost all meaning as she rocked with him to a music older than time.

"Gavin, yes, oh, don't stop." Her orgasm swept her to uncharted heights. She felt his arm muscles trembling from supporting his weight, and heard Gavin's hoarse words in her ear, "Oh, Lindsey, Lindsey," as his body shuddered, and he lay still against her, pulsing inside her.

They lay entwined for a time, luxuriating in the wonderful sensations they had shared. Lindsey's body, glimmering with perspiration, still tingled and every part of her was sensitive to his casual touch. He trailed the back of his hand down her arm and up again to her shoulders, neck, and down between her breasts. She stroked his cheek and with a throaty laugh, whispered, "I know this sounds corny, but that was the best ever."

Gavin chuckled softly. "Just wait." And when she opened her mouth to protest, his mouth closed over hers. His strong arms enveloped her, and his fingers stroked every inch of her with a magical effect. His kisses were soft then demanding. His tongue thrust into her mouth while his fingers probed in the thatch of curls between her legs, expertly stroking. Then his hands were on her breasts and his kisses were moving down her body. His teeth nipped at her navel. Moving lower, his lips and tongue licked and sucked the small sensitive core of her. He gripped her buttocks and her hands were wild and tangled in his hair, unknowingly encouraging his incredible ministrations. Lindsey moaned, her head whipping back and forth on the pillow.

"Now, please, now." She clutched at him convulsively.

Gavin continued to tease and fondle her clit until she was out of her mind. This was pure ecstasy. With another orgasm screaming through the top of her head, her legs stiffened. She arched up to receive his gift of pleasure and cried out in transported joy. Gavin quickly moved up to embrace her, plunging into her anew. They sought each other's lips in another surge of emotion. Finally, they curled into each other, collapsing in complete exhaustion.

Later he lazily queried, "Any better?"

Lindsey laughed. "You've ruined me for anyone else. That was fabulous." And she snuggled closer.

When Lindsey woke at dawn, Gavin was gone.

»Chapter Nine«

As Lindsey was heading out for her morning run in the Virginia countryside, Brad was just finishing a leisurely late lunch on the terrace of the Anar Restaurant overlooking Abu Dhabi Bay at the Emirates Palace Hotel. He'd had an excellent slow cooked stew with sumptuous aromatic spices paired with a nicely chilled Sauvignon Blanc. He could get used to this life, he thought, if he could get everything worked out with Rashid. The stew had tasted wonderful. He'd savored every bite in the opulent surroundings of the dining room, but the image of an irate Rashid remained. When he walked back to his Khaleej Deluxe Suite, the meal seemed to form a leaden lump in his stomach. In his room, he dialed Joe Johnson's number in Washington.

"Yes?" Joe answered, sounding a bit guarded. "Joe Johnson, here."

"Hi, Joe, it's Brad. I'm calling from Abu Dhabi. Sorry it's so early."

"Geez, Brad. It *is* early. Couldn't it wait until I get to the office?"

"No," he said shortly. "I'm worried. Rashid is getting agitated, almost fanatical in his demands. I'm not sure how to handle him. I knew you would have good advice." Brad paced up and down in the well-appointed suite.

"It was your idea to get mixed up with those Arab nuts."

"Fuck that, Joe. You agreed it was a good idea to deal with this group. We provide the information and an accurate training facility model and we, that's you and me, *we* get a lot of money. I'm the one taking all the risks here."

"Not exactly." Joe sounded irritated. "Besides keeping our little friend, Lindsey, occupied with the lawsuit, *I'm* the one with the contacts in the government who made it possible to get our hands on the building layouts we needed for the replica facilities. I've got the State Department's already, but I'm still working on the FBI's. And *I'm* the one who will get the blueprint of the Standard Embassy Design that State will use in training. My ass is on the line, too."

"Okay, okay, but I need something else that will appease this asshole, Rashid. The curriculum for the anti-terrorist maneuvers isn't enough. What do you think we can give him?" Sweat trickled down Brad's face from his temples and from above his lip even though he had set his room thermostat to sixty degrees.

"Well, it would be dumb to give them the layouts to the two agencies' training facilities. We'd never see another penny, and, anyway, that's when we ultimately step over the line. I'm not sure I want to spend the rest my life in prison for treason if we're caught. The Standard Embassy Design that State Department is moving toward would be even more volatile in the wrong hands. State is even building a mock embassy to those new specs, someplace in southern Virginia, so they can do their Capstone Exercise at the end of all their agents' high-threat training."

"But what can they do with those layouts? It won't make them stronger or smarter to train in a replica facility."

"Damn! You *are* a stupid ass. If this group ever wanted to attack those agencies' facilities, it might help just a little to know the floorplans." Brad could hear the sarcasm dripping through the phone. "They would know where to find people when they're most vulnerable. And that's just for starters. If Rashid and his friends ever get their hands on the Standard Embassy Design, the terrorists would have a huge advantage by knowing in advance just where to hit."

"God, I didn't think of that. At the beginning, Rashid seemed like a reasonable guy. He said he only wanted to help his poor country develop a respectable force to keep the bigger countries in the Persian Gulf area from gobbling them up."

"And you believed him?"

"C'mon, Joe, he praised the United States for being so powerful and wealthy. He said he wanted to help his country be strong, like his friends, the Americans. Strong enough to withstand invasion." Brad stood looking out the window at his nine-hundred-dollar-a-day view. He suddenly felt pathetic. Who was he kidding? Rashid and his colleagues were thugs at best, and what he didn't want to acknowledge, but was probably true, they were terrorists.

Joe was yelling into the phone. "What bull-shit!"

Brad steadied himself. "Okay, probably bull-shit, but that's not why I called." He took a deep breath. "Yesterday he started to scare me. He's changed, and it's made me nervous."

"Changed how?" Joe's voice went up an octave.

"Now, he's mentioned a jihad." Brad ran his free hand through his thinning hair and gripped the phone with white knuckles.

"Shit, Brad, did he actually use the word 'jihad?'"

"Yes, and infidels. That's us, right?"

"This is getting way out of control. Let me think about it."

Brad looked at the phone with shock as all he heard was the dial tone.

"You're early," Mary said as Lindsey walked through the glass doors of the office at seven forty-five. "I don't even have your coffee made yet."

Lindsey knew she was grinning. "I was Wonder Woman on my run this morning, and the traffic was fairly light on the drive in. Every traffic signal turned green as I approached. It's just an amazing day."

"Gad, what's gotten into you? Your feet are barely touching the floor and your head's in the clouds. What did you do last night, get laid?" Mary laughed while filling the coffee maker with water.

"Yes, as a matter of fact, and it was incredible." Lindsey was still beaming. "I took your advice and decided to get to know Gavin, you know the mechanic from Laurel Glen."

"You're kidding me. That was fast." Mary made a cup of Earl Grey for herself using the Instant Hot at the sink.

"No, really, I'm not kidding. He actually sought me out at the pub the other night and it turns out he's, in fact, an attorney." Lindsey ran her hand along the top of one of the leather wing-backs in the reception area and waltzed around it.

"A lawyer?"

"Yes, a corporate defense attorney."

"Wait, wait, wait, why would he be a mechanic at Laurel Glen when he's really an attorney?"

Shrugging, Lindsey swayed back and forth with her grin widening. "He said his life had gotten too hectic and he decided to simplify. But who knows?" Lindsey wasn't ready to reveal Gavin's raw emotional confidences. "Anyway, we got to talking about my Brad problem while we ate at Hunter's Head. He has an unbelievable mind, graduated from Harvard Law, and he's thought up a few things we can do about the Brad situation."

"Whoa. Hold on, Lindsey. You're saying you met this mechanic that you originally thought was a smart-ass. It turns out he's really a hot-shot lawyer and he's swooping in to save you from evil Brad and, oh, by the way, also seducing you?"

"That about sums it up." Lindsey was still glowing.

"Would all the optimistic euphoria have anything to do with the *incredible* sex part?" Mary, always the pragmatist, sipped her tea.

"Well, maybe. It was, and I repeat, was a most remarkable evening."

"If you use any more 'marvelous and astonishing' type words to describe this guy, I'm going to throw up."

"Hey, don't make fun of me! It was your idea." Lindsey skipped around the reception desk. Luckily, the receptionist wouldn't arrive for another few minutes. She knew she was acting anything but normal, but she couldn't help herself. Mary was looking at her wide-eyed with her mouth open in an O-shape.

"I've been your good friend for years and I've never seen you like this." Mary poured coffee into the *Head Honcho* cup and handed it to Lindsey. "Let's sit down, if you think you can stop hovering, and you can tell me all about it."

"Mary, you're terrific. Let's go to my office." They walked back to the large corner suite with windows looking out over the Potomac. The view of the Lincoln Memorial, Washington Monument, and the Capitol Building that held the government of the most powerful country in the world, never ceased to inspire Lindsey. "I feel good, Mary. Just sharing my worries with Gavin has lifted a load off my shoulders. What seemed, only yesterday, to be insurmountable problems, seem today solvable. Does that sound silly?"

"No, not at all. I'm glad to have that self-confident, intelligent, positive boss back on the job."

✹

"Hey, Gavin, I don't get these work orders. What is management trying to find out? This just doesn't seem like something George Trenton would want." Jeff looked over the printout, and his eyebrows drooped over his eyes in a frown. "It must be some bean-counter in the finance department pulling the strings. Are they trying to find out if we're working or not?"

"No, I don't think that's it. I imagine they're using the figures for some kind of cost analysis."

"Well, just as long as they're not spying on us. I can tell by lookin' that all the guys are working, and pretty hard, too. There's a lot of wear and tear on the company vehicles, machinery, and then those damn karts. The work is endless."

Gavin could see Jeff wasn't happy. "I wouldn't worry. Darrell, in accounting, told me management wants to keep track of where all the parts go and needs the info for the government contracts. If the big guys in government auditing ever swoop down on Laurel Glen, all the costs will be examined meticulously. You know, they'll want to know which cars, what machinery, which parts for each class. Also, this way management will know when it's time to replace something instead of repairing it."

"Gee, I can tell them that without all this

fancy, new-fangled computer stuff. I know when a backhoe is falling apart and needs to be replaced, or if I can simply put it back together again with a minimum of fuss and expense. I just don't get it." Jeff blew out a breath through his teeth. He looked exasperated and kept the scowl on his face.

"Change is hard, but this might help us know when we need to reorder a certain part. After a couple months of tracking all the parts we'll have an idea about how many of each part we should keep on hand at all times. We'll order fewer times, and have what accountants call, just-in-time inventory. Not too much or too little."

"How do you know all these things, Gav?" Jeff's voice was high and whiny. Not the usual jolly Jeff.

Gavin chuckled. "Oh, I guess I've been listening to Darrell too much. You know he's down here several times a day helping get the system set up."

"Yea, yea. I've seen him. Are you sure he's not in the shop just to check up on us? Nosing around to see if we're working?"

"Nah. Don't worry so much, Jeff. I'm certain management is pleased with how you run the shop. You get everything out and ready on time and keep the wheels rolling, don't you?"

"Yeah," he grumbled. "Okay. Go ahead and get the system set up so that it isn't too hard for my guys to do all this paperwork shit." And he stomped off.

Gavin wasn't going to let Jeff's rare but obviously pissy mood upset him. He'd entered most of the thousand and one parts into the system, and he and Darrell had created a relatively easy method to track the data. Each work order would note the mechanic, vehicle, service performed, parts used, cost of parts, time it took to do each job, and if the vehicle was used for a specific training class. Jeff was right though. Creating exact time periods for certain service jobs was next to impossible. A simple oil change could transform into a complete engine overhaul when the mechanic got into it. Oh, well, he'd have the system up and running by the middle of next week. Then he could get back to working on the cars like the rest of them.

The one advantage of working in the office was that while he waited for different modules of the program to download, he had some time to work on Lindsey's "project."

Of course, Lindsey herself was constantly on his mind. Last night had been...well, indescribable. It wasn't just about the sex, though it had been the best he'd ever experienced. It'd been their confiding in each other. By telling her his deepest sorrow, it had lifted something off his shoulders. He felt they could overcome anything together. He wanted to share everything in his life with her. He'd never felt quite this way about any other woman he'd known. She was warm, funny, level-headed, serious, and sexy as hell. Complicated, yes complicated, but he would take on complicated if that's what it took to be with Lindsey Kelly.

Over lunch he called the investigation agency and made an appointment for Lindsey and himself to meet with a representative at one-thirty tomorrow. Since he didn't have to work the event this weekend at the track, Saturday was open. He hoped the timing worked for Lindsey.

Gavin thought about calling her but decided to wait and call her cell phone when they both were driving home. He was hoping she would want to have dinner with him again. Maybe actually eat this time, before anything else developed. After all, they needed to keep up their strength. He smiled to himself, again remembering the evening before. Yes, that was the best sex he'd ever had. She inspired him to greatness. And he chuckled again.

"What's so funny?" Benny startled him out of his reverie.

"Hey, how'd it go last night? I gotta thank you for taking my place."

"Everthin' was smooth. All five cars stayed to the end. Guess it's 'cause them're gittin' ready for the race this weekend. You workin' the SCCA race?"

"No, but I'm on for the Vintage Races next weekend. Can't wait to see all the old classic race cars. What's it like? Do they really race, or is it just a beauty pageant?"

"Some of the racers really race flat out in them oldies, but others are a bit afeared, since the classics weren't built with as much safety 'quipment."

"Should be fun to watch. I only hope we don't

have any wrecks. I've heard the vintage cars have a tendency to fly apart and leave the driver sitting on the pavement."

"You right there," Benny said with a grin that was missing several teeth. He gave Gavin a good-natured pat on the shoulder. "See ya later, and thanks for thinking of me for the overtime spot last night." Gavin didn't have the heart to tell him he'd been practically last on his list to take his place for the Twilight Testing. He prayed Benny wouldn't find out.

✤

Lindsey was nearly to the toll plaza for the Greenway when her cell phone rang.

The caller ID showed a number she didn't recognize. She usually didn't answer an unknown caller. She waited for voice mail to kick in.

"Hey, Lindsey, it's Gavin. Wanted to talk with you about our appointment with the investiga..."

Lindsey pressed the answer symbol on her phone and the Bluetooth hands free device picked-up. "Oh, Gavin, it's you. I'm on my way home."

"I thought you might not pick up since I've never called you from my cell phone before."

"Yeah, I wasn't sure. I didn't recognize your number. So, you were saying about the investigator?" She braked heavily as the traffic came to a standstill.

"Yes. Are you available to meet with them in the Tyson's Corner area tomorrow at one-thirty?"

"Sure. But aren't you going with me?" She felt

suddenly unsure. She was hoping he had wanted to be with her. The whole investigative angle was new to her. She hadn't even contemplated having her philandering husband, Bill, followed, ten years earlier, since in the long run it didn't matter how many women he had been with. The one she caught him with was one too many.

"I'll pick you up at eleven-thirty, and we can grab a bite on the way." There was a pause, then he added, "Of course, I was also thinking we might need to get together for a strategy session tonight."

Lindsey hooted. "So that's what you call what happened last night?"

Gavin clearly sputtered and laughed. She could hear the merriment in his voice. "We could eat a casual dinner first this time, strategize afterward."

She was wild with excitement, and her heart was racing. She didn't want to look too eager, so she took a deep, soothing breath. "I need to check my calendar, but it should be alright." She couldn't help the giggle that escaped her mouth.

He was laughing, too. "How's seven-thirty? I'll swing by, pick you up, and we could try The French Fox."

"Ooh, la, la, that's more than a casual dinner. How elegant. I'll be ready."

Gavin had dressed with care, deciding on gray slacks, a blue oxford shirt open at the neck, and a navy blazer. He had shined his brown loafers and, contrary to the usual *hunt country* casual dress code, wore socks. He'd picked up some Stargazer lilies at the small florist in Berryville, just as they were closing and was driving into Lindsey's drive at seven-twenty-eight.

This time Lindsey opened the door before he knocked. She stood holding the edge of the door with a saucy look on her face. "Oh, the lilies are beautiful. I love the way they smell." He held them out to her, and she took them from him. She immediately pulled them to her nose, inhaling deeply. Smiling back up at him, she said, "Would you like to come in for a minute?"

"Maybe a moment, to put the flowers in some water, but I made the reservation for seven-forty-five, so that I wouldn't be tempted to get sidetracked." Oh, he was *definitely* tempted. What a gorgeous woman, inside and out.

Lindsey smiled. "Come on in, and I'll find a vase in the kitchen." She was wearing a knee length swingy skirt with swirls in pinks and blues, a light blue silk tank that accentuated her curves, and an over blouse in a darker shade of the same silky fabric. Strappy sandals adorned her smooth, obviously recently pedicured feet. She was the picture of simple elegance.

He watched her fill the tall clear cylinder with water, efficiently clip the stems of the lilies, and slip them into the vase. Then she turned, and her lips curled into a smile, sending a shot of lust through him. She placed the arrangement in the middle of the breakfast table, burying her nose in the bouquet once more. "Umm, they really have a wonderful fragrance. I'll be able to enjoy them every morning while I get ready for work. Thank you for thinking of me."

He hadn't thought of much else since last night. This woman was positively under his skin. From sniffing the lilies Lindsey had a smudge of the rust colored pollen on her nose from a recently open bloom. Gavin reached out and brushed it off with his thumb. "Just a little pollen, my little honey bee," he said laughing.

With astounding control, he motioned back toward the front door. "Shall we go?" There was always later.

The French Fox was crowded with Middleburg tourists and a few locals. Gavin had arranged for an intimate table for two in a corner. "I haven't been here before, have you?" He offered Lindsey the basket of crusty French bread the waiter had set on the corner of the table.

Selecting an end piece from the basket, she said, "Only once, and I can't remember what I ordered, but the restaurant has a wonderful reputation for terrific food and impeccable service." She spread butter thickly on the slice.

Gavin was looking at the wine list. "Red or White?"

Lindsey perused the menu. "I'll probably have one of the veal or fish dishes. Ooh, this Veal Cordon

Bleu sounds luscious." Looking up at him she added, "So either red or white will be fine with me."

In a moment, the waiter appeared. "I'm Maurice. I'll be your waiter this evening. Would you like to hear tonight's specials?" his French accent not quite authentic to Gavin's ears.

"Sure," Lindsey and Gavin answered in unison. Maurice then went on to recite a long and amazing list of appetizers and main course offerings.

"Now, could I get you something to drink while you're making your decisions?"

Gavin didn't hesitate. "We'd like the Cloudy Bay Sauvignon Blanc to start."

"Very good choice, sir." And the waiter vanished into the kitchen.

Gavin crunched into a piece of the crispy French bread. "I had that wine at a wine tasting one time and really loved it."

"I think I've heard of Cloudy Bay. It's from New Zealand, isn't it?"

"Yes, the Marlborough region in the northern part of the South Island."

Maurice reappeared with the bottle of wine in one hand and his other arm wrapped around an ice bucket and stand. After arranging the stand and holder at a discreet distance from the table, he produced his trusty opener, expertly uncorked the chilled wine, poured a taste into Gavin's wine glass and stepped back.

Gavin performed the requisite ritual of swirling, inhaling the nose, holding the glass to the light to check the color, and taking a sip of the light amber liquid. Then nodding to Maurice. "Excellent."

When Maurice had once again slipped silently away, they both sipped the wine.

"Umm. There's a hint of grapefruit. I like it." Lindsey smiled, then said conspiratorially, "Do you think his name is really Maurice, or do you suppose the entire wait-staff assumes French sounding names for the job? He's certainly highly trained."

Gavin snickered. "I was just wondering the same thing. Even his accent sounds a little off. This is definitely a very posh establishment," he said with a wink.

Lindsey giggled, "Oh, here's a bit of useless trivia. Did you know that the word posh dates back to the late eighteen hundreds and is supposedly an acronym for 'port outward, starboard home?' It was describing the shipboard accommodations of wealthy British traveling to India."

"Why go to all that trouble?" Gavin was amused.

"The object was to keep their cabins out of the warm afternoon sun and afford a view of the land in passing. Now isn't that a little-known fact of no interest?"

"On the contrary, I like funny tales like that, and I'm especially delighted by the storyteller." He raised his wine toward her. He did love watching her expressive mouth and her sparkly eyes full of gaiety. It was good to see her happy rather than weighed down by worry.

The ever-efficient Maurice once again materialized beside their table. "Are you ready to order, miss?"

"Yes, thank you. I'll have the micro-greens salad and the sea bass special."

"And you, sir?"

"I'd like to start with the escargot in garlic butter, then the Caesar salad, and for the entrée, I'll have the Chilean sea bass, too."

"Very well." And he glided away.

"I'm hoping I can talk you into tasting at least one of my escargots so that we both have garlic breath." Gavin chuckled and reached across to stroke the back of Lindsey's hand that was rested on the table. Gavin was trying to keep the conversation light, but he could see a pensive look moving into Lindsey's face. "Know any more stories about word origins or better yet the history of clichés. I know one. *To break the ice*, which, of course, means to make a social situation easier. And the history of that is, ta-dah, from the nautical, meaning to create paths that allow ships to move through icy waters." Gavin tried for a breezy deliverance, but he could tell it wasn't working for Lindsey.

Lindsey reflexively flipped her hand over to capture Gavin's stroking one, grabbing on as if he were a buoy keeping her afloat and saving her from a sinking ship. "I'm sorry. I must not be very good company tonight."

"Not at all. I love being with you."

"My mood is so up and down. I'm swinging from one extreme to the other. Being with you makes me feel happy and light-hearted, but then I think about Brad and my business. The doubts seep in, and I feel anxious and upset."

"We can get through this. You've helped me so much, Lindsey, by being a good listener, so let me be a good listener for you."

"I hate to burden you with all my problems when you have an entire boatload yourself."

"Someone, and who could that be, recently reminded me that my problems are history, and now I just need to live in the present and look forward to the future. I get it that your challenges are in the present, Lindsey, so let me help you." Gavin's heart was full to bursting with feelings for this special woman. He wanted to take care of her, but he could never say that to her. In her core she was independent, confident, and downright feisty. He needed to help her find herself again. "We're gonna get this guy so he won't bother you anymore."

"Okay, no more thoughts or talk of Brad Hansen until tomorrow when we're on our way to the investigators' offices in Tyson's Corner." She forced a smile that Gavin noticed didn't quite reach her eyes.

The first course arrived, and Maurice poured more of the crystal-clear wine into each of their glasses. Lindsey ate one of the offered snails that Gavin held out to her on a fork with a piece of bread under it to catch any drips. She laughed at some of his comments, but he could tell she was still thinking about Brad Hansen. When the salads were placed in front of them Gavin decided to get her talking. "Tell me about your times living in Europe. What was your favorite country?"

"Italy!" she said without hesitation and with certainty. "Rome was incredible. I could have visited the Vatican Museum and the Sistine Chapel a hundred times. There's so much history and beauty in that city. And the food! Even their pizza is unique, laden with vegetables like artichokes." She seemed to warm to the subject and Gavin was relieved to see the tightness relax around her eyes and mouth. What a delicious mouth.

"There was a particularly terrific pizza vendor near the Trevi Fountain. Now that's a landmark that comes as a surprise. It's sort of tucked away in a nook where a few streets come together. You're walking down a small street, round a corner, and there it is. It's really quite astonishing."

Gavin sat, nearly transfixed, watching and listening to her animated chatter.

"Have you been to Italy?" she was saying.

"Yes, once. My brother and I backpacked through Italy for a summer during college."

"What were your best memories?" She took a small bite of her salad and gazed into Gavin's eyes.

"We didn't spend too much time in the cities, but I do remember that in Rome we stayed in a youth hostel near the Vatican and rented Vespas to help us cover the sights in fewer days. One night we were at a noted nightspot where a lot of American college students hung out. We talked for ages to these two girls we met there. It got so late that not many taxis were running by the time the four of us left the club. So, being only slightly inebriated, we offered to give them a ride to their hotel on our mopeds. We thought they were completely drunk when they told us they were staying in a nunnery in Vatican City."

Lindsey interjected with, "Get thee to a nunnery," and giggled.

"So, picture these two tipsy gals, clinging to our waists on the back of the tiny bikes. They directed us by hand signals to the right or left and in fifteen minutes we were pulling up in front of a locked door, with a sign over it that said 'Graymoor Sisters Convent.' One of them produced a huge key and unlocked the heavy door. They waved thanks and disappeared into the darkened entry. James and I laughed all the way back to our hostel and for days after, wondered if we'd had dates with a couple of nuns."

Lindsey was fully engaged in the conversation now. "Rome's fabulous, but isn't Florence wonderful, too?" She looked transported. "And my favorite hill town is San Gimignano, with all of its towers. I remember one night we ate at this small, cozy restaurant that was in a renovated wine cave of an ancient palazzo. The sommelier did a cool wine ceremony. My dad ordered a Chianti Classico. The sommelier brought us special glasses. He poured a dash of the wine in my dad's glass, swirled it around for twenty seconds or so, poured the small amount of wine into my glass, also spun it around, and finally poured the few drops not clinging to the inside of my glass into an ordinary glass that he put aside to be taken away. Our glasses were now prepared for the wine."

Gavin nodded. "I'm sure it made the wine taste much better."

"Oh, right—much better." And they both grinned.

The half-eaten salads were whisked away, and the main course set before them. They both continued to relate their entertaining experiences in Italy. Laughing, touching, talking, and ignoring the food. Gavin noticed the knowing look on the experienced Maurice's face as he silently removed the remnants of the meals not being eaten by them. It said I've seen couples in love before. Go for it man!

»Chapter Ten«

Gavin stayed the night with Lindsey at *Sticks and Stones*. After the initial fevered love-making, they slept curled like spoons in her fourposter bed. Lindsey felt completely safe in Gavin's arms and slept without dreaming.

She woke before Gavin and was able to slip from his embrace without waking him. After the coffee was brewing, she momentarily contemplated going for a run but decided on a day off. Chuckling to herself, she thought, hadn't she run a marathon last night? The old girl-talk from grad school echoed in her head. Good sex, good exercise. Definitely nothing like it for getting the heart rate revved.

In nothing but her robe she walked out to the road to retrieve The Washington Post. She loved morning. It was the promise of a new beginning every day. When she got back to the cottage, she heard the shower running and knew Gavin was up. The sudden thought of him set her senses on fire. A little morning surprise might be in order.

Dashing up the stairs and down the hall into the master bath, Lindsey skimmed off her robe and hung it on the hook next to the shower. Then she quietly opened the glass door and stepped in. Gavin had shampoo lathered in his hair and his eyes were closed as Lindsey slid into the warm stream of water behind him. With soap-slicked hands, she rubbed over his muscled back and began to massage his shoulders and neck.

"Umm, that feels incredible." He didn't even sound surprised she had joined him.

"I thought you might like some help getting clean," she murmured stepping closer. "This is a full-service establishment. The housekeeping staff is thorough, and I have heard them described as exceptional." His low throaty laugh sent shivers down her spine.

"I can attest to that." Gavin turned to pull her against him under the steady warm spray of the shower. "Shower sex. I'd definitely call that full-service and exceptional."

The water ran over them in hot, sensual rivulets, rinsing shampoo suds over them both. He kissed her with passion as his fingers probed her slick darkness. His mouth was everywhere. On her ear, her neck, her breasts. God, how could he be touching so many wonderful places at once? She slid her hand in a slow gliding motion along his erection. It was marvelous and hard. She couldn't get enough of him. She leaned into him, rubbing her breasts against his firm chest. The friction was exquisite. She felt like a shameless hussy. Hot, wet, and throbbing.

"Mm, Gavin, your body feels so good. I can't get close enough. I want to crawl inside you." Her breath caught as he raised her, pinning her against the wall, and quickly rolled on a condom that had miraculously appeared from the shower ledge.

Guess she wasn't that much of a surprise—or had he only hoped it would come in handy.

He slipped inside her as he supported her buttocks with his strong arms that also cushioned her body from the hard tile wall. His long, lazy, measured strokes quickened. He positioned his entry to give her the most spectacular pleasure. He had an undeniable aptitude for extraordinary sex. She didn't want to know how he had become so experienced. Maybe it was natural talent. Damn the man, this was phenomenal. She came with an electrical pulse that was nothing short of magnificent. The jolt shot through her body, and she clutched him to her, thrusting her pelvis up to meet his every stroke.

"Lindsey, Lindsey." And she could feel him surge into her. His body trembled and was still. He continued to hold her close. They were both breathing heavily, but as their heartbeats began to slow, he lowered her feet to the shower floor.

"I like surprises." He nuzzled his head into her neck. Guess he had just hoped for her impulse to join him in the shower. She smiled at the warm thought.

Gavin cooked a sumptuous breakfast of western omelets and rye toast. Lindsey poured the orange juice and marveled at his ease in the kitchen.

"Where did you learn to cook?"

"It was cook or starve," he said as he placed the plate in front of her and sat opposite her at the long farm table. The lilies he'd given her the evening before emitted the most distinctive, sweet aroma.

"This is more than survival. It borders on gourmet. Where have you learned all these talents?" Lindsey was thinking back to the shower.

"You have no idea the depth of my experience."

Just the way Gavin made the last statement gave Lindsey an uneasy feeling. What did he mean? He was so good at everything and had conveniently appeared on the scene just when she needed a friend and ally. Was he too good to be true? Was Gavin the caring man she thought she was getting to know? Or was he part of the Brad scheme to undermine her business? A friend to her, or a comrade of terrorists? Suddenly Lindsey was unsure. Was Gavin what he appeared to be or was he using her to help Brad? What did she really know about Gavin Blake?

»Chapter Eleven«

Lindsey was ready at twelve-fifteen when Gavin returned from quickly driving home. They were both more casually dressed for their meeting with the investigators. She had made a couple of turkey sandwiches and added two apples and two bottles of Perrier for the trip into Tyson's Corner. Their *leisurely* morning had cut their time short for the drive to the city, so it would have to be a picnic in the car as they drove.

"I hope we can find out what Brad is up to." Lindsey unwrapped Gavin's sandwich and handed him the first half. She didn't feel particularly hungry but thought she should eat something. She took a sip of her Perrier and a bite of the Gala apple. "I've never hired private investigators before. What do we tell them?"

Gavin finished chewing. "We'll tell them everything we know, then ask what they recommend." He negotiated the new traffic circle at Gilbert's Corner and continued east on Route Fifty. "Mmm, this is good. What kind of mustard did you use?"

Lindsey wasn't thinking about the food. Her thoughts were focused on Brad's activities. She knew she needed to lighten up and give some type of response to Gavin's question. "Oh, it's just a brown mustard I had in the fridge."

"Okay, Lindsey. I can see I'm not going to be

able to distract you with idle chatter, so let's go over what we know so far and what we'll tell the Grant Agency investigators." He finished the first half of his sandwich and glanced over at her. Lindsey felt uncomfortable. Was Gavin really on her side, or was he just pumping her for information? She'd known him for just over two weeks. Sure, he could get her temperature rising and was the sexiest man she had ever known, but what did she *really* know about him. He'd so opportunely appeared in her life, just when everything was falling apart with Brad and her business. Was the timing connected?

"You know more than I do about Brad's movements, so you should go first." She squirmed in her seat and fiddled with the seat belt. The shoulder strap was across her neck and felt like it was choking her.

Gavin looked over at her again. "Are you alright?"

"Fine." She lied.

His perplexed look conveyed anything but belief. "Okay." He concentrated on the road again. "I guess we should start with your telling the investigators about what Brad said he planned to do in the Middle East expansion."

She tried to focus and relax. "He said he wanted to build a training camp in the UAE. Brad thought it would be more cost effective to train closer to the high-threat areas. There's a Training Center just outside Amman in Jordan that a lot of the defense contractors, DoD and State use, but it's overbooked and there seems to be more training opportunities than the Jordanian site can handle. Even knowing those circumstances, the accountants weren't able to verify Brad's cost figures for building a facility, and they determined he had also inflated the income side of the calculations. They felt his hypothetical demand was over-stated." Lindsey continued to fidget with her seat belt.

"You can adjust the point of connection for the shoulder strap. Would you like for me to pull over and make it more comfortable for you?" She could tell he was becoming irritated.

"I'm fine." And she willed herself to be still.

"Alright." Gavin went on. "Then I could tell them about the flight information and his travel dates. They should have some suggestions at that point."

"Maybe I should talk to my dad about all this. I know he knew Brad. Brad was quite a bit younger, but they both got out of their service careers about the same time. Dad was with Delta Force, and Brad was a Navy SEAL."

"You want to call your dad and ask him what to do? I thought you *wanted* to meet with this agency. Now you're not sure?" Lindsey could hear the exasperation in Gavin's voice.

"I'm not sure. Okay? I just thought Dad might have some insight into the situation. He might even have a suggestion on our next course of action."

Gavin pulled off the road into the McDonalds' parking lot. He glared at her. "So, Lindsey, you said you wanted to go with this firm. Now you want to call and cancel?"

"I didn't say that. Let me just take a moment." She felt boxed into a corner. Gavin had been the one to suggest this private investigation deal. Was this a preconceived arrangement that he and Brad had cooked up? Finally, she said. "I think I'll just give my dad a call and see what he has to say. It won't take five minutes." She released the buckle on the suffocating seat belt and stepped out of the VW. Glancing back, she saw the look of confusion on Gavin's face.

Lindsey hit the speed dial number for her dad. He answered on the second ring. "Hey, doll. What's going on?" He always answered her calls with the same greeting.

"Dad, where are you?" Her breathing began to slow, and her confidence began to return.

"I can't say, or I'd have to kill you." He chuckled. "I'm home, in Arlington, hun."

"Da-ad." She groaned, but then in a serious tone said. "I'm in trouble."

"Tell me, baby."

"You know all the mess I've been having with the Brad Hansen lawsuit and how it is impacting the business? Well now it's becoming a lot more complicated." Lindsey paused to think. Slowly she began relating the circumstances to her dad, leaving out Gavin's role. Actually, leaving out any mention of Gavin Blake.

"So, I was thinking of meeting with some private investigators this afternoon, in order to discover what Brad Hansen is doing. What do you think?"

"Lindsey, I think it is a good idea. Where's the meeting and when? I'll be there."

"Well, Dad, I guess I should also tell you about Gavin."

✻

Gavin felt sad and defeated. You'd think at her age, the woman could make up her mind without her father's permission. Didn't she trust him? He tried to stay calm and analyze the state of affairs. Logic wasn't working for him. He knew he was too emotionally involved. Hell, he had to admit, he was jealous.

Lindsey climbed back into the car. "My dad, Jack, will meet us at the Grant Agency."

Damn. Things were going from bad to worse. First, she had to consult her father and now he was jumping right into the middle of this complex situation.

"Fine, I'll let *Daddy* come to the rescue. I can drop you at the agency and just bow out."

"What is this all about. I can't even call my dad, now?" She blew a breath up that made the hair on her forehead puff up.

Gavin's shoulders slumped forward, and he put both hands on the top of the steering wheel. "I'm just saying maybe you'd feel better just letting your dad help you."

"I was just getting a second opinion."

"Okay, and I'm just saying, I believe you'd feel

156

more comfortable if your dad takes it from here." His life had been just fine two weeks ago. Simple and, well, he had to admit, boring. Lindsey had made him feel alive again. But it might be just too painful. Did he really need all these difficulties in his life?

He looked over at Lindsey. She was trying to adjust the stupid seat belt so it wouldn't cut into her neck. Instead of Miss High-Powered Executive, she looked small and uncertain. Gavin reached across her and pressed the button, lowering the connection point on the door frame.

"Sorry, I overreacted. Guess I'm just a little jealous." Gavin drove back onto the highway and waited a few beats. Sighing, he said, "So, fill me in on Jack."

The meeting with Gary and Marisa at the Grant Agency went well. Gavin had to acknowledge that Jack had some good ideas. Hell, he immediately liked the guy. How could he be jealous of a doting father? It was immediately apparent he adored Lindsey and was extraordinarily proud of this remarkable woman. At least they agreed on that point.

They were sitting in a booth at Clyde's, hashing over the plan of attack. "We're gonna bury this asshole Brad," Jack was saying. "And Gavin, your idea of hauling in the big guns to nail this jerk is right on target." Jack took another slug of his Irish coffee. "I knew of Brad Hansen in my Special Ops days. He was much younger than I was, of course, but he had a reputation of being a good guy. Real patriotic." Jack shifted his weight in the booth. "But from what you said, Gavin, I can imagine Brad may already be on the State Department's radar screen." Lindsey was hanging on his every word. "I'll get one of my old buddies at State to check the National Security alerts on Monday."

Lindsey was sitting next to Gavin and across from Jack. Leaning across the table she clasped her dad's free hand. "What else should we be doing?" Her demeanor had taken a total about face. She was once again eager to track Brad's movements to determine his motives. "To be fair, maybe, Brad truly thinks that he can make a living with security training work in the Middle East."

"Who wants to be fair? I think it's something much more sinister," Jack replied. "For him to take the risk of dealing with what is probably a terrorist organization, he has to have a deal that will make him a ton of money."

Jack looked directly at his daughter. "We must assume the worst, then be happily surprised if the attack dissolves. You should know that, Lindsey, since it's what you teach every student who takes your attack recognition training for deployment."

Gavin was content to sit back and watch father and daughter interact. It was so obviously a special bond.

"Would it be legal for him to train operatives

from the Middle East in our counterterrorist procedures?" Lindsey sipped her latte.

"Hell, no! It would be treason to divulge our government's tactical training to any subversive group." Jack turned to Gavin and shot him a wicked grin. In an abrupt change of subject, he said, "Do you have designs on my gorgeous daughter?"

Gavin was caught off guard but recovered quickly. "Damn right!"

Jack hooted with laughter and gave a thumbs-up sign before downing the rest of his drink. "Brad Hansen has met his match."

Lindsey looked pleased. Gavin guessed he'd passed a critical test, but he wasn't sure he was a physical match for a former Navy SEAL or even this slightly aging, retired Delta Force operative. He'd have to rely on his wits.

»Chapter Twelve«

After he got the return call from Joe, Brad drove the ninety minutes to Dubai and caught the late-night Emirates flight back to Washington. Joe had been hopping mad and told Brad to get back to DC, so they could have a face-to-face. No way was Joe going to discuss any more of this over a phone.

Brad walked into Joe's law office the following morning. Looking around at the expensive furniture and a décor obviously executed by a professional, Brad thought Joe must not be doing too bad for himself.

Brad's jet-lag was catching up with him, and his eyes felt irritated and scratchy from the dry air on the plane. Dubai was a damn long distance from Washington—a half a world away.

Serena, Joe's voluptuous receptionist, greeted him with a warm, toothy smile. "Hello there, Mr. Hansen." She drawled his last name and made it three syllables. She wasn't from the South, so he guessed she thought it sounded seductive. "Mr. Johnson is expecting you and will be right with you." He suspected Serena had been hired for her eye-candy attributes rather than her innate intelligence. She wore a very tight, short-skirted business suit with a low-cut blouse that revealed a great deal of cleavage. She ushered him down the hall to Joe's office, and he couldn't help noticing the provocative swing of her hips. *Nice ass*, he thought, *wonder if*

Joe is having a little side action with the sexy Serena.

"Sit down Brad," Joe said pointing to one of the Chippendale wing chairs in front of his desk. "That will be all, Serena. Please shut the door on your way out and hold my calls." When Serena was surely far down the hall, Joe looked at Brad with steam in his eyes and said, "Shit, Brad, what have you gotten us into?"

"Hey, Joe, getting involved with Rashid was just as much your idea as mine. Now it's all *my* fault?"

"Listen, you ass, with a bit more research on your part before we got in bed with this guy, you would have found out who this Rashid character is fronting. Through my contacts at State, I learned he's on a watch list of suspected Islamic State radicals. This means you may have already compromised us if they're keeping a team on him. We are so fucked!"

"Wait, now, Joe. I've been super careful every time I've met with him. We can make it right. What do you think we should do?"

Joe ran his hand through his thinning hair and looked a little wild-eyed. "This is really a clusterfuck. I want you to take the discs with the State's training facility and the Standard Embassy Design blueprints away from my office. Put them in a lockbox under an alias, under your mattress, or throw them in the Potomac. I don't care at this point. I will deny knowing anything about them."

Brad was panicking. "No, Joe, I can't go this

alone. I think Rashid may kill me or both of us if we don't start building the training facility for them in Oman. He knows we have the plans."

"Did you tell him about the Embassy blueprints, too? If you did, we're both in deep shit, because if Rashid knows we have them and we don't give them to him, he'll probably kill us. And if our own government finds out we have the prints and are willing to hand them over to a known terrorist, they *will* kill us or put us in prison for life."

"I didn't tell him about the Standard Embassy Design. I may have alluded to a mock embassy, but he doesn't know if it's the actual real SED design, or not."

Brad took a nervous gulping breath and dropped another bombshell. "Rashid keeps harping on our getting control of Lindsey's company, STLS, so we can look legit to the Omani government. He said we should just 'kill the bitch.' That is a direct quote."

"Oh, that's a great idea," Joe shouted. "Then we can be executed for murder."

"Hell, Joe, I may be pissed at Lindsey for firing me, but I definitely don't want to kill her." Brad was sweating now. "Rashid made it sound like if we didn't get the deal done with the lawsuit and take over the company, or if we didn't eliminate her, his people would."

"Unbelievable! This gets worse and worse. Brad, you need to get out of my sight so I can think about this. In the meantime, you have custody of the discs." Joe thrust the disc containers and the rolled embassy plans at Brad and said, "Now get out!"

Lindsey was euphoric after their meeting with the Grants, and their strategy session at Clyde's with Gavin and her dad had been outstanding. She felt like shouting, YAY! and doing a jig. Now she really thought they might catch Brad at something so horrible that they could use it as leverage to make the lawsuit disappear. Gary and Marisa Grant weren't cheap, but they had a professional organization in place and loads of contacts on several continents to make it happen. Dad was going to do some research on Brad Hansen with some of his State Department buddies. Yes, it was all coming together.

In contrast to her upbeat mood, Gavin was uncharacteristically quiet on their drive home from Tysons. As they drove up the drive to *Sticks and Stones* Lindsey tried to draw him out of his reverie. "What'd you think about the plan that Gary and Marisa formulated?"

"Good, good. Great proposal." He parked in front of her house.

"Want to come in for a wine, and we could discuss it some more," she said hopefully.

His smile looked forced, "Hey, Lindsey, if you don't mind, I think I'll head home. I've been neglecting my house, and I also need to do laundry and mow the lawn. Love to take a raincheck, though. I'll call you tomorrow." With that he walked around the car, let her out, gave her a peck on the cheek, and was driving back down the drive while she stood there looking dazedly after his taillights.

Wow, what just happened?

Gavin did think the plan the Grants had devised was a good one, but after saying goodbye to Jack at Clyde's, he'd realized that Lindsey might be better off without Gavin on the team. Lindsey's father had great contacts at the State Department, and with the Grants working the surveillance on Brad and computer background checks, all the bases were covered. The litigation would probably cease to exist in a few weeks. He just needed to cool it a little.

He still had so much negative baggage. He didn't want to drag Lindsey down while she had plenty of problems of her own. He should stick with his original idea to lead a simpler life and not get so involved in someone else's difficulties. Look where it had gotten him when he had represented that scumbag and tried to help him. Disaster.

When he got home, he put a load of laundry in his stack washer/dryer and changed into yard clothes. Mowing the lawn was mindless, and he hoped it would get his thoughts off Lindsey. Wrong. He couldn't stop thinking about her. Lindsey was so attractive and bright. He could get lost in those big blue eyes. She was successful, and she had made it all on her own. Dynamite in bed, too.

Jeff had been right when he said she was the total package. What would she want with an eight-to-five mechanic? Even though he had been a top-notch attorney once, he no longer practiced. In so many ways, he loved his new undemanding mechanic's life, but if he were to compare their incomes, his was pathetic. He should definitely give her some space now that she had Jack to help her.

Lindsey was stunned when Gavin drove away. She couldn't figure out what had gone wrong. Earlier that day he had told her dad "damn right" he had designs on her when Jack had put it to him. Then right after they left Tysons, he went silent on her. Maybe he was angry about her calling her dad, but then again, they seemed to get along great. She let herself into her front entry and continued to second guess what had just happened. At least Mosby was a constant. He never failed to greet her with purrs and meows. Mosby was more like a dog, all lovey and wanting attention. Not fickle and standoffish like a cat.

She decided going about her routine would take her mind off Gavin and what seemed to be his rejection. She fed Mosby and poured a small glass of red wine. She didn't think it would be a good idea to drown her misery by drinking a whole bottle. Maybe she would give Mary a call and get her take on the situation. She grabbed the phone and her wine and headed to the arbor.

Mary picked up on the third ring. "Hi, whata

ya doing this beautiful Saturday afternoon, Mary?"

"I'm drinking tea, and I'm nearly finished with a good Louise Penny, Inspector Gamache mystery. What's wrong? I can tell something's wrong."

Lindsey began to sob. Her friend knew her too well. For the next half hour Lindsey poured her heart out to Mary. They had been friends for so long, and Mary had always been there for her.

"Mary, I actually thought Gavin could be the one. I haven't let myself feel anything for a man since Bill. Now, I finally decide to trust in someone again, and he just drove out of my life. Literally! What did I do wrong?"

"Well, you don't know that he's gone for good. Maybe he really did have to mow the lawn and do laundry. Give it a day or two."

"But, Mary, you didn't see him. He has been all over me for nearly two weeks. Then something happened, and it was like he turned off a switch and all the light went out of him. I was just getting some confidence back and now this. What should I do?"

"I think we should meet for lunch and go to an afternoon movie tomorrow. Let's try that new Thai place in Leesburg and walk to the multiplex cinema down the street. If we don't eat much for lunch, we could try some popcorn therapy at the theater, and it wouldn't hurt to make yourself scarce. Not play hard to get, just not be quite so available."

"Okay, maybe you're right. I'll meet you at the Thai restaurant at 12:30."

Gavin finished his chores, had some leftover pizza for dinner, and decided to read and make an early night out of it. He was halfway through a Lee Child, *Jack Reacher* novel, and thought that would hold his interest. As soon as Child described Sandy in the novel, all he could see was Lindsey. Damn! This reading deal wasn't working for him. He got up and took a beer outside to get a breath of fresh air. It was dark and clear, so he sat in his Adirondack chair to look up at the starry sky. It just reminded him of one of the first nights with Lindsey when they had watched the stars twinkle on. He realized then it wouldn't be easy to ever get Lindsey Kelly out of his mind. He went into the house, turned out the lights, and finally drifted into a restless sleep.

»Chapter Thirteen«

Lindsey woke early on Sunday morning and decided she needed to go for her normal run to banish the cobwebs from her mind. She had awakened several times in the night only to let her mind spin through the Brad and the Gavin worries. She would slip off to sleep, but then wake two hours later and the spinning would begin again. If she ran a long way and managed to stay awake through the movie with Mary, maybe she would sleep a bit better tonight.

She put on her running shorts and a Laurel Glen Vintage Race T-shirt. Of course, that simply made her think of Gavin again. What was the matter with her? She wouldn't let another charming handsome man, like Bill, get under her skin and ruin her life. She wasn't sure who to trust.

She allowed her thoughts to wander to her problems as she started a steady pace. As always, she would allow herself to ponder negative thoughts only on the run out. On the return she would contemplate only good thoughts. After all, that was her rule. She tried to convince herself the Brad problem was being addressed. He *would* be defeated.

More worrisome was her confusion about Gavin. Tough it had been only a few weeks, she had developed strong feelings for him. It wasn't just his good looks and perfect body—he also had a cool confidence about him. At first, she'd mistaken it for arrogance, but that wasn't it. He made her feel wanted and safe. Why had he rejected her?

Yes, physical exertion was just the ticket to put this mess in the proper perspective. Logic would win out. She thought she'd try for a half-mile beyond the entrance to the Trenton Farm before turning back. There was a large oak tree that marked the two-mile distance.

She saw the normal farm use pickups and the old red Honda Civic. Then she noticed a large black SUV with tinted side windows stopped in an entrance to a farm field. It looked out of place. No one in the Hunt Country had tinted windows. Much more likely to see a government-type vehicle like that one near the CIA in Langley or on 23rd Street in DC, close to the State Department headquarters. She trained agents and operatives every day in surveillance detection among other skills, and this vehicle definitely screamed *out of place*. Was it Brad and his cronies keeping an eye on her?

Damn, she was getting paranoid.

Though she wasn't quite to the big oak she used as the two-mile landmark, she decided it was a good time to turn back. She slowed her pace to regain her breath and tried to follow her "think good thoughts" rule for the return run. She knew there was beautiful nature around her, and she concentrated on listening for the calls of the birds. All she could think of was the black SUV with the tinted windows.

Another old pickup passed her. Then she heard it—an engine revving and coming from behind her. She got right to the edge of the road facing traffic. She didn't think a vehicle on the other side would be a problem. The engine noise grew. She turned and looked over her shoulder to see the big black SUV barreling down the narrow country lane, swerving to her side of the road.

My God, it was headed right for her!

Adrenaline shot through her, and all her senses went into overdrive. Time began to move slowly, and she seemed to be running in a bog. Her body turned sideways, and her hair whipped into her eyes when she looked back at the oncoming truck. She saw the dark fanatical eyes of a man behind the wheel. The sound of the revving engine was a cacophony.

At the last second, she jumped and rolled into the ditch that slanted down to Cromwell Run. She hit the four-board fence at the bottom of the slope with a thud, and was momentarily stunned, as if hit by a Taser. She vaguely registered the roar of the monster truck fading away in the distance.

Thank God, it was leaving. Where she lay, she could smell the wet soil and hear the water babbling over the riffle. Her back and head must have taken quite a hit. At least the fence had kept her from rolling right into the stream. She hurt all over, but she was still alive.

By the time she got back to her house, the terror finally gripped her, and she was trembling all over. First, she went right to her gun locker and retrieved her Glock 43. Then she stripped in the laundry room and took the weapon with her into the bathroom. Setting it next to the sink, she immediately got into a hot shower.

After twenty minutes of high-pressure hot water pouring over her head, she staggered from the shower. Though it wasn't cold in the house, she was still shivering so she wrapped herself in her big terry cloth robe and twisted a towel over her hair. Had she imagined it, or had some crazy person just tried to run her down? She didn't think she should call 9-1-1. The guy was long gone, and the Loudon County Sherriff's department deputy would just think she was nuts. Attempted hit-and-runs just didn't happen in the bucolic horse country.

Her breathing had begun to slow when the phone started to ring. She looked at the caller ID. It was Gavin. "Hey, hope I'm not calling too early. Wanted to touch base and let you know I need to go up to Laurel Glen today to cover for Benny. He took my Twilight Testing the other day, so I owe him one."

Lindsey couldn't help herself. The words tumbled out in a panicked rush, "Some scary guy in a huge black SUV just tried to run me down while I was out running on Trappe Road."

There was stunned silence on Gavin's end. Then he said, "I'll be right there."

Twenty minutes later Gavin was at her door. "I'm here for you. Tell me everything, baby," he said, wrapping muscular arms around her. Lindsey dissolved into his embrace, and he helped her to the couch. "Please, tell me—it will help to steady you."

She wasn't sure about that but followed his lead and related the entire story, gulping breathlessly, reliving the moment. She did leave out her motive, which was trying to get Gavin out of her head by running to exhaustion.

"Where are you hurt? Let me see."

Lindsey let the robe fall from her back. "I hit the fence pretty hard at the bottom of the ditch, and for once I was glad it was a four-board fence. Conservationists around here don't like the four-board fences because the fawns that aren't large enough to jump the fences can't get under or through a four-board like they can the three-board. But if my head hadn't hit the bottom board when my back hit the post, I could have snapped my neck." Then with a final sigh she concluded, "I'm sore, but I'll get over it."

"We may need to go to the emergency room. It's red and already starting to bruise. Should we put ice on it? Let me at least get you something to drink. Do you need a quilt over your legs?"

He was being so solicitous and sweet. "No, I'm fine and 'no' to the emergency room, too. The docs there would probably think you were beating me, and no one would believe the near hit-and-run story."

"*I* believe it." And Gavin hugged her to his chest. Lindsey burrowed her head into the crook of his neck. He smelled fresh, musky, and all masculine spice. She wanted to stay cuddled with him for a long time until the nightmare subsided.

"Tell me again what you remember about the driver. Was it Brad?"

"Oh, no. I just remember his eyes. Dark, but showing a lot of white, like he was a fanatic or maybe manic. The image I have is like a Berserker going into battle, but no horned helmet. The front windshield wasn't as darkly tinted as the side windows, so I saw him clearly right before I took the dive into the ditch. It was definitely not Brad. If I had to choose an ethnic group, I'd say Arab."

Brad looked worried. "Are you sure we shouldn't report it. I'm not trying to scare you, but what if they try again?"

"You may be right," Lindsey said resignedly.

"I'll make the call." Lindsey didn't want him to dial 9-1-1, so he looked up the number for the main Sherriff's Office. The Loudon County Sherriff's Department responded immediately, and they said they'd send out a deputy to take a statement. At least, it would go on record in case something else happened.

*

Though outwardly calm, Gavin was frantic inside. What if something had happened to Lindsey? He was fooling himself if he thought this was a fling. He couldn't imagine his world without her. Even after less than a month, she had become an integral part of his life. He wasn't big into *love at first sight*, but now that he had gotten to know her a little better, he thought this could be the real deal. They just had to make it through this trouble, and then they could envision a future. At the moment, he needed to be here for her.

"Maybe you should throw on some clothes before the deputy gets here. Could add credibility to your statement even if I think you look extremely hot in the robe."

"Gavin, you naughty boy," she said slapping him on the arm. "I'm making a recovery from the attack, but I'm not quite ready for what I'm seeing in your eyes." She smiled with a sparkle and warmth he hadn't seen since he'd arrived. And was glad some color was returning to her face. Maybe she wouldn't let this haunt her. He hoped so.

"Let's get ready for the deputy."

"Come in, officer," Gavin said as he showed him into Lindsey's sunroom.

"I'm Deputy Franklin." He put out his hand in a stop gesture and said. "No, don't get up." He walked over to where Lindsey was sitting and shook her hand. "So, let me hear what happened. If you don't mind, I'll just jot down a few notes. It will make it easier when I write up the report."

"No problem. Please sit down."

Lindsey gave the officer some background about the lawsuit with Brad and told him about the incident.

"The driver looked wild-eyed like he was on

something or, as I told Gavin, a fanatic."

"Did you get a good look at him? Good enough for a description? I could get a sketch artist over here, if you thought it would be of any help."

"I just noticed his eyes mostly. I'd say he was medium build maybe even on the light-weight side. Definitely not a fat man. He had dark hair and brownish skin." Looking at Gavin, then back to the deputy, she fidgeted and tapped her fingers against her leg. "I told Gavin he did look Arabic, but that could be an assumption based on my current predicament."

"Could you see his clothes?"

"Not much help there. It looked like he had on an ordinary open necked shirt."

"Then tell me more about the car." Deputy Franklin was taking copious notes.

"It was a large black SUV, I thought government-issue when I first saw it. Probably a Tahoe, but I couldn't be sure."

"License plate number?"

"Sorry, no, I was busy jumping for my life."

"Oh, guess that was a dumb question. I was just hoping for at least a partial."

Lindsey smiled. "I'll keep that in mind if they try again."

The deputy chuckled. "Glad to see you're feeling better." But to his credit, Deputy Franklin was very professional and didn't scoff at what had happened. "We take threats like this very seriously. Whoever it was may very well try again. You should be extremely vigilant. Do you have an alarm system or a big dog, Miss Kelly?"

Gavin jumped in and said, "I'll be staying on the property until this whole problem is resolved."

Lindsey looked at him and said, "Oh, that probably won't be necessary."

"We'll discuss it. At the very least we'll put some more secure dead bolts on all the doors."

After a few more pleasantries, Gavin went out with the Deputy to the hall.

"Thanks for coming out on a Sunday," he said, "I'm sure Miss Kelly feels safer just knowing you would respond quickly if there were another incident."

"No problem. That's why we're here. As we say —to protect and serve. Hope they don't try again."

While Gavin was with the Deputy, Lindsey thought over the situation. Maybe she should see if Mary would stay with her for a few days while this mess got sorted out.

But as Gavin came back into the room from the front door he said, "You know I'd feel a lot better if I stayed here with you. I could stay on your couch, so that you won't feel any pressure. We could put the relationship on a brief hold. That way our minds would be clear and focused."

"Right. I'm sure, if I knew you were downstairs sleeping on my couch, I wouldn't be tempted *at all* to slip down in the middle of the night to snuggle against your warm hard body." Lindsey and Gavin smiled and gave each other knowing looks.

"You're right," he said with a shrug.

"Gavin, sit with me." When he was seated next to her on the couch, she reached for his hand and held it softly in hers. "I need to tell you, when you got back in your car and drove down the drive last night, I was devastated and confused. Just when I was beginning to let myself trust again and was feeling I had found my kindred spirit, you closed down. I could see it in your eyes. You literally drove out of my life. But, Gavin, there's no going back for me now. I want you. I feel you're a part of me. I'm just not whole without you, though I'm not sure it's fair to you when my world is in such chaos."

Gavin gazed into Lindsey's eyes. His mouth twitched at the corners. "I was thinking I was complicating *your* life and that you would be better off without a mechanic hanging around your neck. I washed clothes, mowed the lawn, and even tried to read, but I was just as miserable and couldn't stop thinking about you."

"We're pitiful, like two love-sick teenagers." She giggled.

Gavin pulled Lindsey to her feet and gave her a gentle hug. "What we need to do right now is figure out what else we can do to calm the chaos. Come sit in the kitchen while I fix breakfast for us."

Gavin maneuvered Lindsey to one of the island stools. He got the ingredients together for an herb and cheese omelet with English muffins and started a pot of coffee. "Orange juice?" he asked while taking the carton from the refrigerator. She nodded, and he filled two small glasses for them. "Okay, where's a pad of paper? While I cook you should start writing down everything that's happened with Brad and any unusual events that might relate. That should help us formulate a plan of attack." Gavin said the last part of the sentence while rubbing his hands together with the look of a mad scientist about him.

Lindsey couldn't help smiling. Gavin had a way of lightening the mood. She swallowed her first sip of the juice, and said, "I'm ready for us to take some action to add to the investigators' efforts, and it's a great idea to start with the facts."

In an hour, the omelets were consumed, the dishes were clean and stacked on the bamboo drying rack, and they had the start of a scheme to thwart Brad Hansen.

"Now I just need to call Mary and fill her in on this morning's events. Why don't you call my dad and see what he thinks of our plan?"

»Chapter Fourteen«

Brad was nearly hysterical when he called Joe on Monday morning. Joe was less than thrilled to hear from him and said, "What the hell are you calling about now?"

Brad took a deep breath to calm his voice. "Rashid just called to tell me that his associates in the States had taken care of our *little problem*. When I asked him what he meant, he just said running on lonely country roads can be very dangerous."

"Shit, Brad, what has your extremist Arab done now?"

"I don't know for sure, but it sounds like his goons hit our friend while she was running and left her for dead. I never wanted all this to happen. God, I don't know what we can do!" Brad's voice had risen an octave as he spoke, and he knew he sounded as panicked as he was.

"Calm down, Brad. We had nothing to do with it, but *you* do need to get Rashid under some control. Let's think what we can come up with to appease him."

"I did what you told me and put the discs and rolled blueprints in a lockbox at a bank in Bethesda. I'll tell you where when I see you. In the meantime, I think we should give him at least some of the plans to the training facility. Maybe not the ones for the Embassy, yet, but something."

"Brad, this is a very slippery slope. Where will

it stop? But let's not discuss this on the phone. Come to my office at 2:00 PM today and we'll decide what to do next."

"I'm a patriotic kind a guy. I've served my country, and now I just want to reap some benefits. Is that too much to ask? I made lots of money for that bitch, but she's the one with the fat bank account, not me. Even drives around in a Ferrari, for God's sake!" Joe sat glaring at him. Brad knew he was ranting and whining again. He tried to compose himself, breathing in deeply as he stared out Joe's office window.

When he looked back, Joe's gaze had softened. "I can see this whole Lindsey situation has driven you nearly mad, Brad. I've known you for years. Do you remember when you came in with your dad the time I helped him negotiate that real estate deal? He was so proud of you and bragged about your assignment to a SEAL unit. You were a hard-working guy in your special forces days."

"You need to pull yourself together. Don't let Lindsey's actions undermine your confidence. So, she fired you. No big deal. You're letting it eat you up from the inside, but instead move forward, Brad. Don't let revenge be your motive."

Brad moved back to the chair and sat down. "Yeah, okay, I'll move forward, but I still want to make a huge amount of money out of this deal."

Joe shook his head slightly and said, "Let's take care of one thing at a time." Always practical,

Joe asked, "First, Lindsey. Did you check the hospitals and the morgue in Loudoun County?"

Brad nodded his head. "Yes, I did that right after we spoke this morning, and nothing so far. Maybe she was just injured."

"We can only hope that's the case," Joe said with a sigh. "OK, so let's talk about what we can do to extricate ourselves from this mess."

"I'm not seeing any way out. We're going to have to give Rashid something."

Nodding, Joe said, "What about misinformation?"

Brad leaned forward in the chair with his arms on his knees, put his hands together and looked at the floor. "It could work, but it would need to be believable."

Then Brad jerked up abruptly. "I've got it," he said in a rush. "What about giving them the layout to that old Mock Embassy they built at Fort AP Hill? I think the State Department is still using it for their Capstone at the end of the Basic Agent training, but they should switch to the Standard Embassy Design for training, soon."

Brad leaned on Joe's desk. Picking up a pen he started tapping it against the desktop. "Yes, I remember being part of the Capstone event. The training is a coordinated effort involving several agencies and they carry out a weeklong embassy riot and hostage rescue exercise. But in the old embassy replica the distances between the outer security walls and the various buildings inside, plus the actual building layouts are not anything like the new Standard Embassy Design. They'll switch to the real embassy replica when construction is finished at their new training facility."

"I like it. I know someone who could get a set of drawings for that old mock embassy without raising suspicion."

Brad stood and started pacing. "Once we have the blueprints, I'll go back over and meet with Rashid. How long will it take for you to get them?"

"Maybe a week. In the interim, keep checking on Lindsey's whereabouts and contact Rashid. Put him off with your strategy to deliver the embassy diagrams within a week or so. I'll continue to put the pressure on Lindsey's attorneys about more discovery in the lawsuit. That should keep her busy if she managed to survive the attack."

Brad raked his hand through his hair for the third time. "It's a plan. Let's hope I can continue to stall him. I don't relish being the one to end up in the morgue."

Brad felt more upbeat and confident than he had in weeks. Now he just needed to stay cool and keep his eye on the prize! He headed into the gym where an hour of running and sweat-inducing weight training would help clear his mind. He'd call the hospitals and search police reports after his workout.

»Chapter Fifteen«

Even though Lindsey felt a bit battered, she decided to try to keep to her normal schedule. She'd leave out the morning run, for the time being, but bright and early Monday morning she drove to the office. Lindsey could tell Mary was full of concern by the way she hovered. "Can I get you more coffee?" "Let me just bring those files into you." "I'll run over to Doug's office and get that information for you. Just sit tight."

Finally, Lindsey couldn't bear the solicitous attitude any longer. "Mary, stop! Sit down with me for a minute."

Mary pulled up a comfy chair in Lindsey's office, tucking one foot under her as she sat. "I know I'm hovering, but I can't help myself. I'm so worried about what happened—even more worried that whoever tried to hit you won't miss next time."

Lindsey could see the concern in her friend's deep black eyes. Lindsey remembered back to the day Mary walked through the door of her tiny first office. She had obviously used a flat iron and some kind of hair goop to help get her thick black curls under control. Today her short, soft natural curls made her look more attractive.

Lindsey smiled at the memory and at her true friend. "Really, Mary, don't worry. I'm taking precautions. Gavin is installing better locks on the house, and I have a local contractor putting in a motion detector system for the grounds as we speak. I'll probably only catch deer and raccoons on the videos, but it makes me feel safer." Lindsey smiled, trying to put Mary at ease. "And," she paused for emphasis, "Gavin will be staying at *Sticks and Stones* this week until we set the plan in motion."

Mary raised her eyebrows and seemed to relax for the first time. "Okay. I'll try not to fret but be careful. No running on country roads!"

"Yes, Ma'am." Lindsey saluted. "So, here's what I found out this morning from my dad. Since Brad has been flying back and forth mostly to Dubai, but occasionally to Abu Dhabi, dad concentrated on those areas with his State contacts. The State Department is keeping an eye on several know terrorists in the region. They showed him a few surveillance videos and a guy dad thought looked a lot like Brad was seen in a couple meetings with one Rashid Abdul-Azim. He's a front man for an offshoot of the Islamic State in Iraq and Syria. He has a legitimate business in Abu Dhabi, so maybe Brad doesn't actually know that this Rashid is a terrorist. In any case, Brad has become a *person of interest* since he's been seen with the Arab terrorist. Dad didn't think the State Department guys knew who Brad was—yet— but he was sure they were working on it."

Mary tucked her hair behind her ear and frowned. "Working with terrorists doesn't sound like the Brad we knew for nearly nine years. He must have changed or become desperate."

"Yeah, maybe he got greedy, because we also

found out from the investigators that Brad has a numbered account in the Caymans. The Grants said when we met with them that it's always important to follow the money."

Lindsey leaned forward conspiratorially. "In the strategy Dad, that Gavin and I have come up with, we have decided to give Brad the benefit of the doubt and assume he started out thinking he was working with just another foreign national group. We don't think he has given away any *state secrets*, yet, but that could change soon. Dad is scheduled to go to Dubai on Wednesday to see if he can figure out what's going on. He still has some local contacts from his State Department days. I'm going to carry on as usual in case Brad is having me surveilled. I don't want him to think he's gotten to me if he did have a hand in the botched hit-and-run."

"Oh, please be careful. I know you know how to detect surveillance from all your training, but this seems dangerous. Can't you stay home for a few weeks until your dad or the State Department can take care of the situation?"

"I'll be fine. I think I'm pretty safe driving between home and the office. There'll be plenty of people on the road. Remember the old saying, safety in numbers. Then on Saturday at noon, Gavin will follow me to the Ferrari Picnic at Laurel Glen for the Vintage Races. That evening, Gavin will be having his old law school friend for dinner at his place in Berryville. I'll stop by there after being at the track. It's only fifteen minutes, and Gavin can follow me home from his house."

"Sounds like you have it all worked out. Now you just have to make it unscathed until the weekend. Remember, no running!"

The pace was demanding with the preparations for the Vintage Race, and Gavin was busting his chops trying to keep up. It was Tuesday and he was trying to act as if his life was business as usual, not in a swirl of turmoil. Actually, the work was helping take his mind off Lindsey and *The Plan* for now.

Laurel Glen had been hosting the race for the beautiful old race cars for over ten years. It was the highlight event of the season. It was also one of the largest, which meant more work for everyone to be ready for the big weekend. The event really started on Wednesday evening as the "big rigs" started rolling in. Gavin hadn't been at Laurel Glen the previous year, but all the mechanics and maintenance guys told him that the track turned into a small city for the five-day event. They said it was a little like a carnival, with a car show of old muscle cars, a drifting demonstration with charity rides, and, of course, the kart track open for business. There were tents for catered events and the corrals cordoned off for the car clubs. Extra workers had been hired to man the gates, to direct traffic and to work the additional concession stands. The entire staff was bustling around with excitement.

Jeff Carper was pumped, too. "Gavin, I need

you to work with Eddie on ambulance number four. It'll be parked outside of the EMS shop. Run down there and drive it back. Eddie will get bay three ready for it." The mechanics were checking over all the safety equipment today. Then tomorrow they would start on the final maintenance of the go-karts. With seven ambulances and three fire-fighting rigs, plus all the maintenance equipment and school cars, there was plenty to keep the eight, full-time mechanics engaged.

Gavin smiled broadly and gave a salute. "I'll get right on it, boss." The jog down to the EMS building felt good and energized him. It was a perfect day, and he had a few minutes to breathe in the fresh air. His thoughts naturally drifted back to the dazzling Ms. Kelly. He was worried but knew that together they would be able to handle the problems. But what a way to start a relationship.

He reached the EMS shop and saw Kevin, one of the Emergency Medical Technicians sitting on a lawn chair in the sun. EMTs did a lot of waiting around, but when they were needed, they hopped into action.

Gavin waved at Kevin and quipped, "Tough job. How's your tan?" Getting up to greet Gavin, the EMT gave it back to him. "So, my man in maintenance, out for a leisurely stroll?"

Gavin snorted. "Hey, Kevin, I ran all the way." He held up four fingers. "Just let Ashley know I'm snagging number four for maintenance."

"Will do, the keys are in it."

Gavin drove the Advanced Support vehicle right onto the lift plates in bay three. As he got out, he said, "Take 'er up, Eddie."

Hopefully, there would be no serious accidents, but the emergency vehicles had to be ready to respond. Two ambulances were stationed at each of the three tracks to ensure a less than three-minute response time. The Glen was noted for its safety record, so the mechanics didn't want to be the cause of tarnishing the reputation. Jeff had instilled the importance of vehicle maintenance in them all.

Gavin stayed busy, so the day passed quickly. Right at five, he clocked out and drove home to pick up a few more things before driving to Lindsey's. He was making spaghetti sauce for dinner. There were just certain times when comfort food hit the spot. He had all the ingredients for the sauce, some fresh angel hair pasta, and makings for a salad. Of course, a baguette and a bottle of Chianti.

When he arrived at *Sticks and Stones*, he let himself in with the key Lindsey had given him. He went straight to the kitchen and started the preparations. Mosby was meowing and winding around his legs, but Gavin thought it would be better for him to wait for Lindsey. He figured he had about a forty-five-minute lead on her, so Mos' wouldn't starve in the short-term.

Now with the sauce on a slow simmer to blend the flavors, and the salad in the big glass bowl waiting in the refrigerator, Gavin went up to take a quick shower and put on some casual clothes that didn't smell like the garage.

⁂

Lindsey rolled in about fifteen minutes late to find the table set with her good china. Now where did he find that? Even candles were ready to be lit and the wonderful aroma of Italian food was emanating from the kitchen. She could get used to this.

Gavin appeared as if on cue and handed her a glass of Chianti.

"Welcome home!" he said and gave her a kiss on the cheek. "Thought you might like comfort food for dinner, so let me know when you'd like to eat, and I'll put in the pasta and heat the bread."

"Gavin, you don't have to pamper me so much. I came through my near-death experience mostly unscathed. I'm fine, really." Lindsey put her wine down and went to him with her arms out. "I do need a hug, though."

Gavin huddled her against him and held her for a long moment. He spoke into her hair, "You just scared me on Sunday. I couldn't think of being without you, so I'm in protective mode, I guess."

"Well, all this is amazing," she said indicating the dining room table. "Very romantic." Smiling up at Gavin she said, "Let me help you finish up. I'm starved." Lindsey picked up her wineglass and they both went into the kitchen.

"Speaking of starved, I think we have one irritated cat on our hands. I figured you should be the one to feed Mosby, since it's the routine, but he's been meowing at me for an hour and I wasn't sure what to feed him."

Lindsey bent over and picked up the complaining Mosby. "I'm home to take care of you now," she said while scratching behind his ears. His meowing turned to purring in a moment. "What a glutton for attention."

With Mosby fed and sleeping at Lindsey's feet, she and Gavin had a relaxed dinner by candlelight. As Lindsey stuffed in the last bite of spaghetti and wiped her mouth with the napkin, she sat back, looked at Gavin and sighed. "That was wonderful! Now, I'm stuffed. I'll need to run two extra miles tomorrow."

"Whoa, that means, I'll have to run two extra miles with you for protection." With a sly grin he added, "I can think of another way to burn calories. Oh, I'm sorry. I promised no pressure while I'm here on *protective service*."

Lindsey chuckled and said, "Why don't we take the last of the wine outside. That arbor and gazing toward the Blue Ridge helps with my relaxation. Now my mantra. "Everything will be okay, everything will be okay." The last was said in a droning monotone.

Gavin laughed quietly. "I thought that was my line."

"I'll do the dishes in a while since you did all the cooking. Thanks, by the way. The yummy dinner was a nice surprise."

"My pleasure," he said pushing back his chair

and standing

They made their way to the side porch and once again sat facing the shadow of the mountains.

"I feel so lucky in many ways. And with you next to me, I'm sure we'll get through this." She squeezed his hand. "Thanks again for all your support. It makes me feel safer."

"Have you heard anything from your dad."

"Oh, yes, he contacted his colleagues in the State Department, and they are setting up the scenario."

"Do they think they can make Brad see his precarious position and convince him to help with the plan to seize his terrorist friend, Rashid?"

"Dad said the agents intend to explain the U.S. law to Brad in graphic terms. From the looks of things, the idiot is possibly violating the ITAR—the International Traffic in Arms Regulations—which requires Americans to obtain special permits before defense-related technology can be transferred to foreign countries. They're going to point out such a violation carries a penalty of just over a million dollars and up to ten years in prison."

"That should get his attention."

"Yeah, and they'll emphasize that the law includes providing military advice or training to foreign units that could be construed as defense services."

"Well, surely that will convince him." He turned to face her.

"He'd be stupid not to grab a chance to avoid

prison for the next decade," she said. "If the agents think Brad willfully violated the regulations, he's a goner, but I suspect he just doesn't know the law."

"I think you're right, but we'll have to wait and see. Now let's relax and contemplate the sky."

"Or each other." Lindsey slipped her hand into Gavin's.

»Chapter Sixteen«

Lindsey maneuvered her freshly repaired and painted Ferrari into the Ferrari Corral at the Laurel Glen track, backed into a spot, and unfolded from the low-slung car.

"Hey, Henley, what a super day, and you've outdone yourself making our corral stand out. You're the best!" Lindsey gave her a big hug. "How did you get this terrific location for our corral and tent? You must have a lot of pull with the management." The special rail side spot had the perfect view on the right to see the cars coming down the chute and through the carousel. From there the club members could watch as the cars raced by, accelerating through turn eight and speeding up the hill and under the bridge.

Henley chuckled. "You're the one with an *in* with the management. George Trenton thinks you hung the moon."

"Not quite. I think he just really likes the Ferrari Club."

Henley Gant had made all the arrangements for the barbecue and had a table set up in the tent with lots of nibbles. Wine, beer, sodas, and water were iced down in big red tubs. The tables had black and white checked table clothes with large red geraniums in the middle of each. Ferrari flags flapped in the wind at the corner of the tent. Everything looked very festive.

B. L. SCOTT

Gazing around at the setup, Lindsey looked at Henley. "You sure know how to throw a party." Lindsey thought it was one of Henley's best attributes, but she didn't say it out loud. Henley was known as the Perle Mesta of Laurel Glen among her Ferrari Club friends.

Lindsey grabbed a water from one of the tubs and walked back to Henley. "I'm really looking forward to a day of racing and relaxing with friends."

"Lindsey, I'm so glad you could make it. I was afraid your car wouldn't be repaired in time. It looks like they did a perfect job. It's good as new."

"Yes, I'm thrilled with the repair job. Looks great, and I'll see if it handles the same at high speed the next time I'm on the track." More of the club members were arriving and Lindsey turned to greet Tim Nelson, the president of the club.

"Hi, Tim. I thought you were racing one of your vintage Ferraris."

"Threw a rod. So just a spectator today. Might be more fun anyway." Tim's total self-confidence and ease around everyone overshadowed his gnomish stature. He was an amazing guy.

"One of our own, Jake, is racing a 735 S Sport Prototype in the pre-1960s class," he said.

"That should be exciting to watch. Are there very many of that model around anymore?" Lindsey was switching to her car-head persona, and the tension of the past week was easing away.

"Not many, but we'll have to ask Jake when he finishes his qualifying round preparations. He should be back any minute."

Lindsey chatted with her club friends and soon was totally immersed in the hubbub of the sports car world. Everyone was talking about driving to Lime Rock in two weeks, and Lindsey joined in, joking about the competition of the event. She knew she wouldn't be in Connecticut for the Lime Rock Ferrari Meet, but tried not to think of where she and Gavin would be in two weeks. She needed to keep her mind focused on the present—breathe deeply and think vintage races.

Just then George Trenton entered the tent and greeted everyone with a hearty, "Hey, welcome to Laurel Glen." Trenton had been the track owner for nearly thirty years, and he looked energized and younger than his sixty-seven years. The vibrant business must keep him young, Lindsey thought. His tall, straight stature gave him an air of self-assurance.

"George, great to see you." Tim gave Trenton a manly slap on the back. "It's a wonderful turnout for the races. Stay a while and have a beer."

"Thanks. Don't mind if I do." He made his way toward the beer tub. "Yes, we lucked out with the beautiful weather." George turned to Lindsey. "How's my favorite beltway bandit?" he asked jovially.

"Hi, George." She gave him a brief hug. "We're staying busy. Hey, I may have a class next month that will need driver training and a little shooting range time. Think you can squeeze me in?"

"We can always squeeze you in. Call Chris next week and set it up. Just tell him I recommended he make some room for you," he said with a wink.

George fished through the icy tub and found a Michelob Light, popped the top, and took a long swig. "I've been meaning to ask you about something I heard." He pulled Lindsey to the side and lowered his voice. "At the end of this last week we did a firearms recertification class with a small group of deputies from Loudoun County. One of the deputies mentioned he had visited a home next to my farm to take a hit-and-run report. He just wanted me to be aware of the possibility of some unsavory sorts in the neighborhood. Was he talking about you?"

Lindsey felt a little embarrassed, but answered truthfully, with a quiet, "Yes."

"Are you alright? What's going on?"

"Well, uh..."

"Why would anyone want to run down a nice person like you? Maybe it was just a mistake," he interrupted.

"No mistake, George. The more I think about the incident, the more I believe they were *trying* to hit me."

George patted her on the shoulder. "Lindsey, you must be terrified."

"I'm hangin' in. What makes me think this was real is I'm having some serious trouble with an ex-employee and think he may have something to do with the attempt. The guy is suing me for breach of contract and seems to be trying to put me out of business. Some of his foreign associates may be attempting to expedite the process."

"Whoa, that's awful. Let me know if I can do anything to help. I'll be looking out for any strange folks in the vicinity. I certainly want to keep my next-door neighbor safe even if our 'doors' are a mile apart."

"I'm confident I'll be fine," Lindsey said without much conviction.

"I hope you'll call at the first sign of trouble."

"You have already done so much for me. I probably wouldn't be in the business I'm in if it hadn't been for your mentoring and encouragement."

"Nah, you're smart. But glad to be of help."

George threw his empty can in the trash and with a wave and a cheerful "good-bye," he was off to the All-British Cars' Corral nearby. He was the consummate businessman. He had told her many times, "You have to have customers to make a business thrive. So be good to your customers."

Tim came over to Lindsey. "George has really made a super business out of this place. I heard it went through several owners and bankruptcies before he bought it in eighty-seven."

"Yes, he was clever to blend the racing on the weekends with training during the week, but it took a lot of time to find all the clients he has today. He once told me he was an overnight success in twenty years." Lindsey grinned.

"Right." Then Tim wandered off to talk with a few members about the logistics of the Lime Rock weekend, and Lindsey walked over to ask Henley if she could help with anything.

Henley simply said, "Lunch is served!"

They all ate the barbecue with enthusiasm and watched more racing and the afternoon melted into early evening. With thanks and promises to see each other soon, the members began to drift off.

"What can I do to help clean up, Henley? You always try to do everything."

"Yeah, I'll help, too," Tim said.

Henley flashed them a smile. "I like to organize parties—you know that—and it makes me happy to do it. This club is a big part of my life, but the clean-up is my least favorite part. Thanks for offering to help."

"Glad to do it," Tim and Lindsey said in unison, then laughed.

"OK. Everything is disposable, so let's just roll up the plastic tablecloths around the debris and carry each one to the big trash can at the back of the tent. We'll have it cleared in no time."

"You have such a generous heart. I hope you know how much all the members appreciate your planning skills and all the work you do for the club." Lindsey grabbed the other side of the plastic cloth and folded into the middle as Henley was doing the same on the other side of the table.

"It makes me feel good to be a part of the organization."

When the debris from every table was deposited in the big trash cans, Tim left with a thumbs-up gesture as he drove toward the gate. Lindsey helped pack up the remnants of the food and decorations to put in Henley's car.

"I'm sorry I won't make it to Lime Rock, Henley, so in a few weeks after the meet why don't we get together for lunch in town. Your foundation office is somewhere inside the beltway, isn't it?"

"How nice. Yes, I'm located in Ballston."

"Great, I'll call you after the Lime Rock Ferrari meet, and we'll pick a date and place." Lindsey smiled warmly at Henley. She thought it would be great to get to know her better. She only hoped all her troubles would be solved in the next few weeks.

»Chapter Seventeen«

Lindsey was a little apprehensive leaving the track on her way to Gavin's, as most of the spectators had already left and the country road to the highway was deserted. She ruefully shook her head at her caution and asked herself, "what can happen in a fifteen-minute drive?" She hadn't seen anyone following her.

Then she jammed on the brakes, heart racing. A black SUV sat in a driveway ahead. Was she still being shadowed?

Her tightly held muscles relaxed when she noticed stickers on the windows for a local high school and a Redskins flag flying out of one of the back windows. Lindsey inhaled deeply. There didn't seem to be enough oxygen in the air. She knew she was being paranoid and overly cautious.

The lights in the homes along the country road were blinking on as te day began to fade. The few cars coming toward her had on their headlights. Suddenly, some idiot in an old pickup came zooming up behind her with his bright beams on, the reflection from the rearview mirror momentarily blinding her. He was really tailgating. Was he trying to get into her trunk? What a jerk.

Her attention jumped from the trailing truck when bright lights topped the rise in front of her—in her lane! She didn't have a second to think. It was a gut reaction. Some part of her extensive training kicked in. She scanned the roadside, and finding a clear path into a field, drove off the road and narrowly missed the head-on collision. The bump as the Ferrari bounced over a shallow ditch threw her against the door, and the sound of the dry field stubble scraping against the undercarriage of her car reverberated in her ears.

The large black SUV quickly cut back to his side of the road and sped on. The tailgating pickup kept moving toward the main highway. Neither vehicle stopped to see if she was all right.

Adrenaline pumped wildly through her veins. She was gripping the steering wheel as if she was fused to it. Peeling her fingers from the wheel, she sat back and leaned her head against the seat. That's when she began trembling uncontrollably. She squeezed her eyes shut, hugged her arms around her waist, and willed herself to settle down.

Was it just someone in a hurry? Or was it another attempt on her life? Why was this happening to her? Brad couldn't be so vindictive he wanted her dead.

No, this had to be an accident. The driver of the SUV wouldn't have *wanted* to hit her, though her low-slung Ferrari was no match for a huge SUV and wasn't designed for off-road forays. The fear began to subside and was replaced by another emotion—anger. She wouldn't succumb to their scare tactics. With her temper rising, she blew out a large breath, released it slowly, then put her foot on the gas pedal, and drove slowly back onto the road.

She was still afraid, but she was alive.

✳

She felt nothing but relief when she pulled into Gavin's driveway ten minutes later. The car incident had to have been a fluke. She wouldn't mention it.

Lindsey had had no trouble finding Gavin's bungalow in Berryville, and she was favorably impressed by the tidy, low, white clapboard structure with dark blue shutters. It was like a safe beacon in the storm. Breathe. Was she back to normal?

Stepping out of the Ferrari she saw the two men standing around the grill in the side yard. Seeing Gavin's muscular athletic body in his tight jeans and short sleeve polo gave her a tingly feeling low in her belly. Her anxiety started to ebb. She exhaled in a rush, her attention completely riveted to the handsome man intent on flipping burgers. She guessed she needed to control her urges until this mess was behind them, but what she wanted was to drag him into the house and have her way with him. Sadly, that wasn't possible at the moment.

Gavin had been a perfect gentleman since the incident with the hit-and-run, but she was wishing he wouldn't hold back any longer. Maybe he was losing interest. She couldn't keep him out of her mind. Blowing out another long breath, she walked over to the two friends.

"Hi, you must be Tom?" she said.

Gavin turned to greet her, taking her into a quick embrace. Turning back to his friend and extending a hand, he said, "Meet Tom Duncan. I've been telling Tom about you and your problems with Brad Hansen. Hope that's ok with you. Tom has a logical legal mind and may have some pointers for us on the lawsuit side of the problem."

Tom was an attractive guy maybe an inch shorter than Gavin. He had a youthful appearance and a teenager's exuberance exuding from every pore. Lindsey thought he must be a very content and happy man. She reluctantly stepped away from Gavin. "No problem. I'm sure he will keep the conversation confidential—attorney/client privilege or something like that."

"Yeah, sure, my lips are sealed." Tom made a zipping motion across his lips then produced a wide impish grin, which made Lindsey think they may have been talking about something other than Brad Hansen.

"I'm just taking the burgers off the grill and everything else is ready for us on the backyard picnic table. Potato salad and all the fixins' for the burgers. It's such a pretty evening, I thought we'd eat outside." Gavin led the way to the backyard, burgers in hand.

Tom followed and added, "Great idea." Was Lindsey imagining it, or was Tom trying a bit too hard to be upbeat.

Hoping to ease the situation and change the direction of the conversation away from the Brad Hansen mess, Lindsey linked her arm in Tom's. "Gavin has told me a lot about you. Can't wait to hear of all his, let us say, *indiscretions* in his college years."

Laughing, Tom led her to the picnic table. Gavin had gone to a lot of trouble to make the dinner a special occasion. He'd even adorned the table with a dark blue cloth and a pot of daisies.

The sun was setting across the valley, and the evening was starting to cool. The final rays of the sun filtered through Gavin's hair emphasizing his fine profile. Lindsey's attraction to this kind and caring man was overwhelming her. She reached for his free hand and squeezed.

They talked about everything and nothing while eating the casual meal.

"You should have seen Gavin as an undergrad at Penn." Tom chuckled. "He was always pulling pranks. Hey, remember the time, Gav, when we put the 'Just Married' sign on the back bumper of Professor Jenkins' Volvo. Since he always backed into his parking spaces, he didn't see the sign for three days. When his wife noticed it, we heard he had hell to pay." Tom snorted. "Luckily, he never knew who did it."

With nearly all the food on the table devoured Gavin got up to clear.

"I even 'made' dessert," Gavin said with air quotes accenting the *made*. "The famous Cow Puddles from the Berryville bakery," he laughed. Everything about the evening was easygoing and Lindsey relaxed. She wasn't thinking about Brad, for once. Gavin consumed her thoughts. What a good-looking man. Oh, no, she was obsessing again.

Over dessert Tom and Gavin talked about Tom's wife, Carla, and Gavin asked about the upcoming birth of the baby. Tom exhibited all the traits of a proud father-to-be, and Lindsey suspected she would have been subjected to ultrasound pictures, if he'd had them handy. Lindsey was content to listen.

Then, for the second time in the day, she went through the ritual of saying good-bye to friends, and they all promised to get together soon, but with Carla next time.

Gavin followed Lindsey home, and after feeding the cat, they checked the surveillance camera footage together. Only a mother possum with her three babies trotting along behind her crossed the drive. "Aw, aren't they cute?" She smiled up at Gavin.

Lindsey closed the surveillance program on her laptop. "I'm beat. Let's call it a day," she said, standing and heading to the stairs. "But I'd love some company. We could just cuddle." She spoke in a low, seductive voice then raised one eyebrow as if it were a question.

Gavin sighed. "I think I'd better stay on guard down here on the couch. If I get close to your exquisite body, I can't promise to be content with just snuggling."

"That's what I was thinking." Lindsey arched her back and tossed back her thick streaked hair and gave him a leering glance.

Gavin went to her and held her close. "You know I want you. I just don't want to muddle the situation. Just a couple of weeks longer and our strategy will be set in motion. Then our problems will be behind us."

"I hope so," she said pulling back and looking deeply into his intense brown eyes. "Yes, I hope so."

He gathered her to him again and leaned in, but if he'd meant to give her a brotherly kiss on the cheek, she changed the trajectory by meeting him open-mouthed. Her tongue slid between his lips and gave a flutter. She pressed into his hard body and felt his immediate response.

"Minx," he said, stepping away from her. His hand moved as if he were going to playfully swat her on the butt, but he seemed to change his mind. Lindsey wished he had less control.

Reluctantly, she turned to the stairs. Looking back, she said, "See you in the morning. Let's skip the run, and I'll fix waffles for breakfast. We can read the Sunday Post and act like a normal couple before we call Dad and find out the latest."

He managed a smile. "Night," he said, looking chagrined.

She hoped he was as frustrated as she was.

Brad let the phone ring eight times. Joe's sexy receptionist, Serena, must be checking her makeup again, and not at her desk. With exasperation, he was about to hang-up when an obviously irritated

Joe picked up the receiver and barked, "Yes?"

"Hey, Joe. It's Brad and...

"I can tell who it is," Joe huffed. "With the first words out of your mouth, I got it. So, what do you want now?"

Joe must have been having a bad morning, but Brad chose to ignore his mood. "I've got Rashid all prepped to receive what I told him was the *important and essential information*. Did you get the plans for the old Embassy design?"

"God, you idiot. I told you to watch what you say on the phone." Joe's voice dripped with derision. Brad was getting pissed at Joe's constant disdain. So, he'd said *embassy*. So, what? Joe was acting pompous again. Brad had plenty of experience in covert operations, but right now he was under a lot of pressure. He knew the more nervous he got, the more lapses in protocol. He would need to defuse the situation and get Joe under control.

Continuing his diatribe, Joe hissed, "Let's just say I think I have what you want."

Brad was beginning to feel he had two people to placate—Rashid *and* Joe, so he used his soothing voice to say, "Oh, yeah. Didn't mean to slip up."

The rant quickly faded, and Joe took an audible gulp of breath. "When will you fly back to pick up the package?"

Brad sensed they were back on equal footing. "I have a flight scheduled for early in the morning, and I do mean early, like two-twenty AM. I should be there just before ten."

"Good," Joe said. "Just come directly to the office. Do you have the return flight booked, too?"

"I'll leave tomorrow night. That way my brain won't ever get on DC time, and I'll be back in Dubai before I'm even missed." Brad paused for emphasis. "I don't think Rashid's guys are following me anyway since he knows I needed to travel to collect the paperwork."

"Rashid wouldn't waste his time following you. I just hope no one in *our* government is watching you meet with our friend."

"Nah, haven't seen any tails."

"Well, you wouldn't, if they're any good at their job," Joe added with a note of annoyance in his voice. "See you tomorrow."

»Chapter Eighteen«

Gavin and Lindsey were still at the kitchen farm table when the phone rang. Lindsey moved the landline phone to the table between them.

"Hey, Dad. So, what time is it in Dubai?"

"It's seven in the evening. I wanted to give you guys time to have a leisurely breakfast before I called. It's eleven there, right."

"Yep." Lindsey fidgeted with the buttons on the phone. "I'm going to put it on speaker so Gavin can hear, too, Dad." She peered at the phone and finally punched a button. "Okay, I think it's on speaker now. Tell us what's happening," Lindsey said with a nervous laugh.

Gavin had noticed that Lindsey had been on edge all morning waiting for Jack's call. He had tried to put her at ease, but nothing was working. The conversation over the waffles with fresh berries and lots of syrup had been light, but there was a shadow over Lindsey's eyes.

Maybe to get into action on *the plan* would calm her. She was such a stunningly attractive and intelligent woman, but this trouble with Brad had shaken her confidence. He wanted her with every breath, not simply for physical desires, but to share everything with her—mind and body. They would get through this problem and their relationship would come out stronger for it, he was sure.

Jack began to explain, "The State Department

agents have been tailing Brad and Rashid for days and have drawn up quite a case against Brad. They feel they can get him to cooperate once he hears the alternative."

"What's the timing?" Gavin asked, taking control of the conversation. Lindsey was obviously unsettled. He'd give her time to collect herself.

"Gavin, you and Lindsey should fly over this next weekend and we'll set the plot in motion. We should have Brad in a safe house by then, and the agents want you here, Lindsey, to remind Brad of the patriotic guy he once was when you hired him over eight years ago."

"I'll do my best to appeal to his sense of honor," Lindsey replied, seemingly calming with the plan of action.

"And I want you here, Gavin, to watch over my girl, and, of course, lend your legal opinion on whether Brad has already stepped over the line."

Lindsey leaned toward the phone. "We'll call you as soon as we get the airline reservations. Where are you staying? I hope someplace not too expensive, if there is such a thing in Dubai."

"I'm at the Asiana Hotel. It's fairly close to the airport in the Deira area, near Port Rashid. It's about a hundred a night and very nice."

"Okay, we'll try to book there, too."

They signed off with the agreement to call with all their arrangements as soon as they were finalized.

Lindsey was reenergized after the call from her dad. Gavin could see the sparkle in her eyes. He hoped it was because she could see the end of the ordeal in sight. He was certainly looking forward to finishing this mess and getting on with life. His vision for the future included many shared years with Lindsey. He longed for that to be her vision, too.

They had shifted to the sunroom. Lindsey sat on the couch with one leg under her facing Gavin at the other end of the couch. "Do you think our strategy will really work?" Lindsey softly asked.

"I think the State Department would like it to work. Your dad said they've been trying for a while to get more information on this guy's terrorist cell. What's his name?"

"I think he said it was Rashid Abdul…uh something. Well, I'd better get busy making the arrangements for the trip. And I think we should come up with a story on why we're going to the UAE. It's pretty extreme for a mechanic to take leave to go to Dubai." She got up and got her laptop from the side table and sat back down on the couch a little closer to Gavin.

"Yeah, that *is* a bit out of character for my present position. Guess I could just not mention where I was going, and not show up, but that might make it even more mysterious." Gavin put his hand to his forehead and rubbed his brow while he thought. He looked up. "I know, maybe George could send me over for something to do with either his racing or training business."

"I don't know what that might be. Do you think we should confide in Mr. Trenton? Maybe he could think of something legit," Lindsey offered.

"Since he has his security clearance for all his government contracts, I'm sure he can keep our conversation confidential. He didn't get where he is today by blabbing his private business dealings."

"Well, it's Sunday, and even if he did go to the track to make sure the weekend racing event is going smoothly, he should be back to the farm soon."

"Maybe by the time you finish our flight and hotel reservations he'll be home. Pretty convenient that he lives next door." Gavin smiled. He was glad Lindsey seemed more like herself.

"I'll get to work on the arrangements," she said, opening her laptop.

"Do you want me to help?" Gavin snuggled up to Lindsey and caught her around the waist.

"Ha, I don't think I need *that* kind of help."

Gavin shrugged. "Aw, I just wanted to be near you." He got up and headed toward the porch door. "I'll get out of your hair."

An hour later, Lindsey found Gavin, reading a paperback on the patio.

"I have us booked business class on the Emirates flight Friday night, arriving Saturday morning. It took most of the points I've accumulated on my American Express, but I think it will be worth it. With a nearly thirteen-hour flight it will be nice to be able to stretch out and sleep."

"Were you able to get us in at the same hotel as your dad?"

"Yes, we're all set." Lindsey scooched in next to Gavin on the bench and he put an arm around her shoulder. "I'll be glad when this is all over."

"Hmm, ditto that thought." He drew her closer. "I like it that your dad thinks I can take care of you." Lindsey stiffened. "But of course, you can take care of yourself. I'll just be an extra pair of eyes and ears," he quickly added.

"Shall I call George Trenton now to see if we can drop by for a visit?" Lindsey asked.

"I'm ready when you are."

George was waiting at the door when they drove up. He was nearly as tall as Gavin, and as usual, his hair was a tangle of white as if he'd been running his fingers through it all morning.

"What's up with you two?" he asked. "You sounded sort of vague on the phone Lindsey. I didn't know you even *knew* Gavin."

"We, eh, met at the track. Can we come in? What we have to discuss is rather sensitive," she said with a tense laugh.

George showed them into his den. An abandoned coffee cup and strewn papers suggested George had been enjoying a relaxed Sunday afternoon reading the Post and working the crossword puzzle.

"So, what's this all about?" George asked as they were all comfortably seated.

Lindsey began. "It's a bit of a long story, but you'll need to hear everything, so you can understand our situation."

"What's this *our*? First, I didn't even know you knew my mechanic, now you're in some *situation* together?"

Lindsey changed her position on the couch and looked wide-eyed at Gavin. He could see she was at a loss of how to begin.

"I'll start off with the truth about my background," Gavin said. George looked puzzled but remained silent. Leaning forward with his elbows on his knees, Gavin began. I'm not only a pretty good mechanic, I'm also an attorney," he blurted out.

"Well, that explains a lot. You seemed a little more savvy about computers and business in general than the average mechanic," George said, leaning back in the chair.

Gavin's ears and neck started turning red, and he looked down a moment. "I'll give you the short version." Clearing his throat, he began, "After I graduated from Harvard Law, I spent two years with the Public Defender Offices in Richmond. Subsequently, I was a corporate attorney with Carter, Clooney & Davis in their DC office for nearly ten years, specializing in government contracts. Then something went terribly wrong involving a case from my idealistic years in Richmond. It was so serious it made me reevaluate my life.

I decided it was best to stop being a lawyer. I didn't want to make the same mistake twice. Now, for a few months I've been enjoying a simpler life as a mechanic at Laurel Glen, until I met your friend, Lindsey, at one of the Twilight Testing sessions." He looked over at Lindsey and he could read the sympathy in her eyes. He knew that she knew how difficult it was for him to tell of his past.

"I'll take over the saga here," Lindsey said. "I think I mentioned at the Ferrari meet that I'm in some trouble because of the firing of a business associate—actually, a lot of trouble." She stopped to take a deep breath and gather herself. Every time she had to tell how threatened she felt over Brad's actions, she started to shiver. She wrapped her arms around herself and continued.

"His name is Brad Hansen and when he left my company's employ, he may have gotten in bed, so to speak, with the wrong sort of people in the Middle East. We think he started out thinking he was going to be the next King of Blackwater, like Erik Prince, who has made millions training foreign nationals in Asia. Apparently, Brad's original idea was to provide training to a client in Dubai or Abu Dhabi. It seems to have gotten out of hand, and now the State Department is involved. Brad has been identified meeting with the head of a known terrorist group associated with Islamic extremists."

George held up his hands looking concerned and interjected, "Whoa, whoa. Why are you still in the middle of it since he no longer works for you?"

"I don't want to be, but we think his associates were the ones who tried to run me down on Trappe Road. For some reason, Brad and these Arab guys want my company."

Lindsey's voice rose another octave, and she continued in a rush. "Brad has sued me for breach of contract, and the legal bills are killing me, but we think instead of waiting for Brad to bankrupt me and take my company when I'm on the ropes, this group he is dealing with are in a hurry. With me gone, it would be relatively easy for Hansen to buy my company for pennies on the dollar." Lindsey buried her face in her hands, and a few tears ran down her face. Then she abruptly sat up rubbing at her eyes. "Oh, I told myself I wouldn't cry. It's just that I'm so worked up about this whole mess."

Gavin broke in and picked up the story. "I got involved when she asked for my help. I told her about my legal background, and she thought I might be able to find something we could use against Brad to call off the lawsuit. I started digging. Through my contacts in the government security industry, we found that Brad was spending a lot of time in the Middle East and was living pretty high on the hog."

Lindsey jumped in and said, "That's when my dad got involved."

"This *is* complicated." George said turning his head from Lindsey to Gavin and back to Lindsey. "What does your dad have to do with all this?"

"He is a former special forces man who later had a career with the State Department. He's the one who asked all the right questions with his contacts at State, and they let him know that Brad was a *person of interest* in an operation they're conducting in Dubai."

Lindsey took another big gulp of air, "So, with the help of the State Department agents working on the operation, we have developed a plan. That's where you come in, George."

Gavin met Lindsey's eyes, and she felt her confidence returning. She continued. "The scheme requires that Gavin and I travel to Dubai and Abu Dhabi to persuade Brad to help the State Department agents entrap the leader of this known terrorist cell. They're hoping to snag the 'big fish' who is above Brad's contact." Lindsey was on a roll. "I'll be there to remind him of the terrific patriotic guy he used to be, and Gavin will be there to determine if Brad has already stepped over the line, legally. If he has divulged anything that impacts national security, he could spend a whole lot of time in prison."

Gavin went on, "It could be a win-win situation. If we could help Brad get out of his dilemma, he would probably be so grateful, he'd leave Lindsey alone."

"Our problem is Gavin doesn't have a legitimate reason to go to the Middle East. I'm sure the guys in the mechanics' shop wouldn't think a *thing* of seeing Gavin take time off to fly off to Dubai," she said with a wry smile. "We thought you might be able to come up with a reason with all your ties to government contracting and racing. Does anything pop into your mind?"

George rubbed his chin. "Hmm, let me think. When will you be going?"

"We leave Friday night."

"Whew, you waited until the last minute, didn't you?"

"Everything's been moving quickly ever since the attempt on Lindsey's life," Gavin said.

George sat quietly for a few minutes, tapping his index finger to his hips. He puffed out a long breath, and said, "Well, I have a friend at Yas Island Marina Circuit in Abu Dhabi. It's the track where they hold the Formula One race in the United Arab Emirates, but the race is the last one in the season so won't be until November." George paused again to think, his hand to his chin. Then looking up and with an *aha moment* look on his face he burst out, "Maybe this will work. The track has the Yas 3000 Driving Experience. I could sign up for that, and Gavin could go along as my mechanic."

"That just might do," Lindsey said, brightening.

"No one would think that was out of character for an eccentric old coot like me to go to some exotic place on the spur of the moment." He chuckled.

Lindsey jumped in. "I could put out the word through my business contacts that I am going over to check on one of my contracts with the State Department Diplomatic Security Division. That way it wouldn't seem funny for me to be meeting with State Department officials at the Embassy if need be." She lowered her voice and looked directly at George. "But I hate to draw you into this disaster. It could be dangerous, George, if the wrong people know I'm there. Anyone associated with me could also be harmed. Are you sure you want to get so tangled up in this?"

"Hell, I've always pushed the envelope. Couldn't have been a champion racer if I didn't live life on the edge," he added with a big grin. "Besides, I've lived a great life. If anything happens, I can't say I've missed a thing."

"Ooh, I hope it doesn't come to that," Lindsey said.

"Once we get there, I'll leave all the cloak and dagger stuff to you two," George said with a glint in his eye.

"Okay, I'll email you with our flight times so you can be on the same flight. Might seem more realistic for you and Gavin to travel together."

"And I'll call my old friend in Abu Dhabi and see if I can book the Driving Experience. Gavin won't need to go with me to the track. That will just be our cover story here," he said with a wink.

Gavin and Lindsey headed back to *Sticks and Stones* with a final wave to George, who had a decidedly lighter spring in his step than when they had arrived.

"I think he's enjoying this," they both said at the same time and laughed.

When Gavin got out of his VW back at *Sticks*

and Stones, he glanced over at the Ferrari parked by the garage. He frowned and walked closer to look at what seemed to be chunks of dried grass stuck in the grill and around the wheel wells. "Hey, Lindsey, what's this?" He pulled some of the debris from her car.

Gavin saw the red rise in Lindsey's cheeks. She ducked her head and looked up at Gavin from beneath her hair. She shrugged. "It's nothing. I had a little mishap on the way to your house last night. Took a short detour into a field."

His brows came together forming a deep furrow. "What does that mean? Did you fall asleep? You know you haven't been getting the best sleep lately."

"No. That wasn't it. I didn't want to worry you, but now that you've noticed you'll bug me until I tell you all about it. Come on in, and I'll recount the whole story."

Gavin followed Lindsey into the house, glancing back at the Ferrari one more time before he closed the door. They sat at the kitchen island sipping hot tea before either spoke. "Okay, enlighten me Lindsey. You're such a good driver. I'm curious to know what could have made you leave the road."

Lindsey sighed. "It's difficult for me to replay the incident in my mind."

Gavin could see Lindsey was visibly shaken as she told him about the near miss involving the SUV and old truck. He got up and went to her side of the island, pulling her up into his arms. He was upset she hadn't mentioned it sooner but didn't want to alarm her with his theory on what really took place. It sounded like another attack to him.

He spoke softly into her ear. "Lindsey, I wish you'd told me sooner, but I get it. You didn't want me to worry." He pulled back and looked directly into her deep blue eyes that were glistening with unshed tears. "I *want* to worry about you. I don't know what I'd do if one of these crazies hurt you."

"I'm sorry, Gavin. I think I was just trying to convince myself that it was an accident. Someone in a hurry, or texting, or something," she finished lamely.

"It sounds more serious to me, and even though it didn't happen in Loudoun county, I think we should call Deputy Franklin. He'll know what to do."

✿

She was drained from the afternoon with the deputy, but it felt good to get it off her shoulders. Deputy Franklin had told them the department would file another report which would help in a conviction, if they ever caught the perpetrators.

After dinner Lindsey cornered Gavin. Putting her hands on his hips and looking straight into his absorbing brown eyes, she said, "Hey, you, I've really been missing you. I know you made a promise so things wouldn't get more complicated while I'm involved in this tight spot. But I need you and," with a formal bow said, "I desire your company."

Wrapping her arms around his waist and hugging him to her she murmured, "I think not being together is causing even more turmoil and tension. Please come to bed with me, if only to hold me until I fall asleep." She hated sounding so desperate, but it was the truth—she did need and want him.

"Lindsey, I thought giving you space was what *you* wanted. I didn't mean to be the cause of even more anxiety."

"I miss you." Lindsey smiled up at him.

"Every night I've had a hell of a time getting to sleep, knowing you, my darling girl, are right above me, snuggled beneath the duvet. I want you more than anything."

"Looks like we've changed the game plan," she whispered in a low sexy voice.

They went hand-in-hand up the stairs. When they reached the bedroom, each slowly undressed the other. Fingers trailed across sensitive skin as buttons and hooks were released. His light kisses moved across her shoulders as her bra strap slid off. Her hands gently caressed his erection as his jeans fell to the floor. The slow erotic movements added to the anticipation. Pulling back the quilt, Gavin lifted Lindsey into the bed and lowered himself beside her.

It was a night of slow and sensual love making. Each in tune with the other's pleasure. In the wee hours of the morning, they slept.

»Chapter Nineteen«

The rest of the week flew by. The preparations had been made for the trip and the expectations were building. Lindsey arranged for Rusty, an old codger and one of George's stable hands, to feed and care for Mosby. Mary had everything under control at Lindsey's office and would stall the attorneys while she was away.

Gavin reported that the guys at the mechanics' shop thought he was crazy to go so far away from home. But he said he didn't mind, and he'd take one for the team and go with George on his sudden bizarre trip to visit his old friend in Abu Dhabi. He told them he thought it might be fun to see another country. They didn't guess he'd been to scores of countries all over the world.

Lindsey was putting the last-minute paraphernalia into her carry-on with her cell phone tucked to her ear. "Mary, have Hank check with Chris at the track about the driving and firearms training modules for Triple Shield. George said he had cleared it with Chris, but we need to be certain."

"I've got it under control." With a snicker Mary continued, "We'll do our best to struggle along without you for a week but be back soon. We'll miss you." Then Mary's voice became raspy with emotion. "Take care of yourself and come back safe."

After she got off the phone, Lindsey zipped

her carry-on and rushed down the stairs. Gavin was loading the bags into his car for the trip to Dulles International. They'd asked George to ride with them, but though they were neighbors, George said he'd have his driver take him to the airport. George was a bit of an odd bird, Lindsey thought.

She locked the house and strode toward the car. Gavin looked up and smiled. His whole face lit up. Lindsey could see he was genuinely happy to see her.

"You have everything? Passport, tickets?" Gavin asked for the third time.
"Got it."

They were ready for the adventure. She hoped it would only be an adventure and turn out with a happy ending.

They found George in the Emirates Lounge having a bourbon on the rocks. He waved them over. "Hey, Lindsey, Gavin, join me for a drink. We have about an hour before we board."

"Sounds great," Lindsey said. Was she being a little too enthusiastic?

When the hostess appeared, Lindsey ordered a Sauvignon Blanc and Gavin requested a Michelob. Lindsey moved closer to Gavin on the banquette seat and took his hand. She looked around the airy space and commented, "This is a great way to wait for the departure."

George, who had flown Emirates many times, seemed happy in the surroundings, too. "This is really the Air France Lounge, but they partner with Emirates in several locations. Wait until you see the Emirates Lounge in Dubai. Since it is their main hub, it's a massive elaborate place."

Lindsey glanced at Gavin. "Yeah, I'm looking forward to the return."

They sipped their drinks, and Lindsey tried to relax and be in the moment. Surely the strategy would go smoothly, and they *would* be waiting in the Emirates Lounge for the return, soon.

Before they knew it, their flight was announced. They gathered their things and took the short walk to the gate. When they boarded the huge plane, they were directed to their seats.

"Wow, these are more than seats. They're pods! We can enjoy music, movies, fine wine, then stretch out for a good night's sleep," Gavin said with wonder in his voice, like a little boy with his first bike. "I travelled business with the law firm many times, but this is definitely a notch above the norm. Fun!"

"Let's start with the champagne. Might as well take advantage of all the perks." Lindsey elbowed him in the ribs. She was trying to match Gavin's playful mood to keep things light and easy. Inside she was still troubled. Her mind was spinning. What if Brad wouldn't cooperate? Or even worse, what if his associates were still out to harm her? What if he was able to get control of her company? So many what ifs. And, of course, there were the whys. Why was it so important for Brad to take her company? Revenge, or something else?

"Earth to Lindsey...you have a thousand-mile stare in your eyes. What is it?" Gavin asked.

"Guess you know me too well by now," she said with a sigh. "I was thinking mostly of why." She shrugged carelessly. "I can't figure out why Brad and these Arab nuts want my business."

"I think they *need* your business for some reason. Otherwise they wouldn't be going to such extremes."

"Well, maybe Brad will shed some light on the why, if we can convince him to come back to the good guys' side."

"I say tonight we should eat, drink, and be merry, or at least eat, drink, and go to sleep," Gavin said with a chuckle in his voice. "We'll have plenty of time to worry about this when we arrive in Dubai."

Jack, Lindsey's dad, had been in Dubai nearly a week working with the State Department agents and a few of the officers of the United Arab Emirates Armed Forces. Major Khalifa Al Hamadi, with the UAE forces, had been instrumental in smoothing the way for their operation. Now they were ready to put everything in motion.

Jack and the State agents had it timed to the minute. They'd left a note at the front desk of Brad's hotel and hoped he'd think it was from Rashid summoning him to a meeting. Brad was to go to a certain address in Abu Dhabi at exactly eleven PM.

The address was for a warehouse close to one of Rashid's known holdings. Brad should recognize the location. Also Brad surely was used to getting ultimatums from this Rashid character. Jack was depending on it.

The agents, stationed at the hotel, radioed that Brad had left the Emirates Palace promptly at ten thirty. Phil and Harry, the other pair of State agents, were in the pick-up car by the warehouse. The idea was for Jack to utilize his special forces training to capture Brad. They'd pull in after Jack had "neutralized the suspect." At least that was the term the agents used. He was on his own if anything went wrong.

Jack hoped his training would automatically kick in when he needed it. "It's just like riding a bicycle," Harry had told him, right before dropping him off in the alley. *Right,* Jack thought. Now here he was in a doorway alcove across the alley from the warehouse entrance indicated in the note.

It had taken some doing to get into the back entrance to turn the light on inside, but it was essential that Brad think someone was waiting for him in the building. With any luck, Brad would be focused on entering the building and not hear Jack approaching.

⁂

Her arms were tied to her sides and she was confined in a small, dark, hot space. She wasn't able to move. Where was she? Her panic was rising. Lindsey woke with a racing heart. The blanket was tangled around her, and she was on her side in the Emirates' sleeper-seat with her nose pressed to the side of the pod. Adjusting her position, throwing back the covers, and retracting the footrest portion of the bed, she glanced at her watch.

Damn, she'd only been sleeping for three hours. She needed more sleep if she were going to be alert on arrival. She turned toward Gavin and could see he was breathing deeply, peacefully asleep. She didn't want to wake him with her tossing and turning, so she decided to get up and walk back to the bar area. Maybe if she had a small nightcap, it would make her drowsy and she could still get a few more hours sleep.

One of the flight attendants was acting as bartender. "Hi, my name is Brenda. Could I get you something to drink?"

Brenda was attractive, and Lindsey pegged her age at about fifty. The experienced flight attendants usually worked business or first class. Lindsey nodded. "Sure, that would be great. A big glass of ice water to start, then if you have Brandy & Benedictine, I'll take a small glass."

The server bent over and looked at the stock under the countertop. "I believe it's down here somewhere. Yes, here it is." Brenda popped up from behind the bar with bottle in hand. "I'll get you that water and then let me pour you a small drink." She reached for one large highball glass and also a small crystal snifter from the shelf behind the bar.

Lindsey perched on one of the barstools.

"Thanks. Sounds great. Make the B & B a very small amount please." Lindsey looked around the space that was the full width of the wide-bodied plane and as long as it was wide. Laughing, she tried to make a little conversation. "This is a really nice setup. Looks large enough to have a cocktail party for all the business class passengers."

Brenda smiled warmly and nodded. "Yes, it's a very generous bar area. I like working the bar. It's a way for me to meet a lot of nice people from all over the world. Where are you from?"

"I live in the Virginia countryside west of DC." Lindsey warmed to the idle chat as it took her mind off the reason for the trip. It was relaxing her. Maybe she would be able to get back to sleep after all when she went back to her pod.

Brenda looked beyond Lindsey. "May I help you, sir?"

Lindsey turned to see a bleary-eyed George walk up. "Hi, Lindsey, can't sleep either?" Turning to Brenda, he said, "I'll have a Courvoisier."

Smiling up at George, Lindsey said, "Well, I had a funny dream that woke me and thought a small nip might help me get back to sleep."

George settled on the stool next to her. "I never sleep well on a plane, or at all for that matter. Must be my age." His lips pouted out and down at the corners, then just as suddenly he brightened and smiled. "But I've built in a day to recuperate before I get on my friend's racing circuit in Abu Dhabi. Should do the trick."

The three of them conversed about light topics, and Lindsey was padding down the aisle back to her seat within fifteen minutes. She felt warm and fuzzy. Nestling between the bed cushion and the covers, she was asleep in three minutes.

Lindsey shook Gavin when the plane began the initial descent into Dubai International. "Hey, sleepyhead, are you going to sleep all day. You're missing a delicious breakfast and the view of a spectacular city."

Gavin was immediately alert and pushed the buttons to make his bed turn back into a chair. "Gosh, you should have poked me earlier."

"You still have plenty of time. It's really strange, the plane flies over the city, then out over the desert nearly into Oman, and turns to land from the east."

"How do you know that?"

"Oh, I was here a few years ago with Dad. It was smaller then, but the plane came in from the desert side that time, too."

"Okay, thanks for the wakeup call." Gavin pushed the shade higher.

"I asked the flight attendant to keep your omelet in the warmer until you were ready." She leaned over Gavin, her breast brushing his arm, and pointed out the window. She spoke with an excited childlike quality to her voice, "Look. Can you see that tall building that resembles a giant sailing ship? Amazing, isn't it?"

"Yeah, sure, great view." He looked back at her. "Yes, very nice view. I'm starving, in more ways than one," he said wiggling his eyebrows up and down, "but I'll settle for breakfast. I'm ready to eat." As if on cue, the breakfast was set on his tray table. Then without another word he grabbed his fork and dug in.

Lindsey marveled that Gavin could eat just about anything and not gain a pound, and, oh, what a nice distribution of those pounds. He was one purely perfect, male specimen. She never tired of looking at him.

She hoped everything would turn out well on their Dubai adventure. It would be nice to get to know each other in a more conventional way without all the tension. Crossing her fingers, she prayed the plan would work.

Lindsey started gathering everything she'd taken out of her carry-on. It seemed to have exploded in her seating space. She and Gavin both had bedhead, but they would shower and dress in clean clothes when they got to the hotel.

"Do you know what I did with my hat? It's the peach colored one I got at the Gold Cup Races at Great Meadows."

"Maybe it's in the overhead or stuffed in one of the many hiding places in your pod."

"Oh, here it is," she said. She brushed her hair back into a ponytail, put on the cap, and pulled the tail through the opening in the back of the cap in one fluid motion. "Good to go."

✿

Oh, yes, she was magnificent in whatever she wore, Gavin thought. He was falling hard for this complex woman. Good to her core, but she could light his fire in just one look with her naughty sexy lopsided smile. He would have to hold that thought.

Gavin finished his breakfast and prepared for landing, too. The pace was about to pick up, and he wanted to be ready. He was so glad he'd been able to sleep. Hopefully, he would be prepared to help protect Lindsey. Of course, she didn't think she needed to be protected. Sometimes she was overly independent, but he had to admit she was a remarkably capable woman. Still—he'd keep her close. He didn't know what he'd do if something happened to her.

»Chapter Twenty«

Lindsey loved it when everything was going according to schedule. She and Gavin had said good-bye to George at the airport, promising to keep him up-to-date on the events that were unfolding. After showering and dressing at the hotel, they waited for Lindsey's dad in the lobby. They didn't want to look like tourists, so they were in clean but a bit raggedy khakis and neutral T-shirts. No coral-colored vacation tee with "*Aruba – The Friendly Island*" printed on the front for this trip. Lindsey had a hijab with her, which wasn't necessary in the up-scale areas but would be useful where they were going. She even had a long skirt tucked into her tote to cover her slacks during the transfer into and out of the safe house.

"There he is," Lindsey said, pointing. "I can't wait to hear what all has happened."

Jack walked with a jaunty strut as he approached them.

"If your swagger is any indication of how proud you are of yourself, the plan must be going well." Gavin tipped his head, squinted his eyes and grinned.

"Glad you're safe, Dad," Lindsey said, giving him a big hug.

"Yeah, everything went extremely well last night. I had to knock Brad on the side of the head with my blackjack, but he wasn't out long."

Jack said grinning. "Guess I still have it, the special ops' skills, I mean." He subconsciously stood up straighter and puffed out his chest. "The State guys helped me load him into the back of the SUV, and we got him quickly to the safe house. We've let him sweat since last night, but with your arrival, we're ready to launch stage two of the plot."

"Any sign of Rashid and his cohorts?" Gavin asked.

"We have Rashid under surveillance, but we haven't seen him meeting with anyone." Jack said. "Also, we have Brad's cell phone, and so far Rashid hasn't tried to contact him since the snatch."

"That's good," Gavin said. "We have some time to question Brad before we put the rest of the plan in motion."

"Okay, so why are we standing around here? Let's get into action," Lindsey put in.

"Let's load. I have an old sedan pulled up in front." Jack said while moving toward the entrance. "We can talk in the car."

Brad was still groggy, and his head ached like a son-of-a bitch. It must have been the blackjack he vaguely remembered seeing right before everything went dark. He pushed himself up with his back against a cement wall and looked around. He was in a windowless room that smelled dank and moldy. Must be in a cellar. A single, bare light bulb hanging from the ceiling illuminated a rickety staircase off to the right and nothing but filth and rat droppings around him in every other direction.

Where the hell was he? He could be in BuFu, Egypt for all he knew. Of course, whoever took him would have had to drug him if they'd taken him to another country in the middle of nowhere. Though his head hurt, he didn't seem to have a drug hangover. So, he was probably still in the Emirates.

He didn't know how long he had been out. Shit, he didn't even know who had taken him and more importantly, why. Maybe Rashid and his gang had figured out he was stalling. He was screwed if they had the intelligence to tap his phone and knew he was trying to give them bogus blueprints. His mind was racing. He'd never been in so much trouble.

When he was on a SEAL team, it was just that, a team. He had his buddies to rely on. They worked together. This time he had fucked up all on his own. He really didn't want to die. He just dreamed of making the big bucks training some foreign nationals. Stupid, stupid, stupid. How had he gotten tangled up with this group? If he was completely honest with himself, it was his own damned fault for this cluster-fuck.

Yeah, he finally had to acknowledge Rashid and his buddies had to be terrorist. If *they* didn't kill him, his own country would. Damn, now that was an awe-inspiring notion to contemplate, and not in a good way. He was getting worked up again. If Joe were here, he'd tell him to settle down, but Joe wasn't here. Joe was never here on the front line.

That pussy had no idea of the strain he'd been under in dealing with these erratic hostile bastards.

He felt disoriented. He had to do something, but he couldn't move around very easily with his hands and feet shackled.

"C'mon, Brad, no one is coming to rescue you, so start thinking," he muttered to himself.

He could butt-walk like an inchworm over toward the stairs. Maybe he'd hear something, like bits of language, so he could work out who was holding him. It seemed eerily quiet. There was no sound of movement from upstairs. Were they ever coming to interrogate him, or would he be left in this cellar to rot? God, he was terrified, but he had to try to remain under control. He had to think.

Jack was weaving in and out of the traffic like a native. Dubai had the worst rush-hour traffic —and it was rush-hour twenty-four-seven—but he seemed relaxed, talking and avoiding other cars at the same time.

"We are holding Brad in one of the Agency's safe houses on the outskirts of town near the Sonapur work camp," Jack said. "Sonapur means City of Gold in Hindi, but, ha, that's a laugh. It's a town of nearly 200,000 pitifully poor, mostly Indian, migrant workers. The workers who have done well, relatively, live in single-family hovels in an area just before you get to Sonapur. That's where we're headed. We'll be there soon, so let's talk over the strategy."

✿

Pulling in beside the ramshackle house, Jack spoke again with a smirk on his face. "I can imagine Brad is supremely pissed by now since he has no idea who has taken him or where he is. And it's been just over twelve hours."

"Good. Let him sweat," Lindsey said under her breath. Then in a louder tone, "He has been a pain in my ass for a long time. I wouldn't mind hanging him by his toes."

"Now, Lindsey, be nice," Jack said.

"You sound like Mother. Hey, this guy has caused me a lot of grief. It's payback time."

She arranged the hijab around her head and neck then pulled the skirt over her khakis as she got out of the car. The property looked dilapidated from the outside but was totally reinforced and modernized on the inside. Her dad had said the cellar holding Brad was heavily insulated, so they weren't worried he'd overhear their conversation. In fact, the entire house was nearly soundproof. Wouldn't want any neighbors hearing strange sounds coming from within.

All four of the State Department agents were there, rotating guard duty. Two were in the hall leading to the stairs of the cellar and the two from the pick-up team were in the kitchen, which opened into a dining and living area.

"Hey, guys, how's our guest?" Jack asked with a shit-eating grin on his face.

Phil, the one her dad said was the head of the

team, levered out of his chair to welcome the new arrivals. He was a big guy, but Lindsey could see he was all muscle. "Good to finally meet you two. Jack's told us a lot about you." He shook their hands. "Welcome aboard." He looked back at Jack. "Oh, and to answer your question, Jack, our guest hasn't made a peep. We have him in our deluxe accommodations on the lower level. Our microphones in the cellar have picked up some groans, incoherent mumbling, and rustling. That's all."

A second agent smiled at them and came over to the group from the sink in the kitchen. He was a smaller wiry guy also in superb physical shape, with a Navy Chief's anchor tattoo on his left forearm. "Nice to meet you, Gavin, Ma'am," he drawled nodding at each of them. "I'm Harry, Phil's partner."

Phil slapped Harry on the shoulder. "Our Harry, here, is from Dallas. Bet you couldn't tell." Then motioning to the hall, he said, "The rest of the team's at the listening station. You'll meet them later." *All men*, Lindsey thought. She would just have to be the exception. She wasn't missing this, and she *was* an essential part of the project.

"We were just having a sandwich. Want anything before we get started?"

Jack glanced to the kitchen counters. "Yeah, Phil, that sounds good. What do you have?"

"A turkey sandwich okay? Not a lot of variety in the stores around here. All the makings are still out on the counter."

"I'll make 'em." Jack busied himself in the kitchen. He found three paper plates and dealt out two pieces of bread onto each plate. Then he put some mayo on the six slices of bread, stacked the turkey on three, and slapped the other three slices on top.

"Voila, instant lunch," Jack said with a flourish. "Mind if we join you at your beautifully appointed table?" Lindsey knew her father. He was trying to make light of the entire operation by being flippant, but of course, he was usually a bit of a smartass. This time it did seem to have the effect of lowering the tension in the room.

"We've got tea or bottled water and chips if you want some." Harry added in his soft southern voice.

"Sounds great," the three newcomers said. "I'll take a bottled water," Lindsey said and the other two put up a hand and nodded since their mouths were already full.

Lindsey, Gavin, and Jack sat at the kitchen table eating ravenously.

"It's been a good while since we had breakfast on the plane," Gavin said, talking around his partially full mouth. "And since the strategy includes your being captives"—he nodded at Jack and Lindsey—"you'll probably have meager rations for a time." Gavin chuckled.

"Pretty funny!" Lindsey said and nudged Gavin in the side.

When they had finished, Gavin drew Lindsey into the front hall. "Are you sure you want to go through with the mission? It's pretty dangerous, especially for a woman. We have no idea how Brad will react. You know Jack could probably be just as convincing on his own during this part, and he knows all the tactics of an interrogation."

"I'll be fine." Lindsey pulled her arm away from Gavin. "I can take care of myself."

As if unaware of her change in mood, Gavin continued, "Just don't let Brad get to you. Stare him down, and remember he was once your employee. You were in charge."

Lindsey bristled. "You're treating me like a helpless ninny—which I'm not. When did you become the boss of me?"

Gavin backed off and stared at Lindsey. "I'm just concerned, but I can see you're in your *independent woman* mode." Gavin shook his head and put both his hands out in front of him, palms facing Lindsey. "I'm sorry. My concern brought out my protection persona."

Lindsey shook her head. "Just leave me alone so I can collect myself."

"Yes, ma'am." Gavin turned and walked into the hall.

Lindsey watched his retreating form. Maybe it had been a mistake to pull him into her troubles. Like a typical male, he was taking command and trying to solve all her problems. Her business hadn't become successful on its own. She could handle Brad and this whole operation without being second guessed by Gavin. Why had she even brought him on this trip?

Lindsey took a deep breath and walked back into the kitchen where Jack was discussing some of the finer points of the operation with Phil. "Well, I went over the first phase with Lindsey in the car, so, we might as well get started," Jack said and nodded his head toward Lindsey. "She's here, so guess it's time to bind our hands and throw us down the stairs into the cellar. Well, maybe not throw, just guide us to the stairs. We'll take it from there. We'll stumble the last few steps. Hey, Phil, for authenticity you could say something interesting in Arabic, like 'get down there, you American whore.'"

Phil laughed, but quickly became dead serious. He put on his agent demeanor and practiced the phrase in a low guttural tone. All four of the agents assigned to this task force were fluent in Arabic and several other languages that could come in handy in this part of the world. And, yes, this was not a game. Everyone here was taking a dangerous risk.

Phil and Harry finished tying Lindsey and Jack, then put a black hood over each of their heads.

"Feel ok? Not too tight? Sorry we had to put on the hoods, but it needs to be as realistic as we can make it."

"That should do. Whew, they're pretty stinky." And then Jack got completely quiet and with intensity said, "It's a good plan, guys, so let's follow it. Okay—ready?"

The door rattled at the top of the stairs, and

Brad nearly peed his pants. They were coming. Oh, God. His heartbeat ratcheted up again, just when it had finally reached a more normal rate. He began to hyperventilate.

No, he could do this. He'd had the training. He drew in a breath and concentrated on the floor a few feet in front of his shoes.

The next thing he knew, two people, their hands bound in front of them, and heads hooded, tumbled into the dirty space at the bottom of the stairs. As soon as the door slammed at the top of the stairs, the new arrivals rolled over and managed to pull off the hoods.

"God, those smell awful. They must soak them in goat pee," Jack said, peering around the room.

This was definitely not what Brad had envisioned.

"My, God, Lindsey, what are you and your father doing here?"

Lindsey seemed dazed. Then her head snapped, and she did a double take on Brad. "You! So, you're behind this, you asshole. Great work! Now you got me involved with terrorists and kidnapers. What's going on?"

Brad blinked his eyes as if trying to get his brain wrapped around this new development. Now, at least, he knew his own government wasn't holding him. It must be Rashid and his group. Hell, a much worse scenario.

"It's not my fault you're here, and, anyway,

I didn't know they were terrorists when I started working with them. You were the one who drove me to it. You wouldn't let me develop the training facility over here for foreign nationals. Hell, on top of that, you fired me!"

Lindsey slipped down and propped her back against the wall on the other side of the room. "Wait, you can't blame this one on me, Brad. I had the good sense to see there was no profit in your little scheme." Cocking one eyebrow up, she widened her eyes at Brad. "So, how do you think your idea is working out for you now, pal?"

*

Lindsey didn't have to play a part. She was furious. This idiot had nearly driven her company under and turned her life upside down. Not to mention he had to be the one who was responsible for her nearly being run over by a crazy person. Damn it, she would save her business, even it meant she had to strangle this asshole.

Lindsey turned away in disgust. She took a breath and tried to calm herself. Brad was still sputtering something about *not his fault*. Lindsey just shook her head.

In the practice scenario Jack was to keep the pressure on Brad, so after a brief silence Jack spoke. "Nice to see you, too, asshole," he said sarcastically. "Thanks for pulling us into your unsavory business. What kind of shit is this? You're not the Brad Hansen I used to know if you're in league with terrorists."

"C'mon, Jack, I didn't ask you guys to get involved."

Jack kicked his boot against the wall just missing Brad. "Well, when you had someone nearly kill my daughter in that hit-and-run, I got involved."

"Now, Jack, that wasn't me. You can't prove I had anything to do with it. I even told Rashid to back off."

Wagging his finger, Jack said, "Ooh, slipped up, Brad. That little statement just proves you were in on it."

"No, I..."

Jack got right in Brad's face. "Yes, Rashid Abdul-Azim. We know all about your deal with Mr. Rashid." Jack's teeth were actually bared. Lindsey could tell he was just as infuriated as she was.

"How can you know anything?" Brad croaked. "Rashid is a legitimate businessman. I'm just helping him develop a training center so his group can protect their country against aggression."

Jack backed off and went to Lindsey's side of the room and leaned against the wall. "Shit, do you really believe that garbage? You should hear yourself. You sound like a politician trying to justify helping the Taliban. You know as well as I do that *'legitimate businessman'* is pure hogwash!" Jack yelled using air quotes for legitimate businessman.

Brad blanched. "Okay, okay, that's what I thought at the beginning, but I have to admit I suspect, now, that he's not really totally aboveboard."

"That's an understatement!" Jack shook his

head slowly.

Lindsey jumped into the fray. "Okay, this crap isn't getting us anywhere. We can discuss all this in a minute, but first we need to see if we can get out of this mess without dying."

"Right," Jack said.

They spent some time untying each other, then all took a seat on the floor leaning against the wall.

Lindsey began. "The State Department has had you under surveillance for weeks." Brad's head whipped up, an incredulous look on his face, but Lindsey didn't give him time to interrupt. She went on. "The agents have caught you numerous times meeting Rashid Abdul-Azim. Now they have a tail on him, too. He is a known terrorist and works with an extremely violent terrorist cell out of Syria. He isn't the head of the cell, though, so the agents have stayed back and didn't bring you in, hoping you and Rashid would lead them to the person in command."

"Oh, I never thought it would lead to all this," Brad said putting his hands to his face. "Some of this is sheer bad luck. It's really not my fault."

"Quit whining, Brad," Lindsey snapped.

Jack took up the story. "After the attempted hit-and-run, I got drawn in because I don't take kindly to someone trying to harm my baby. I started checking with my colleagues at State about what you were up to, and that's when we found out about Rashid. The State Department guys figured you were in way over your head, but you're an American citizen, and must be protected, even if you *are* a treasonous bastard." Jack propped himself back against the moldy wall. "They have enough on you to put you away for many years, but the State Department agents seemed to think they can use you in trapping Rashid. Bait, so to speak. If you're lucky, and if you agree to help them, they might go easier on you."

Brad sat up straighter and brightened. "Really, you think so?" Lindsey could see throwing him that lifeline was the right strategy. There was hope in his eyes when he added, "Sure, I'll help them. You know I'll help them." He was nearly pleading.

Jack motioned toward Lindsey. "State thought since you and Lindsey had a history, albeit a checkered one, she could motivate you to do the right thing. They just got me as an added benefit."

He frowned and shook his head. "But that arrangement got blown all to hell when Lindsey and I were taken from a sidewalk near our hotel and stuffed into a filthy van."

"What I haven't been able to understand, Brad, is why Rashid and his gang want to get rid of me," Lindsey said.

Brad sighed. "I think they thought, with you out of the way, I could buy control of your company. STLS would then be a legitimate front for their, let's say, not so legal activities. At the beginning, I truly thought it was an honest training contract. As it progressed, I started feeling uneasy about some of the requests, but I didn't know how to get out of it."

Jack made a derisive sound. "Sure."

"No, really, Lindsey, Jack." Brad looked from one to the other, his hands balling into fists. "I was so angry when you let me go from the firm that I was determined to get back at you. I was going to show you. I went a little crazy. But I never wanted to physically harm you."

"Well, that's comforting." Lindsey rolled her eyes.

"Building my dream training facility, with someone else footing the bill, was just too good a deal to turn down. I got caught up in proving I was better than you."

Lindsey frowned. "When did you change from the patriot I thought I knew to a mercenary asshole? Or were you really that greedy from the beginning?"

Jack took over the conversation. "Okay, enough of the recriminations. Let's work out what to do now. The good news is that several people, namely State agents, know we are missing. With any luck, someone may have even followed us and knows exactly where we are."

Lindsey cut in. "Right! Thanks for the rosy version, Dad, but in reality, they may know we're gone but have no idea *where* we've gone."

"Yes, that's true, too," Jack said with a sigh, "but we need to hope for the best and plan for the worst. Let's work on a strategy."

Tom and his partner, Nick, were sitting by the

listening station. The two agents were subordinate to Phil and Harry but had been chosen for their heavy field training and their fluency in Arabic. Gavin sat with them at the table while Phil and Harry stood nearby leaning against the hall wall to hear what was said in the room.

"Seems to be going as designed," Gavin said with a smile.

"That Brad is a piece of work. I'd rather burn him for treason than bargain with him," Nick said, the words coming out in a low growl.

"But maybe we'll catch the big fish this time," Tom added.

"Yeah, maybe." Phil shrugged his shoulders, obviously unconvinced.

Being the most serious-minded of the bunch, Harry tried to focus the group on the immediate task.

"We need to get ready for the rescue. When Jack and Lindsey have all the information they think they can squeeze out of him for now, they'll give us the sign. We need to listen carefully and be ready to act."

Phil took charge. "Tom, you and Nick need to get into your terrorist garb. You'll have your heads wrapped, and when we knock you out, your faces will be looking down. Brad won't be able to see who you are if he manages to catch a glimpse of your bodies."

"Hey, I thought we were taking positions on the floor up here, maybe a little fake blood soaking through our head gear near the temple for a more realistic touch, but I don't relish being bonked on the head," Tom said.

"Yeah, yeah, we really won't hit you guys since the scuffle to gain control of the terrorists' position supposedly takes place before the cavalry rides in and saves the day. They can't hear anything up here, so, you're right, Tom. We won't do any bonking."

"Thanks, but, really, Phil, 'the cavalry rides in?' Please." Tom groaned and punched Phil on the arm.

Ignoring Tom's jab, Phil continued, "It'll be getting dark soon. Lindsey has her watch on, so she'll know when the time is right for the mock escape to the car. Wouldn't want the neighbors being curious about a daring daytime snatch."

»Chapter Twenty-One«

Lindsey rubbed her wrists. The restraints hadn't been that tight, but she had still lost some feeling in her hands. "Now that we're untied, we can be ready to rush the guard if one of them brings us food," she said.

"We could bang on the door to see if we could entice them to open it," Brad suggested.

Jack stood up straight, shoulders back with his hands on his hips and said, "They're probably giving us time to sweat. They want us worrying what they might do to us."

"Well, it's working," Lindsey muttered. "I'm scared shitless." She recognized her dad's Delta agent stance. He was really getting into his role.

"I don't think they'll open the door until they're ready," Jack said. "But while we're waiting, Brad, why don't you fill us in on your deal with Rashid."

Lindsey was going over the progress in her mind. The scheme had been, first, to ridicule and debase Brad, followed by trying to gain Brad's trust, then, finally, to coax Brad into revealing the deal with Rashid. The more information, the better. So, they were in part three and Lindsey hoped the agents upstairs were listening and taping the conversation. She thought about Gavin. He was also right upstairs, but she had to block out thoughts of him for now.

Coming back to the present, she noticed there were dark circles under Brad's eyes and Lindsey thought he looked much older than he had a few months earlier. Still she couldn't muster much sympathy for the fool. He had always seemed so confident that it bordered on arrogance. Now he appeared to be a broken man. His blustering when he worked for Lindsey must have been a cover-up for his insecurity all along.

✻

Brad cleared his throat. "First, did you get a look at your captors?"

"Nah," Jack said, "but when they spoke it was Arabic. They also smelled worse than a herd of goats. Real nice guys, I'm sure."

Brad was getting sick of Jack's sarcasm, but thought it best not to say anything since they were obviously blaming him for the fix they were in. And this mess sure as hell wasn't his fault. He needed to explain in words even this smartass, pea brain would understand. He blew out an audible breath and began.

"A few months before I left STLS, I was making some routine calls to some of my old SEAL buddies. I got a lead from one of them that a group was searching for a project manager to build a training facility in Oman. Well, I jumped at the chance to accomplish my goal of running a training compound close to the action in the Middle East.

"I flew to Abu Dhabi, where the group was based, and met for the first time with Rashid. He

251

seemed like a normal Arab businessman, and we hit it off. We discussed the facility and the training that would take place there. He asked if I could make the training villages and urban areas truly authentic, and I assured him I had been in many high-threat areas of the world and could make it realistic. I explained I knew facility layouts, so the men could practice counterthreat drills in 'real' buildings. So, he told me to draw up a proposal.

"That's when I broached the idea with you, Lindsey, about building the training facility out of the U.S. You said you'd get some numbers together and get back to me. You know the history there. The more I pushed, the more you put on the brakes. I thought you were being unreasonable."

"Yeah, I remember that period," Lindsey said. "I thought you were losing it."

"Well, I should have lost it, the way you were treating me." His voice had risen. He paused while he looked down at his hands and as he resumed speaking, brought his tone back to a more reasonable level. "You showed me spread sheets with break-even points, fixed costs, overhead, and lots of other numbers until I was cross-eyed. I knew in my gut it was a good deal but couldn't convince you. I told you it was a project we shouldn't pass up. Looking back, I can see I was acting desperate, but I didn't want to give up."

He sighed and drooped forward. "Right after you fired me, I had a conversation with my attorney who encouraged me to continue doing what I already knew how to do, namely security training. You know, Lindsey, I made you plenty of money over the years. I thought I had done a good job. I was in a state of shock over being fired. Paralyzed. I also felt super pissed off with you. I couldn't do anything for a few weeks."

Brad could see Lindsey clenching her teeth. She was holding back something. "Did you have something to say, Lindsey?"

"Yeah, I was biting my tongue not to say, 'quit whining' again."

Brad grimaced, trying to ignore the comment. "Oh."

Taking a deep breath, he continued, voice rising. "Hey, you forced me into doing this with your stubbornness. I took the initiative and came up with a real moneymaker, and all you did was hit me with spreadsheets and... And after I'd made you a shitload of money, you fired me. Fired! Like some third-rate, pissant stooge. Okay, I might have been wallowing in self-pity for a short time, but finally the anger helped me overcome the feeling of rejection. I got ahold of myself and decided to get back in the game. I was going to show you, Lindsey.

"So, I contacted Rashid and, to explain the time lapse, I told him I had been ill. I let him know I would be in Abu Dhabi the following week. I was riding high with the new direction of my life.

"I met with Rashid dozens of times, and the plans went forward. We met mostly in a rug shop he owned or in my hotel room, rarely in public. I was a tad curious about the secrecy, but the money flowed into an account in the Caymans, so I thought everything was going smoothly. Then he said they were having trouble securing land in Oman for the camp, and he asked if I could purchase the land through my security company." Brad paused and ran his hand through his hair.

"Well, then I had to tell him I was working on my own and didn't have a United States security company backing me. That was the first time I saw the real Rashid. He went into a tirade and threatened me. He said I'd have to have a legitimate, reputable, security company behind me or I would have to return the money."

"Did you ever do a background check on this guy?" Jack asked shaking his head.

"No, I guess I was in too much of a hurry to make the big bucks," Brad said in a low voice. Feeling embarrassed, he looked down, then picked up his head and stared into the far corner to avoid eye contact. "I just wanted to build the training compound. There were two reasons. One, I thought it was a great idea and, two, because I wanted to prove to Lindsey my idea was right. In hindsight, probably not the best motivation." He looked at Lindsey with the best apologetic look he could muster.

"Right, twenty-twenty hindsight," Lindsey said. But the look on her face was more like *what a dumb-ass*. He chose to ignore the sneer.

Brad nervously tapped his hand against his leg. Looking right at Lindsey, he all but whispered,

"You were always the smart one when it came to business. You did an extensive cost-benefit analysis for every project, which was always too cautious for my taste. But this time, Lindsey, I didn't want to believe you were right on my one big opportunity.

"The cash was rolling in, and I was important to Rashid and his group. I was going to build the training facility and show you. It was after Rashid's first rant that the alarm bells started going off, and now, confined in this cellar, it's obvious it was all too good to be true."

Brad looked around at the dismal surroundings and shook his head. "The only thing I could think to do was to stall Rashid. I flew back to DC the next day to meet with my attorney and partner, Joe."

Jack cut in, "Joe who?"

"Oh, I thought I mentioned him before. It's Joe Johnson. Lindsey's met him. The earlier breach of contract lawsuit was his idea, so I could get the money I deserved and to get back at you." Brad glanced over at Lindsey. "But when I told Joe the whole story, ending with my encounter with Rashid, he said there was one way to get the backing of a genuine company."

Brad paused and took a deep breath before continuing. "He said I should up the ante on the lawsuit to include damages. It was millions. A figure designed to unnerve you. You would either give up and hire me back, or the company would be weakened by a lengthy lawsuit, go under, and I could acquire it for pennies on the dollar."

"You scheming, son-of-a-bitch. I can't believe you plotted against me like that. We were a good team once, friends even, but you've changed Brad." She just glared at him with a look of disappointment on her face.

"Okay, okay, I see that now. I was just so angry. It messed with my reasoning." He paused and sighed, rubbing one hand to his wrinkled brow. "Do you want to hear more of this disaster saga? It keeps me from thinking about who's on the other side of the door."

"Yeah, sure."

"Okay, so a week later at the next meeting with Rashid, he mentioned the FBI's training camp at Quantico and also about a Mock Embassy being built by the State Department. He asked if I could get blueprints for those facilities and replicate them in Oman? I told him I could probably get my hands on the plans, just to placate him. I thought if I said no, he might kill me then and there."

"You're right on that count," Jack jeered. "Didn't it dawn on you, at that point, your Rashid might not be a businessman wanting training to protect his country?"

"I wasn't thinking straight. I was panicking. I called Joe, and he said to come home immediately since we shouldn't discuss this type of thing over the phone. Flying back and forth so much, I was tired and jet-lagged. I felt overwhelmed."

Lindsey stared at Brad. "You're making excuses again."

Brad defiantly stared back. "Do you want to hear this or not?" Lindsey just shrugged.

Brad went on. "Joe and I knew we couldn't get the layout for the FBI complex, and even if we could, we wouldn't give them to Rashid and his associates. Rashid made it clear at our last meeting that he wanted the site plan to the mock embassy based on the Standard Embassy Design that the State Department is using to replace old embassies. He somehow knew they were building that design for training somewhere in the states."

Jack's head whipped around, and he practically shouted, "You don't have those blueprints, do you?"

"No, no, but Joe was able to get the plans for the old Mock Embassy that's at AP Hill in Virginia. It's where the State Department's Basic Agents operate their week-long Capstone exercise at the end of their training."

"That's not much better. Have you passed them to him yet?" Jack asked.

"Not yet. We were supposed to meet this weekend."

Brad noticed Lindsey surreptitiously look at her watch, look up at Jack, and give a slight nod. What was that about?

Jack cleared his throat and spoke in a loud voice. "Well, it looks like he couldn't wait. Now he has all of us, and it's time to pay the piper!"

»Chapter Twenty-Two«

"There it is!" Gavin shouted.

"Okay, everyone, let's execute the plan as we practiced," Phil said calmly. "Brad's going to pay the piper, for sure now. Tom, you and Nick take your places on the floor at the top of the stairs. By the way, love your terrorist garb. Quite stylish!" He smiled. "We'll hood Brad before we bring him upstairs, but he may be able to catch a glimpse of what's on the floor, so we need to be convincing. Harry and I will be the rescuing agents. Gavin, you need to stay in the kitchen while the operation goes down. Wouldn't want Brad to inadvertently see you. After we leave in the car, you three tidy up the place and get the interrogation room ready."

"It should definitely be an improvement over that musty cellar," Tom added.

"Gotta treat a fellow American to more genteel hospitality than he has been receiving from those terrorist bastards," he said with a chuckle.

"Aw, couldn't we get a little nasty during the interrogation?" Harry smirked.

"I promise you, it will be a lively conversation."

Phil threw back the door to the basement with a bang, yelling at Harry, "Go, go, go!"

Harry rushed down the stairs with his gun stretched out in front of him, swung it around the corner to see three startled faces, and yelled, "Clear!"

Phil barged into the cellar. "Are you the only ones down here?"

Jack said, "Yes."

"Am I glad to see you," Brad said breathily

Phil glared at him. "Maybe you'll change your mind on that later."

"Well, I'm certainly glad to see you two agents. What took you so long?" And Jack chuckled.

"Long? We were damn fast considering all the logistics. We saw them take you and Lindsey, so were able to follow, but it took us a while to get the operation set up." Phil crossed the room toward Brad. "Looked like there were only two of them here when we did the heat scan of the house. It showed only two signatures on the first level. We just weren't sure what we would find in the cellar. Harry and I decided we could handle two guys with the element of surprise on our side."

Harry joined Phil in front of Brad.

"Brad Hansen, you are under arrest and will be detained on suspicion of treason." Harry barked, in his best Navy Chief's tone. He pulled Brad up, jerked his arms behind his back, and cuffed him.

"Now, wait, wait, I didn't do anything wrong. You can't do this. I'm an American citizen."

"That's why we haven't used lethal force on you. The guys upstairs weren't so lucky. Terrorists and kidnappers don't receive the same courtesy."

Brad struggled, but Harry easily slipped a

rope around his waist, hooded him with a nice clean hood, and began manhandling him toward the stairs. Brad probably outweighed him by thirty pounds, but that didn't faze Harry.

Ignoring Brad's protests Phil said to Jack and Lindsey, "C'mon, we need to get out of here. We're meeting the other agents at a safe house closer to town."

Muffled, but still a raspy, panicky shout came from beneath the hood. "You can't treat me like this. I'm an American citizen. Don't I get one call to my attorney?"

Phil only laughed and pushed Brad up the stairs. "Shut up, you asshole!"

Brad couldn't figure out what the hell was going on. He thought he had been rescued and was safe, but instead these guys were treating him like a criminal. When they made it to the top of the stairs out of that horrible foul-smelling cellar, Brad was able to take a deep breath of slightly less acrid air. As they led him down what seemed like a narrow hallway, he stumbled against what he sensed was a body on the floor. God, these agents weren't fooling around. His life was going to shit.

They hustled Brad into what had to be an old sedan. The upholstery felt ragged, and some errant seat springs poked him in the butt as he slid to the middle of the seat. It also smelled worse than the cellar. Two people squeezed in the back on either side of Brad. He assumed it was Jack and Lindsey.

They drove on and on, some on rough roads, some in traffic. He tried to count the left and right turns. It was hopeless. He'd never figure out where he was.

Leaning toward the larger body mass next to him, he spoke in a conspiratorial mumble, "Jack, can't you convince these two in the front to uncuff me. This hood is ridiculous. I'm not a flight risk."

"No can do, Brad. At least your hood looks cleaner than the one's the terrorists used on us. Consider yourself lucky. Treason is a serious charge. We won't be able to interfere."

"Please, Jack, Lindsey, help me." Now he was begging and practically sobbing. He had really fucked up this time.

From the front seat Phil roared, "If you don't shut-up, you jerk, we'll knock you out with a little shot. You may not like the side-effects. When you wake up, you'll vomit repeatedly and have a severe headache. Wanna keep yapping?"

Brad went silent.

Harry contacted Tom to let him know they were five minutes out. This time they pulled in front of the house, so the entrance would seem different to Brad.

Phil got out and opened the back door of the sedan. Lindsey slid out and started toward the house. Phil reached in and yanked Brad's arm. "Get out you shit. I can't believe we're putting our lives on the line for the likes of you." He shoved Brad toward the front door and the others followed.

"Yoo-hoo, is anybody home?" Jack's attempt at some levity fell flat.

Phil continued down the hall to the designated holding room. When they were in the room with the door closed, Phil removed the hood. "Here you go, Brad, your home away from home. A nice clean room, with your very own cot—a pillow even." Then he clapped Brad on the shoulder, went out, and shut the door.

Phil met up with the others in the kitchen. "He's shitting his pants already, but we'll let him contemplate his future until tomorrow. We might give him some water and a bite to eat if he's a good boy." He turned to Lindsey and Gavin. "It's getting pretty late. You two should be dog-tired from your overnight travel. Let's say we take it up in the morning."

Tom, who Lindsey thought of as the team clown, was standing on the other side of the kitchen near the stove, his tall lanky form silhouetted by the streetlight glow coming through the window. He threw a white towel over his crooked forearm and bowed slightly. "Or you could stay for a gourmet dinner. We're having filet mignon with Béarnaise sauce, baby roasted potatoes, and a Caesar salad on the side. I thought a nice Cabernet Sauvignon would complement the selection."

Phil scowled, "C'mon, Tom, we're all tired. Quit the funny business."

"Okay, okay, lighten up, Phil. Nick and I will go out to get something for the four of us. Any preference? Just don't be too picky. There's not much choice in the local stores."

In a robotic tone Phil clicked off a list. "If they have frozen pizza, get that, but if not, a chicken, some rice, an onion, various peppers, and a couple of cans of green beans would do." Phil pulled out a chair at the kitchen table and lowered his large frame onto the inadequately built piece of furniture. He made a shooing motion with his hand toward Tom and Nick.

Gavin looked toward Lindsey and Jack. "I don't know about you two, but I'm beat. I'm not sure why since I mostly sat around today while you were busy with Brad. I vote we head out."

Jack nodded and started gathering his things. "I'll be the chauffeur and drive us back to the hotel." Turning to the agents he chirped, "You guys have fun tonight!"

Looking around at the fatigued faces of the team, Phil sighed. "We'll discuss the schedule again in the morning. Oh-eight hundred fine with everyone?" They all agreed. Phil gave the departing group the high sign. "Have a good night."

Great. Here he was *again* being held prisoner. He couldn't believe his own country was treating him like this. Brad was sitting at the small table with three other chairs around it. At least this was cleaner and more comfortable than his last cell. He looked around. That bunk Phil had mentioned didn't look half bad.

He remembered back to his training days. In case any of the SEAL team was ever captured by the enemy, the training had included experiencing some pretty nasty terrorist techniques for getting prisoners to talk. That way they would know what to expect.

Surely, these guys wouldn't resort to that. And anyway, he had told Lindsey and Jack most of what he knew. But the one thing he hadn't mentioned was worrying him. He hadn't told them about giving Rashid the State Department's curriculum. They surely couldn't know he'd hacked into his old office system and found the lesson plans stored in the director's files.

God, if they found out, that might be enough for the charge of treason to stick. How could he endure the ridicule? Worse, would he survive doing time in a federal prison? The information he had passed didn't seem serious enough that he'd be executed, but he'd probably pay a hefty fine and, of course, there was the stretch in jail. Was five years the minimum? He could hope for leniency. Hell, he'd beg for leniency. What did Jack say about going easy on him if he cooperated? He wasn't sure what he could do to cooperate.

The waiting was killing him. He'd been cooped up in the holding room for what seemed like hours now. Maybe he should bang on the door. No, Jack had said they would appear in their own sweet time. Of course, he was talking about Rashid's men. His own country wouldn't let him sweat too long,

would they

In the middle of that thought, the door cracked open, a tray of food slid in and the door clicked shut again. At least he wouldn't starve. After devouring the small snack, he sat staring at his hands folded on the table. He was tired, apprehensive, and miserable. What would be next? Totally worn out with tension, Brad decided to rest on the cot for a while. Everything would be better after a little rest.

Jack drove, with Lindsey in the passenger seat and Gavin sprawled out in the back. They all were unusually quiet. Dead tired, he guessed. Jack was mulling over tomorrow's operation. He didn't want to alarm Lindsey and Gavin, but he thought there needed to be a better way to ensure Lindsey's safety. Right now, she was bait. In the terrorists' eyes, Lindsey might be unessential, disposable. It seemed a little dicey to him. She was, after all, his baby girl. He knew Gavin wanted to keep her safe, and it was obvious he cared for Lindsey. And Jack could see it was mutual. Lindsey's face lit up whenever she looked at Gavin. Jack thought Gavin was a fine fellow, so if Lindsey thought he was *the one,* Jack would be happy.

They were back in town by eleven PM, but the congestion was still horrendous. They finally arrived at the hotel, pulled into the parking garage, and all piled out of the car.

Though Jack was anxious about tomorrow's

strategy, he spoke casually. "We should just take it easy and get some rest tonight. Then we'll be fresh to tackle the operation in the morning. If all goes well, this time tomorrow it will all be over, and we'll be packing our bags to go home. So, if it sounds okay with you, let's meet in the morning around six-thirty in the coffee shop downstairs. That should give us enough time to get out to the safe house by eight."

"That'll be fine." Lindsey smiled at her dad and used their old way to sign off for the day, "Good night, Dad, and sleep fast." Jack's heart was full of love for this amazing young woman who also happened to be his daughter.

Gavin could tell Lindsey was still pissed. She'd ignored him back at the safe house and hadn't spoken a word on the ride home. She started to walk off, but he grabbed her arm. "Hey, I'm sorry, Lindsey. I didn't mean to doubt your ability to handle the operation."

She turned to face him. "Gavin, you treated me like I was a bimbo. It always hits a nerve with me, whenever anyone assumes I can't handle a situation because I'm a woman." She shook her head. "I can't see this relationship going any further if you continually act like I need protection. Remember, I'm the one who trains agents in counterterrorism techniques."

He took a step toward her, and she took a step back. "Lindsey, please." He held his hands out to her. "I admit I underestimated you. It's probably because I have no capabilities in this field. I know you're the one with the experience. But do you really need to be on the front line facing Rashid?"

Lindsey looked down. "I don't know. I know I don't *need* to be here, but I *want* to be here and involved in the project. Maybe I just need this to prove something to myself."

Gavin stepped forward and he took her shoulders. She didn't back away this time. "Would you give me another chance?" He took her in his arms and whispered, "I'm just worried, and I've grown quite fond of you, you know. Really, more than just fond." He grasped her even tighter to his chest and kissed the top of her head.

She put her arms around his waist and buried her head in his shoulder. "Oh, Gavin, I'm sorry I snapped at you. I'm tired and especially anxious about the next part of the plan."

Gavin pulled back and looked directly into Lindsey's beautiful, dark blue eyes. "You've rehearsed it. I'm sure you can do it, but please don't take too many chances with my best girl." He pulled her to him again and breathed in her scent. "I love you, Lindsey Kelly."

Gavin could see a spark in Lindsey's eye. Was she thrilled to hear Gavin's declaration, or still angry? He knew he had picked a bizarre time to bring it up. Then she snuggled closer and murmured, "I love you, too. Definitely an improvement over the first time we met," she said, trying to lighten the mood. She lifted her chin and straightened her back. "I'll do my best to come back to you. It's in my best interest, too."

Gavin took Lindsey's hand and swung her arm playfully. He whispered into her ear, "This may seem like bad timing, but I seem to be getting a new energy. I'm desperate to grab your body and make wild passionate love to you."

Lindsey gave him a quirky smile then chuckled. "I was thinking the same thing. Race you upstairs."

Out of breath, they reach the door and Gavin rummaged in his pants pocket for his key card.

"I've got it," Lindsey cried out waving her card in the air. They burst through the door, and Gavin slammed it with a backward kick of his foot. Grabbing Lindsey around the waist and pulling her to him, he pressed his back against the door, panting. They'd left the room in some disarray when they'd rushed that morning to cleanup and change. And with the *Do Not Disturb* sign on the door, the maid hadn't been in. Geez, hadn't that morning been light years ago? So much had happened during the day.

But now Gavin's mind was not on the messy room or the coming takedown strategy tomorrow, his mind and body were focused only on Lindsey. He drew her closer, kissing her on the neck and move on to her luscious lips. Pulling back, he whispered, "I'm drunk on love for you. I love you so much and think about you morning, noon, and night. It's been hard not to reach out and touch you for this whole day. I want you now...and forever."

Lindsey's body molded to Gavin's, and he knew she could *feel* how much he wanted her. Her hips pressed forward and moved sensually against his erection. "I can tell another part of your body loves me, too," she said with a giggle.

She ran her fingers through his hair and brushed her lips to his. Moving her hands over his back and down to the waist of his khakis, she fumbled with his belt buckle. He kissed her deeply and her response was immediate. Her lips parted, and he teasingly explored her mouth with his tongue. Oh, she tasted so good. He stepped back just enough to pull her shirt over her head and toss it toward the bed.

She succeeded in her effort with his belt and his pants slipped to the floor. He quickly stepped out of them and kicked them to the side. He was losing control. He couldn't get her clothes off fast enough. He magically undid her bra with one hand while he tugged at her slacks. She started on the buttons of his shirt but abandoned that and nearly tore his shirt off, briefly breaking the lip lock to pull it over his head.

They were both breathless, kissing and stroking while they stripped each other. Naked, they tumbled into the unmade bed continuing the frantic lust for contact. Skin to skin, he moved against her smooth perfect body.

Her hands were all over him, and she was

grinding her hips into him like a wanton. Her abandon only intensified his passion. He kissed and nipped her neck. He circled her nipple with his thumb, gently squeezing, then kissed his way down to her breast and took over the stimulation with his tongue. Her soft murmurs were turning into moans of pleasure. She lifted her pelvis, inviting him in. "Oh, Gavin, I want you inside me. I can't get close enough to you."

His brain momentarily came out of the passionate fog enough to reach to the bed side table drawer for a condom. Holding the packet, tearing the foil open with his teeth, and rolling the condom into place, he slid into her in one smooth motion. She inhaled audibly as he entered her, meeting each of his strokes with an equally forceful thrust. Their now slick bodies were rocking with the frenzied act of love.

"Lindsey, Lindsey, I'm almost there. Come with me."

"So close, yes, yes!" Her body arched and stiffened, and she gasped his name.

Gavin made one final thrust and joined her in the ecstasy.

Luxuriating in the moment for a few heartbeats, the tension of the day forgotten, they drifted into sleep and embraced oblivion.

Hovering on the edge of wakefulness, Lindsey felt Gavin lean over the bed and gently run his hand down her cheek. Joining her back in bed, he kissed her on the temple, on the side of the neck, nipped her earlobe, and whispered, "Time to wake up, sleepyhead."

"Ooh, already?" Squinting her eyes shut, she stretched. Lindsey finally blinked several times and shifted in the bed toward his caresses. She breathed in the clean scent of him. "You've already showered, and you smell delicious, mmm." Nuzzling into him she realized he still wore only the towel from his shower. She reached under the towel finding his very excellent erection. "Wouldn't want to waste this," she murmured stroking the length up and down and then teasing the head.

"I think we have time," he said breathily. Lindsey marveled at his expertise in lovemaking. He gently parted her legs and finding her pleasure spot began stroking softly. He brought her to near orgasm before slipping on a condom and gliding into her.

She was hot and wet and welcomed him while wrapping her arms and legs around his strong lean body. Her fleeting thought was wondering how she got so lucky to be loved by this kind, caring man who was also a stunning example of manhood. Then the explosion burst through her and she was lost in the moment. Gavin pressed in several more times and collapsed on to her, his heart pounding in his chest against hers.

»Chapter Twenty-Three«

They had to hustle but were finally dressed and ready for the day. Gavin glanced Lindsey's way, with the grin of a satisfied man. "Well, that was a pleasant surprise this morning."

Lindsey put a few extra items in her bag and gathered her long skirt and hijab for the day's operation. "Yeah, I think our morning exercise set me up for the day. I feel I could conquer the world." She beamed at Gavin.

He pulled her in for a quick squeeze. "If that's what it takes to make you the conquering Wonder Woman, I'll certainly oblige the lady any time." He knew he also still had a silly grin on his face. So, this was what pure bliss felt like. He'd take an extra helping. He was anxious for this day to be over, and he was hoping for success. Then he and Lindsey could start their life together.

"We'd better get going. We're already five minutes late to meet Jack."

They grabbed a quick breakfast with Jack then hopped into the car for the arduous trip through the traffic to the safe house. Each of them was lost in thought. Lindsey felt the pressure rise in her when she considered the operation. Her throat was dry and tight. Everything was riding on her ability to carry this off.

After an hour they pulled into the drive, got

out, and filed into the house.

From the hallway they could hear Phil and Tom in a heated discussion about everyone's position for the takedown.

"I'm the agent in charge for this little op, so it will be my way or the highway." Phil was adamant, practically shouting. Tom went silent. He was leaning against the wall with one foot behind him on the paneling, studying his fingernails, when the three entered the room.

"Looks like you've started without us," Jack said, beelining it for one of the chairs at the kitchen table. Lindsey and Gavin settled onto the two stools at the counter.

Ignoring what they had overheard when they came in the front door, Lindsey tried to project a light tone. "So, what's happening? Everyone sleep well?"

Phil was all business. "Hi, you three. We're just going to serve our friend some breakfast and get started with the interrogation after that."

Handing Nick the tray full of food, Harry clapped him on the shoulder. "Here's Brad's breakfast. Just put it inside the door quickly and don't say a word."

"Will do."

Gavin couldn't help noticing the strained mood. Was everyone just tired or was something wrong.

Phil was drumming his fingers on the table. "We won't give him quite enough time to eat. Then we'll go in and start the interview. That should throw him off balance." Phil went back to conversing quietly with Harry about the questioning.

Gavin sat glumly on his stool at the kitchen counter. He felt left out of the strategy session. Yeah, he wasn't an agent, but he had good ideas and instincts. The day had started so well, but it was going downhill in a hurry. He glanced at Lindsey who was slouched over the layout of the pick-up point, running her finger idly on the map. Maybe she was feeling the same thing. He got up, went around behind her, and began rubbing her shoulders.

"Mmm, that feels wonderful. Don't stop."

He pulled her tawny mane back and continued massaging the tension away. He said as casually as he could, "So, when will you call Lindsey and me in? Our part in a nutshell, I think, is where I look as though I'm pondering whether he's committed treason, then she tries to convince him to help with the scheme to apprehend the fanatical leader of the faction. Right?"

Phil and Harry turned to Gavin. "Oh, yeah, that's the gist of it. We'll pump him for most of the information we already know. Jack and Lindsey got a lot of stuff we can use. We'll question him on that, first. He'll be wondering how we got the poop on him. Then we'll drop the surprise. That should really set him off. We want to paint a very bleak picture. At that point, Harry will excuse himself and bring you guys in."

Harry took up the tale. "Then you two will

play the good cop, bad cop scenario that we discussed. Okay?" Harry's southern, good ole boy accent was somehow comforting.

Gavin answered, "Yeah, okay, fine."

Phil stood. "Time to get started."

※

"Alright, Brad we'll go over it one more time. When did you figure out you were aiding a terrorist?"

Brad sat stiffly in the straight chair. "C'mon guys, I didn't know he was a terrorist when I started the project. I thought it was just a contract for training foreign nationals. Can't a guy make some dough? It's capitalism."

Phil shouted, "Stop it. We know you've met with Rashid dozens of times, starting even before you left STLS. We know what you've given him and what you've promised him. You, my friend, are in deep shit."

"I didn't know, I didn't know." Brad's bluster dissolved. He was almost in tears.

Harry got up and leaned against the wall. "Quit stalling. We've heard all your bullshit. Was it when he demanded the U.S. embassy designs, or was it when you told him you weren't associated with a security company? Did that set Rashid off? He probably didn't like you lying to him, did he? Well, neither do we!"

Brad did a double take, his head snapping to where Harry stood. "Where are you getting all these reports?" The sweat trickled down his back and pooled under his arms. They knew so much. It wasn't looking good for him.

Harry pushed away from the wall, shaking his head. "He's not cooperating, Phil. Maybe we should give him back to Rashid and his henchmen."

"No, no, I'm cooperating." Brad was wild-eyed. How would he get out of this mess?

Phil ignored him. "Get the others and bring another chair."

Harry left the room.

In the five minutes of silence, while they waited, Brad became even more agitated, rapidly bouncing his right leg under the table and drumming his fingers on the table.

There was a click, and the latch released. Lindsey, Gavin, and Harry pushed open the door. Harry brought in the extra chair. Phil turned scowling at the new arrivals. "Maybe *you* can give him some idea of what he's in for." Phil huffed out a breath, obviously exasperated.

Brad didn't wait for the interrogation to start again. He spoke in a pleading tone. "Lindsey, tell them. Please, tell them I wouldn't do anything to harm my country."

"I'm not sure about that anymore," she said, sighing audibly. "The Brad I knew once, wouldn't, but I'm not certain, now."

Harry motioned for everyone to sit. "You, of course, know Lindsey, and this is Gavin Blake with the Justice Department. He's here to help you understand your legal situation."

Brad turned to Gavin. "Oh, so, Gavin, you're going to represent me, like be my advocate?"

Gavin leaned toward Brad glaring. "Not exactly."

Sweat had soaked Brad's shirt under his armpits and around his neck. "Then what?" His voice was high and reedy, and his head swung from side to side. He looked frantic.

Gavin spoke in a matter-of-fact, even tone, "I'm here to explain your rights. When you've told me your version"—he cleared his voice—"hopefully the truth, about your relationship with Rashid Abdul Azim, I'll determine if the government has enough evidence to charge you with treason."

If it were possible, Brad looked more deflated. He paled and stared down at the table, slumping over. "Oh, no. God, no, how did I ever get into this mess?" He buried his face in his hands.

Phil scanned the group and spoke in a tired voice, "One more time Brad. When did you know Rashid was a terrorist?"

Brad was quiet for a moment. The others could see he was completely defeated. "Okay, I suspected something was wrong when he started asking for more authentic replicas of actual existing training facilities." He exhaled, shaking his head. "And I guess I knew for sure when he started talking about a jihad and attacks on the infidels."

Phil huffed. "Nice. He really said that?"

Gavin ignored Phil. "That's a start Brad, go

on."

"I got really frightened the time I told him I didn't work for a security company any longer. He exploded, ranting and threatening me. I truly thought he might kill me."

"What about State's training curriculum?"

"What? How did you...okay, yes, I gave those to him to stall him while I returned to Washington for the old mock embassy plans. That wasn't bad, was it? I didn't think it was that bad."

Phil angrily flew in, shaking his head as if in disbelief. "You didn't realize it would jeopardize our agents? Having the terrorists know the agents' moves in an attack would give the advantage to the fanatics? God, this is unbelievable! You really are a dumb shit."

In a calm monotone Gavin continued, "How did you get the lesson plans?"

Almost in a whisper he said, "I hacked into STLS. I helped set up the system years ago, so I knew how to get in the back door."

"And when did you hand them over to Rashid?"

"I can't remember exactly, just shortly after I pulled them from Hank's files—Hank Atkins, the Director of Training, who took my place. A matter of a few days after that."

Lindsey stood up abruptly glaring at Brad. "This might be good news for you. It's the timing." Brad looked blank, but Lindsey continued, "Hank noticed the breach of his files and told me about it, but we hadn't met with State's representative about the curriculum changes, yet. We were meeting that afternoon. Knowing they were completely changing the protocol, we dismissed it. You may have passed on obsolete information."

Gavin went on, "It's still serious. If the curriculum *had* been updated, then it would be a matter of national security, and you thought they were the real deal. In your trial for treason, your defense attorney might bring up that you passed *mis*information. It would just be a matter of interpretation."

Brad was visibly shaking. "Trial for treason? This news from Lindsey has to help. Doesn't it help?"

"Well, Brad, it might help, but there's also the embassy layouts. Where are they?"

"I had them with me the night I was hit on the head and taken. Maybe I dropped them and they're still in the alley. Please, Lord, let them be in the alley. They were just the old mock embassy layouts. Not the new Standard Embassy Design. Not that bad, right?"

Gavin was somber. He looked grimly at Phil. "I think it's enough. Are you ready to inform him?"

Brad stood up and abruptly grabbed at Phil's shirt. "No, no please don't charge me!"

Phil pushed Brad's hand away. "We need to confer. Let's go." And they left Brad staring after them.

"Great performance Gavin. I think we have

him sufficiently softened." Phil talked over his shoulder as he made his way back to the kitchen. "Maybe even terrified."

Tom and Nick were playing gin rummy when the others walked in. Tom looked up. "How'd it go?"

Gavin sat at the breakfast bar again. "Great. I think we have him completely panicked. Now, Lindsey has to convince him to be part of catching the big fish."

She sucked in a deep breath, pulled out a chair next to Tom, and collapsed into it. "I think my job will be easier now. Thanks guys. But it was supremely intense in there. I'm exhausted."

"Brad is most likely *way* more drained," Harry chimed in. His soft southern voice held a tone of some sympathy for Brad. "I don't think he got much sleep. There were lots of rustling sounds of tossing and turning in the night."

Lindsey stretched her neck from side to side to relieve the tension. "How long should we wait?"

"Not long. We don't want him to have a heart attack." Phil lowered his considerable bulk into the last chair at the table.

"Okay, just give me a few minutes. A soft drink would hit the spot right now. Do we have any cokes?"

Nick put down his cards and got up. "I think we still have a few left." He rummaged in the kitchen closet that held a broom and some supplies. "Yeah, here's one. Catch." And he tossed the coke to Lindsey. "It's not very cold, sorry."

Tom was checking the paperwork from the agency. "Do we need to go over the pick-up scheme again?"

Lindsey shook her head slowly, scrutinizing the group around the kitchen. "I can't take in much more just now. Maybe later, but I wouldn't mind talking about the call to Rashid since that will be next."

Jack sat at the kitchen table with Lindsey. He turned toward Phil. "Hey, Phil, sorry to butt in, but while we were gone over night, did we miss the part about the phone call and the reason for Lindsey's demands?"

"Nah, we haven't gone over that yet." Phil cleared his throat. He was all business now. "Okay, people, let's get back on track."

Gavin moved to Lindsey and stood behind her, absently stroking her arm.

"Alright, when Rashid calls, Brad will tell him about Lindsey. She'll react with anger about the attempted hit-and-run, saying she must meet with the head of the cell."

Jack cut in. "I think we should make a change there concerning the reason for Lindsey's demand to see the head honcho."

"Why change?" Phil sounded irritated. "We have already arranged the pick-up with the CIA agents. Since we're involving more than one agency, it would be hard to alter the strategy at *this* late date."

"That part wouldn't change, but I've thought

of a way to nearly guarantee Rashid's boss showing up."

Phil was all ears, now. "That would be nice. What's your idea?"

"Well, Brad revealed some crucial information." Jack sat up straighter. "It's obvious the terrorists are willing to provide payoffs for intel. The evidence—Brad's large bank account in the Caymans. I think we can use that."

"How so?"

"Since the terrorist don't have a clue about Lindsey's character, why not portray her as being a money-mongering bitch, just as mercenary as Brad. She could say she wants in on the deal." Jack stood up and started pacing, gesturing with one hand then the other. "She could demand to meet the big shot of the cell to work out the transaction, since she's the CEO of the much sought-after legitimate company. Sorta' like head honcho to head honcho. That way we might snag the leader of the organization."

"That could work," Phil said. "But it would be adding an additional risk to Lindsey. What do you say, Lindsey? Could you be convincing in that role?"

Lindsey leaned forward resting one elbow on her knee with her chin in her hand. "I think I could easily play a tough bargainer, because I've had to be tough in some of our contract negotiations, but I'd be nervous about convincing them I'm a greedy money-grubber. I'm a terrible liar. The terrorists might see through it."

Leaning back, Lindsey looked up at Gavin. He

sat down and took her hand. "I think she could pull it off, but I'm not thrilled about the added danger. Before this idea, we were going to have her demand to see the guy trying to steal her company."

Jack turned from his pacing. "I think this is actually safer. If she just shows up for a meeting, she'd be disposable." Jack looked right at his treasured daughter. "She needs to be indispensable. *She*," and he emphasized she, "would be the only one who could personally negotiate with her Omani government contact. They wouldn't get the land for the facility in Oman without her."

Lindsey smiled at her dad. "Sounds good. I like the idea of being essential. And it *does* seem safer." She scratched her cheek absently and looked back at Phil. "What do you think, Phil? Can you find a name for me to use for this supposed senior administrator in Oman?"

"We could make that happen. Yes, I'm warming to this change in the game plan."

Lindsey explained the operation to Brad again, and concluded with, "I think Phil went over all the details, and I've given you my take, so do you have any questions?"

"I just hope I can convince Rashid that you're for real, Lindsey. What if I can't persuade him to bring his boss when I make the call? He's a loose cannon, a crazy fanatic. I've never been able to predict his response."

Phil was leaning on the edge of the interrogation table, completely relaxed. "Just follow the script. You need to give it your best shot, Brad. If the head of the cell doesn't show, the CIA *might* be able to sweat the name out of Rashid. At least, you better hope so." Phil was using the *give him hope then snatch it back technique* to keep Brad off balance.

Brad looked worried, and even thirty minutes after the team had returned to the interrogation room, the perspiration was still pouring down the sides of Brad's cheeks and neck. He shifted in his chair and wrung his hands together. "You truly think Justice will give me a break since I'm cooperating? I know I fucked up, but please give me this chance to redeem myself."

Phil scowled at Brad. "That's the idea, Brad. Once this is finished and if it goes well, we'll put in a good word for you."

Brad was swaying back and forth, shaking his head. "I don't know what I was thinking. Maybe if Lindsey hadn't fired me, all of this wouldn't have happened. I thought I was training the good guys. Justice surely can't punish me for conducting what I thought was a legitimate business deal."

Lindsey was losing patience with the simpering idiot. "You're whining and making excuses again, Brad—trying to blame me for something that is fully your responsibility. Just stop."

Phil got up, cutting off the conversation. "No time like the present. Let's get started. I'd like to do the meet early tonight if we can arrange it."

⚜

The phone was on speaker. Lindsey wanted this to work. Brad was clearly a basket case. She hoped he could pull it together. Rashid could not get the upper hand.

Brad's voice shook. "Hello, Rashid. Hope I'm not getting you at a bad time."

Rashid's heavily accented voiced boomed into the room. "What do you want, you incompetent ass? Where are my embassy blueprints you promised?" His voice rose to a shout, and he said again in a menacing tone, "Where are they!"

"Th—th—that's part of why I am calling you. Also, I've f—found a way to get the land in Oman."

Shit, he was blowing it, Lindsey thought. He had to calm down. She looked at Brad and pressed her hand, palm down toward the table several times and mouthed *relax, stay calm.*

He nodded. "We can start building right away. No more delays."

Rashid cackled. "Did you finally kill the bitch?"

"Oh, no, no, she's here with me, now."

"In-ter-est-ing." Rashid drew out the word into four distinct syllables. "I guess our little scare tactic brought her to her senses."

"Well, not exactly." Brad sighed, loudly. That was in the script, good. He had sounded like a nervous wreck at first but was warming to his role. *Keep it up, Brad*, she thought.

Brad continued. "She got wind of my work with you and wanted to get in on the deal."

Lindsey steadied herself and spoke in a calm low tone. "Yeah, Mr. Azim, I think I can help you out with the negotiations for the site in Oman. For a price, of course." She paused to let that sink in. "I've talked with Najib Abdul-Hakam, my government contact in Oman. Heard of him?"

Rashid grunted. "Maybe."

"Well, I've done some business with him in the past, and he's amenable to seeing me about the land. Brad and I haven't had too much time to talk, so do you already have a particular site in mind?"

"Yes, yes, Brad knows where." Brad was shaking his head and mouthing *no I don't.*

Lindsey needed Rashid to think she was letting Brad take the lead, at least for now. Clearing her throat, she went on, "I've hired Brad back into the firm. Now, he's the man I depend on to head the new facility, but I'm the *only* one who can deal with the Omani government people. Najib has never met Brad, and it took me a long time to gain his trust."

Rashid just grunted again.

"I need to meet with you and your boss to work out the details and decide how to transfer the money for the property, and, of course, there's my fee."

Rashid broke in, yelling, "I'm not going to deal with a woman, and neither will our leader. All women are whores and can't be trusted." He was getting worked up. Excellent, that's what she wanted.

Lindsey lowered her voice to a manlier tone

and spoke forcefully. "If you think we will ever build this facility and reveal the rest of the classified information needed to make it a reality, you *will* need to do business with me. I expect to be paid handsomely, too, at least as much as you've given Brad."

"We'll see about that," the terrorist hissed through his teeth.

Lindsey didn't back down, "Listen you asshole, the information we have should interest your leader very much! Do you want to please him? Maybe I should talk with him directly. Leader to leader, so to speak."

Rashid raised his voice. "Bitch, I don't have to deal with you."

Lindsey shouted even louder. "You won't get what you want without me!"

Under his breath Rashid said, "whore," but it was purposely audible. Then he said, "I'll get back to Brad after I've spoken to the *Mudabbir*."

Lindsey leaned toward the speaker phone and spoke in a low stage whisper, "We need to hear back from you soon."

Brad jumped in stuttering, "C—call me at this number. My cell phone has no reception..." Then they heard the click as Rashid cut off the call. Brad pulled the phone away from his ear and stared at it.

Phil snorted and rolled his eyes. "That went well."

»Chapter Twenty-Four«

Lindsey noticed that while the team waited for Rashid to call, each one handled the stress differently. Jack was pacing again. "Maybe we pressed too hard. These Muslim fanatics hate women. It will probably be a miracle for them to meet with Lindsey."

Phil seemed unaffected by the wait. He was making a sandwich from last night's left-over chicken. "Yeah, you're probably right, but these crazies seem fixated on having the replica training facility. I think they'll eventually agree to meet."

Harry and Tom were playing gin while Nick idly watched. Lindsey thought of Nick as the quiet, shy one. He rarely spoke and when he did, it was only a few words in his south Louisiana drawl. She wondered if he ever had an opinion, or if he was simply a man of action.

Harry looked up. "I think they'll *have* to deal with Lindsey to get what they want. They're just trying to rationalize how to do that and still save face."

Jack stopped and turned to Harry. "That could be right. Let's hope they decide soon."

The agents had released Brad from his holding room but were keeping an eye on him. He seemed lost in thought, just sitting and staring through the blinds of the front living room window. Lindsey guessed he was finally coming to terms with his precarious position.

Lindsey sat with Gavin on the old couch in the corner of the kitchen, talking quietly. Then Gavin got into the conversation. "Phil, what's your take on whether this *Mudabbir* will show?"

"I don't know, Gavin. We might get lucky."

"Rashid called him THE *Mudabbir*. Is that some kind of a title?"

"These nuts use all kinds of names for their leaders. This one I think means enlightened or powerful one in Arabic. We'll see if 'oh powerful one' shows up." Phil made a flourish with his hand in front of him while bowing, as if meeting royalty.

Gavin laughed. "Maybe he'll arrive in a royal sedan-chair, or is that only in India?"

Lindsey twined her fingers with Gavin's and squeezed. "I just wish they'd go ahead and call. I'd like to get this over with."

Gavin looked into Lindsey's eyes, and disengaging his hand, drew her into a crushing hug. "Everything will be alright. The agents will have you in their sights every moment."

Lindsey didn't know whether he was trying to convince her or himself. "I sure the hell hope so."

At first Lindsey had been fired up with the prospect of nabbing a terrorist, but now her enthusiasm was waning. She snuggled closer to Gavin to whisper in his ear, so others wouldn't hear. "It's starting to sink in. I know I'll be in a hell of a lot of danger during the operation. I'm not sure I can face down a known terrorist. This waiting is killing me."

She pulled back slightly and looked up into Gavin's warm brown eyes as a single tear slid down her check. She wiped it away with the back of her hand and continued. "I'm frightened Gavin. I know I have to go through with it. There's no going back, but I'm still anxious."

Gavin held her gaze and responded in a whisper. "I think you can do it. You're strong and brave —beautiful, too." He drew two fingers down the side of her face in a soft caress. "I think that bravery is having those emotions and yet not backing down."

Lindsey gave a short laugh. "But, Gavin, this isn't a play where I'm acting a part. This is real life. What if I can't convincingly carry off the tough bitch role?"

Gavin gave her a comforting hug. "Brad and the other trained operatives will be right there. I'm not sure the plan will work without you, but if you're not confident you can pull it off, then you know you can back out. The CIA will just have to figure out another way to catch the big fish." Gavin kissed her softly and murmured, "I love you so much. I'm behind you whatever your decision."

Lindsey rested her head on Gavin's shoulder and began thinking of the pros and cons of the operation. She felt Brad was committed to the scheme, but mostly to save his own skin. She wasn't sure she could count on him in a pinch. On the other hand, he was a trained special ops guy. Surely, some of that training would make him aware of the situation.

Her breathing slowed while she tried to convince herself she could do her part. *Okay, what are my strengths?* She'd taken most of the Triple Shields courses, but she was no agent. One of the courses she had taken in Arab culture awareness and their body language, might come in handy. She knew she needed to act subservient, but it wasn't in her make up. Her parents had raised her to be self-sufficient and assertive. She wasn't sure she could be convincing as a shrinking violet. But then could she act the ruthless greedy bitch role? *I'm waffling. Get a grip and stay focused.*

She and Brad had practiced the meet scenario, but now they had to make it happen. If she didn't go through with it, the whole mission would be blown. Lindsey took a deep cleansing breath and gathered her resolve. *I can do this.*

Lindsey turned her head to Gavin's ear and whispered, "I'm in."

Gavin had his eyes closed. Was he sleeping? Then he squeezed her around the shoulders and said, "That's the spirit."

It was mid-afternoon, and they were all weary of waiting. Jack and Gavin had taken a short drive to the local store for some coffee, soft drinks, and snacks. They'd been back for a few minutes and had stacked all the supplies on the cabinet top near the refrigerator. Looking up at Phil, Jack asked, "Have you heard anything from Rashid?"

Phil was calmly playing solitaire at the table. "Not yet, but we're assuming the operation will go forward. I've been in contact with the CIA's team. They are holding us responsible, their words, for getting Rashid and his pal squarely on the X." Phil gathered up the cards and slapped them in the middle of the table.

"We all know what that means. It's where the terrorists always want their mark when they go in for the kill, but this time we're going to turn the tables. We'll insist on the meet location, then call Rashid and switch it at the last minute. That should ensure the operation goes down in the isolated spot we've chosen and, hopefully, they won't have time to put any of their own snipers in position."

Phil stood up. "The CIA arranged for the site that's on the fringe of Dubai's old town, but away from the tourist area. It's mostly streets of large warehouses and storage units with a few small businesses sprinkled in. Very little foot or vehicle traffic. The CIA owns a spice shop and warehouse there, which they use as a front in some of their scenarios."

Brad, who was sitting a little away from the group on the lumpy couch cut in, "Whose operation is it? State Department's or the CIA's?"

Looking over at Brad for the first time during his briefing, Phil answered, "The State Department will be there to protect American citizens: Lindsey, Jack, Gavin, and you. The CIA will be in charge of, again in their words, 'apprehending enemies of the United States on foreign soil in matters of National Security.'"

Phil glowered, forming a worry crease between his brows. "The CIA agents always have to be the important ones, the smug bastards. Nevertheless this time we're the bureau bringing the game to them. The CIA folks don't play well with others. Now even *they* have figured this one out. Working with us is essential. Rare, but cooperation occasionally happens." Phil's eyebrows drew together, deepening the crease between his eyes. "Needless to say, I'm not crazy about working with them either since they're a bunch of know-it-all macho shitheads, but we've been instructed from on high to make it a joint effort."

"Gee, Phil, what do you *really* think about The Agency?" Tom mocked.

Chuckling, Phil went on, "They'll also get *all* the credit if it goes as arranged." His eyes shot up to the heavens and he shrugged with his hands up. "It is what it is."

Lindsey was intently listening to the operational part, but wasn't interested in the legendary riff between the State Department and the CIA. "Right. Is this where we emulate Doris Day and break into 'Que Sera, Sera (Whatever Will Be, Will Be)'?'" Lindsey rolled her eyes. "I'm a little more interested in what's next after we meet at the site."

Phil sobered and continued, "Okay, The Agency will have two snipers in place on the top of the adjacent warehouses, as well as two undercover agents sitting in front of that spice shop I mentioned. There will also be an agent leaning in a doorway close to the pick-up point."

Phil pointed at Harry. "Harry and I will be hanging out across the street from the agent in the doorway. We'll be acting as if we're meeting to conduct a business transaction. A lot of hand shaking and back slapping. Nick and Tom will be waiting with Gavin and Jack in our own van to pick up Lindsey and Brad, if necessary. We may possibly add Jack to the mix in the ground team." Phil paused to stare at Tom just a beat, who sat impassively at the table. "If it all goes to hell, the CIA snipers will be there to take out the terrorists and we'll get Lindsey, Brad, Jack, and Gavin to safety."

He put his hands on his hips. "Of course, the preferred scenario is for the CIA to rush in at the appropriate time, neutralize Rashid and his entourage, rendering them helpless, and drive off with the bad guys. Nick will drive the van in from its location in the alley and whisk all of us away. At that point, we'll be out, and The Agency will take it from there."

"Sounds good in theory, but it may be easier said than done," Jack said, throwing his hands in the air.

Phil went over to Jack and put his hand on his shoulder. "Everything'll be fine, Jack." Looking around at the others he said, "Why don't we take a quick break and have a coffee or something? Maybe some of those snacks you picked up? Then we'll go over everything again."

Lindsey jumped up. "I could go for coffee. I

didn't have time this morning for my usual quota of caffeine." She moved to the coffeemaker and said, "I'll make some fresh. How many want coffee?" Lindsey prepped the pot and saying, "be right back," left the room for a pit stop.

Lindsey was drying her hands when she heard two men speaking in the hallway. She recognized the voices of Tom and Nick. She didn't mean to eavesdrop, but they sounded so intense, she was loath to interrupt. Tom was speaking. "I think we're all pretty tense about this op, but I wanted to apologize and admit I was out of line for second guessing your authority earlier."

Lindsey opened the door a crack and saw Phil slap Tom on the shoulder. "Nah, Tom, I'm the one who should apologize for jumping down your throat. It's really not like me. I like to stay open to everyone's ideas. I think I'm just overly anxious about all this. There's a lot riding on everything going right. If it's a clusterfuck, it'll be on me, but I know I can count on you. If all of us on the street go down, and there is that possibility, it will be crucial that you and Nick get everyone else to safety." Tom smiled, but the smile didn't reach his sad eyes.

They all took the break to get circulation back in their legs by walking around. Lindsey hadn't meant to eavesdrop, but what she'd overheard was unsettling. The exchange between Tom and Phil, the look on Tom's face, and the bit of conversation, "Clusterfuck...all going down," sounded ominous. She was beginning to see this was serious, dead serious. She only hoped she wouldn't be the dead one.

Her hands began to tremble. She was getting worked up again. *Stop it.*

They took their original seats. With coffee in hand, Phil stretched his neck, looking up, down, and rolling his head around on the axis of the neck. Lindsey thought the strain was catching up to the usually calm Phil. He remained standing at the head of the table. "Okay, guys, let's get back at it. I had a short chat with our Agency counterparts over the break, and there's been a change in the meet setting. It's good *we're* flexible."

Gavin sat forward on his stool and gestured to catch Phil's eye. "I hope the change includes what I'm supposed to do. Where do you want me in all this?"

Phil slapped his forehead and frowned. "Geez, Gavin, I really hadn't forgotten you, but you've basically played your role," and he hastily added, "which was extremely important." Phil pointed toward Brad. "I think Brad will agree. He's especially pleased that you have determined his actions only *bordered* on treason, and lucky for him, he unintentionally passed misinformation, so didn't cross the line."

Brad brightened. "Yeah, Gavin, thanks for explaining the finer points of the law, even if I now know you're not actually with the Justice Department. Pretty sneaky." He laughed. Then looking around the quiet room at each of them, he sobered and in a solemn voice said, "I'm truly sorry for the irresponsible role I've played in this mess. I can only hope that since I'm totally on board to make it right, Justice won't throw the book at me."

Gavin slipped down from the stool, walked over to Brad, and sat on the arm of the couch. Nodding his head and looking right at Brad, he reached out and bumped him on the shoulder with his fist. "I'll have to admit from everything I heard about your 'Evil Brad' antics, I was prepared to hate you, if only for Lindsey's sake. But I believe you may be back to the Brad that Lindsey and Jack knew in the past. I think, now, with your legal problems, it will all come down to explaining your actions. Your chances are good."

Brad took a deep breath and blew it out with a whoosh. Grinning like a Cheshire cat, he spoke with emotion, "Gavin, you really think so? I'm so relieved and grateful for a second chance."

Phil jumped in. "Oh, congratulations! I'm glad everyone is feeling so warm and cozy," he mocked in a singsong voice, "Just don't break your arm patting yourself on the back, just yet. We've got to pull off this difficult mission first."

Lindsey felt some of the fog of tension lift. Gavin had a way of defusing the situation and bringing people together. He might make an amazing mediator in adversarial lawsuits, if he ever went back to the law, though she wouldn't push it. She'd be more than happy to be with a savvy mechanic, too. Whatever he decided would suit her just fine. Her thoughts were soaring ahead to the future, but she needed to stop. Focusing on today was vital. She told herself, *live in the present and breathe.*

Phil clapped his hands together, smiling he said, "Now class, let's go over these changes."

The room got completely still, and the light mood was replaced with the group's total concentration. Jack sat down at the table. "Alright, Phil, we're ready."

"Okay, people." This time it was Phil's turn to pace. "The CIA felt, and I agreed, we needed more experience on the front line at the meet. So, we're adding Tom to the group."

Tom looked up abruptly. "What?"

"Yeah, you Tom. Your reputation as an agent who thinks well on his feet in difficult situations is legendary." Phil paused and nodded at Tom. "You and Jack will pose as Brad's and Lindsey's business colleagues. All of you will be dressed in casual garb except Lindsey. She'll be covered completely in a chador and hijab. Only her face will be seen so they can tell it's her."

"Where will I get the chador?"

Phil motioned toward the back hall. "We have plenty of gear here for you to choose from."

Lindsey sat back, sighing, and grimaced. "Sounds like fun."

Phil continued, "The idea is to have Lindsey look submissive, a more traditional woman's role in their culture. You'll let the men in the group take the lead, Lindsey. It was felt that it might calm the situation."

Lindsey nodded. "I agree. The first call to Rashid got a little heated. Now I think it's important for everything to go as smoothly as possible."

Jack continued the update. "Everyone on the ground will be armed with a canister of pepper spray. Not your over-the-counter type, but a weapons-grade spray more like bear spray. Its range is up to thirty feet. Pray you don't have to use it but sprayed in the face the burning will immobilize a man for nearly a half hour. We want these dudes alive, so their discomfort is of no concern. They can't talk if they're dead." Phil paused, then added. "You've all had training with the weapon and know the precautions. Be sure you're up-wind from the subject, otherwise you'll dose yourself. Tom will be the one to determine the need and so will probably be the only one to use the spray. The rest of you will have it as a defense only. We'll demonstrate this particular mechanism a little later after the briefing."

"The other part of the change involves the van. We'll tell Rashid during the phone conversation to expect a dark grey paneled van with the spice warehouse logo on the side. They will more than likely arrive at the site in a car, so we want to drive in, too. Nick and Gavin will pull to the curb on the opposite side of the street from the meet spot. Gavin will be the door man and the four of you will get out. Lindsey you'll be last and lag behind the men."

Phil motioned toward Brad. "At the time of the call, Brad will suggest they wire Lindsey's fee to his numbered account, which is now being moni-tored by the CIA. You will make it clear there will be no meeting until the seven-figure funds are re-ceived. So, at the meet there won't be as much for Lindsey to say. Brad will lead the discussion about contacting the Omani representative. He will, of course, stress your importance with this contact, Lindsey."

Phil took a deep breath. "Any questions on what I've covered so far?" He looked around the room.

Gavin raised his arm. "I'm glad the van will be closer to the gang if, as you said Phil, everything turns to shit."

"Yes, and with Nick at the wheel he can pull across the street between our team and the terror-ists, load, do some high-speed backing, and get the hell out of there." Turning to Nick, Phil hooted to break the stress. "Woohoo! Weren't you at the top of your class on the high-speed backing maneuver?"

They all laughed then, and Tom ribbed Nick. "Yes, he was great at backing out of all sorts of situ-ations. Usually it involved backing out of paying for dinner or a date with someone's sister."

Nick looked sheepish and spoke softly. "Nah, I actually *am* a great driver in reverse. It's a talent," he said with a chuckle.

Phil brought the group back to order. "Let's move to the call. Is everyone clear on the phone conversation? Brad, you and Lindsey have the dia-log in your hands, but you should still go over it, so you sound natural."

Lindsey stood and motioned to Brad. "Okay, Brad, why don't we go to one of the back rooms to practice. It will be easier without this rowdy audience. Bye-bye." She waved at the others, walking toward the door to the hall. "Ooh, and I can pick out my attractive new wardrobe." Hitting Brad on the shoulder she spoke directly to him, "Then we can go over the script.

»Chapter Twenty-Five«

Gavin was consumed with worry for Lindsey. He kept imagining the worst-case scenario. What if it all went south? The terrorists could shoot the whole group. It *shouldn't* happen because they needed Lindsey and Brad. Lindsey to negotiate for the land in Oman and Brad to gain the information that was crucial for building the training facility. But was he just rationalizing? Even though the operation should run smoothly, it could ultimately turn all to hell. He watched her leave the room with Brad, and he couldn't imagine living without this remarkable woman. Not only was she intelligent and brave, she was gorgeous inside and out. She was capable of anything.

He thought back to the morning. He couldn't believe how responsive she was. Just thinking about her made him begin to respond. His pants were becoming a little tight and uncomfortable. Damn, now was not the time. He had to have faith they would have a lifetime to explore each other's minds and bodies. He wished he could do more to ensure Lindsey's safety. He would just have to listen to and believe in Phil.

It was nearly four o'clock when the call came through. They all gathered around the phone in the kitchen and Brad put it on speaker before answering.

"Hello."

Rashid was quietly subdued when he spoke. "Okay, we're ready to negotiate. My *Mudabbir* has agreed to speak with Lindsey and possibly meet when we exchange the Embassy plans."

"Excellent, Rashid. I have a copy of the blueprints for you. We'll keep a copy, too, for the construction phase. Let's discuss Ms. Kelly's fee for her expertise in acquiring the site for the training facility."

"The *Mudabbir* would like to hear directly from Ms. Kelly." They looked at each other, shocked. What game were they playing? They thought women were second class. Men were in charge. Rashid had said they wouldn't negotiate with a woman. Why would a Muslim man want to negotiate *directly* with a woman, especially a powerful leader of a terrorist cell? Something was off.

Lindsey spoke with perfect calm. "I'm here."

A cultured British voice began. "Ms. Kelly, how nice to finally speak with you. Your stellar reputation precedes you."

They were all baffled. Who was this *Mudabbir*? Lindsey didn't let the shock throw her off. She pulled it together, sucking in a deep breath. "And you, *Mudabbir*, what is your name?"

He chuckled. "Ah, no, Ms. Kelly, my name is unimportant. My cause is the reason I am speaking with you."

Phil was busy on the computer streaming

the recording of the *Mudabbir's* voice to both the State Department headquarters and the CIA chief. They would, of course, both tap into the NSA database. This was revealing news—a British-speaking *Mudabbir*. With the search engines blazing away they might be able to narrow down the possible identity of the *Mudabbir*. Maybe a British-born Muslim? Phil tried to identify his accent, was it Scottish... Welsh... Irish... or English? He finally decided possibly the North of England. He passed a note to Harry. The accent—what part of Britain?

Harry listened carefully as the conversation continued. Lindsey spoke next. "Alright, Mr. *Mudabbir*, I believe I have some information and some contacts you may find worthwhile."

"Hmm, yes, very interesting. And you Ms. Kelly, a woman of impeccable integrity, are you willing to betray your country for money?" He spoke with a smile in his voice.

Lindsey didn't find it particularly amusing but went on. "Yes, for the right price." She paused for emphasis. "I have been working very hard, Mr. *Mudabbir*, for many years and can't seem to get ahead in my male chauvinistic country. Men succeed far easier in the United States just like in Muslim countries. They refer to it as the *glass ceiling* for women. So, now I'm ready to take my share, get what I deserve, and then get out. I think I could be very happy living as an expat in Central America or on some tropical island."

"You sound like you have it all organized.

What will it take to commit treason, Ms. Kelly?" The derision had seeped into his tone.

Lindsey didn't miss a beat, "What made you betray your home country?"

"That is of no concern to you, Ms. Kelly." There was an edge to his assertion now.

"To answer your question, Mr. *Mudabbir,* I think five million US will tide me over. Does that seem reasonable to you?" She was beginning to enjoy toying with this asshole. She knew the more she could get him to talk the better chance the voice experts would have to pinpoint his origin and maybe even his name.

"That's a bit steep, Ms. Kelly. Would you consider less?"

"No, that's my number Mr. *Mudabbir.*"

He paused as if pondering. "Well, I believe we could make that happen. I'm looking forward to meeting the invincible Ms. Kelly in person. My men assured me they had taken care of you, but here you are." The smile was back in his voice.

"It will be my pleasure to meet you. If you will kindly put Rashid back on the line, Mr. Hansen will take care of conveying the details about our meeting location and he will also give Rashid the wiring instructions for my fee. We can discuss the construction layouts and funding for your training camp when we meet. Until then, Mr. *Mudabbir.*"

She hit the mute button, so she could let out a huge breath. She slumped forward onto the table. "Almost there." They all gave her the "way to go" fist

in the air, then Brad hit the mute button again to re-
sume the call with Rashid.

"Kelly, that was brilliant. This *Mudabbir* guy
wasn't what any of us expected, but you didn't let
it intimidate you. You changed the script on the
spot, and your impromptu chatter and demeanor
worked even better." Harry was effusive in his
praise. "You did fine, too, Brad."

Phil walked back into the room and took a
seat at the head of the table. Everyone could tell
he was excited. "The voice recognition guys have it
narrowed down to two!" He turned the computer
screen to the group and flashed the two photos onto
the screen.

He pointed to the one on the right. "This dude
is really unbalanced, well, we could say a complete
fanatic nut case. He was born in Wales to an English mother and Pakistani Muslim father. He was
educated in England and attended Cambridge but
left before he finished to join the cause. His name is
Salah Udeen Masoud." Phil raised his eyebrows. "It
looks like *mom* didn't have much of a say in the naming of her son. Anyway, his last whereabouts were
in Syria stirring up the rebels. With the turmoil in
Syria, the Brits have lost track of him."

Pointing to the second photo, Phil continued.
"Our second candidate was born in Yorkshire to a
Syrian immigrate mom and an Irish-English father.
His name is Ian Davis. The father had steady work
while Ian was young, so he attended excellent pub-

lic schools, meaning private schools in England, and went on to Cambridge, as well. His father was a recovering alcoholic and shortly after Ian left for University, dad lost his job and went back on the bottle. With no support from home Ian applied and won scholarships, full ride, for the last three years.

He was one smart young man. He finished near the top of his class at Emmanuel College. It's one of the oldest and most heavily endowed colleges at Cambridge but is quite selective in its scholarship program. He left England about three years ago and now has a home in the south of France and a luxury apartment in Dubai." Phil smiled pointing his finger at the group. "Bingo! I'm liking number two, myself. What do you think?"

Jack tipped back in his chair and gave the two thumbs up sign to Phil. "That's impressive. Tons of info in under thirty minutes. I'm with you. The guy on the phone didn't sound crazy at all. Maybe crazy like a fox, but it appears he's made a very lucrative business out of terrorism. Nice guy!"

Tom added, "Ooh, la, la. French digs, too! I'll bet on our man Ian."

Harry put in, "It's all in the computers. NSA collects an amazing number of conversation snippets from all over the world. There are keywords that just don't slip by the computer programs."

They were all congregated in the kitchen. There was a lot of good-humored banter. Lindsey was listening but at the same time considering the next step. She motioned Gavin to join her by the couch. He somehow gave her confidence simply by being there. "Do you really think I handled it okay? I went way off script, but it seemed right."

Gavin took both her hands and squeezed. "Let's sit." He eased her back on the couch and rested one arm behind her. Facing her and still holding one hand loosely he looked directly into her eyes. "You were amazing!"

She threw her arms around his neck, hugging him to her. "Thanks!" She didn't want to make a scene in front of the others, so she pushed back from Gavin and settled back on the sofa. "I hope I kept the *Mudabbir* talking long enough for a true identification. He was so smug on the phone, calling *me* a traitor when *he's* the one who's the traitor."

"It doesn't matter about the labels, and anyway, we all know you aren't betraying your country but helping at some considerable risk. Don't let him get to you."

Lindsey noticed Phil was back on the phone and had been for quite a while. She hoped he was getting more information on the two potentials. The more they knew ahead of time the more they could be prepared.

Finally, Phil hung up rubbing his forehead and looking troubled. "It just got more complicated. Gather round everyone."

With the look on Phil's face Lindsey thought it couldn't be good news. But being her usual glass half full person, she said as cheerily as she could muster, "What's up?"

Most of them once again sat at the table while Gavin and Lindsey perched on the stools.

Phil was glum when he dejectedly said, "There's a ninety-eight percent probability our man is Ian Davis, and I have some unpleasant particulars on his background and methods. The most important thing I've learned is he is an extremely dangerous character, a real pro."

There was a general groan from the room.

Phil continued, "Here it is. Davis is a successful broker of terror. The profile suggests he is unemotional and believes that everyone is expendable. After all, he would say, 'it's just business.' He was active in the IRA movement in his early career, where he learned his bomb-making skills. But then decided to link up with the radical Muslims about four years ago.

"He has a very persuasive personality and has convince numerous idealistic fanatics to blow themselves up to attain 'spiritual enlightenment.'" Phil looked up. "He works mostly with the Islamic State of Iraq and Syria, also known as ISIS. I'm sure you know ISIS is a Sunni militant group which, for the most part, attacks Shias, but our Ian probably doesn't care one way or the other if a Muslim is Sunni or Shia. He's been credited with at least three high fatality suicide bombing incidences in the last few years. The search engines have also uncovered two occurrences of small personal vendettas where he efficiently eliminated rivals."

The room went perfectly still, and all eyes were on Phil.

"I'll go over the bombing attacks first." Referring to his notes he read, "in January 2016, ten German tourists were killed in the Sultanahmet District of Istanbul. A Syrian refugee with ties to the Islamic State carried out the attack. The site was near the Blue Mosque in the square of the German Friendship Fountain. In warmer weather the large square is usually packed with tourists. Luckily, it was a cold winter day. The explosive belt used by the attacker was Ian's signature, both method and materials.

"In April 2017, forty-seven Coptic Christians were killed and one hundred and twenty-six injured in two nearly simultaneous bombings in Egypt, one inside St. George's Cathedral in Tanta and the other outside St. Mark's in Alexandria. The latter is the historic seat of the Coptic Papacy. In both cases, the explosive belts detonated by the zealots were, once again, most certainly the work of Ian Davis.

"In July 2018, two hundred forty-six were killed and two hundred injured when four suicide bombers hit on the same day in Southern Syria. The deadliest was in As-Suwayda when one of the terrorists drove a motorcycle through a street market and blew himself up. ISIS claimed responsibility and it proved to spread mayhem across a country, already devastated by the civil war. The suicide belts that exploded in all four cases were the work of Ian Davis."

Phil blew out a breath, and his shoulders slumped forward as if there was an ox yoke on his neck. Looking up he said softly, "Are you getting the picture? Mr. Davis is not a nice person."

The room began to buzz with comments. Phil made a cutting off motion across his neck. Everyone immediately got quiet. "There's more," he said.

"There are the two known *and* witnessed small events involving our Mr. Davis that have been reported. In each case, he personally met with his adversary. On these occasions, he was flanked by two bodyguards with a smaller young man also accompanying him. All were in traditional Arab robes.

"Both of the bystanders made similar comments about the young men. Each said he looked glassy-eyed and walked dazedly with a beatific smile on his face. When Ian touched the saintly young man on the shoulder and motioned him forward, he walked ahead as if in a trance. Ian lingered behind until the boy was near the intended victim. Then the explosive belt in each instance was detonated by remote control.

"The explosive force was projected only forward with a predictable outcome. Ian and the bodyguards calmly walked back to their car, got in and drove away." Phil bobbed his head. "He's one *cold* bastard!"

Brad spoke rather nervously, "Do you and all the agency heads think we can still handle this?"

Shaking his head Phil answered Brad, "They think the objective to capture Ian and Rashid can still be accomplished, but the mission techniques and actions will have to be altered."

"How can we change the mission two hours before the scheduled meet?" Harry asked.

Questions were flying around the room. Everyone seemed to be talking at once. Phil held his arms in front of him, palms out. "Hear me out. Not that much will change. Just wait."

Phil left the room and, in a minute, returned with an easel and an oversized pad of paper from the supply room at the back of the house. He set up the easel at the end of the table, placed the pad on the easel, and flipped the cover back to show a blank page. Then he took up where he'd left off. "It will mostly be adjustments in the positioning and the timing."

On the paper, Phil drew a large version of the meet site. "Here's the street. Nick will park the van, which is armored, by the way, here by the left curb. That means it will be heading toward the stream of traffic, if there were traffic. The sliding door of the van will be facing the middle of the street." He drew a rectangle by the curb. "There will be a three-car length space and a row of two cars and a truck parked in the correct direction in front of the van." He drew in the other vehicles with similar rectangles. Just in front of the van but on the sidewalk, he made a large X. "There will be two agents in Arab garb sitting at a small table in front of the spice shop, drinking coffee. They will be able to see the meet site between your van and the first parked car." Phil made a sweeping motion from the spice shop entrance to the middle of the street.

"These are the two warehouses the CIA will use for the snipers. Here and here." He marked buildings with X's that were about a hundred yards in front of the State Department van. "Then, with some luck, Ian's entourage will arrive from the direction of the sniper locations and park here with the snipers behind them." He put another X behind the truck in the row of cars parked in front of the van and about halfway between the van's spot and the sniper positions.

"To help ensure Davis arrives from our preferred direction, for the twenty minutes or so before the scheduled meeting time, the CIA will have a large transport truck backing into a loading dock, here. He put another X on the map. This will inhibit access from the opposite end of the block. Once Ian's vehicle is parked, the truck will depart to give clear access for Nick's famous backing maneuver." Phil looked at Nick and smiled for the first time during the lengthy explanation.

The team let out a collective sigh. Tom cocked his head to one side studying the diagram. "I trust we will go over this scenario a few more times?"

"Yes, of course. As many times as it takes for everyone to feel comfortable with the strategy, but there's more." Phil cleared his throat. "Now for the action part. We're ditching the pepper spray and the entire team will wear Kevlar vests. The four of you on the ground team will exit the van as we planned before. Gavin will open the sliding door, and all will get out, Lindsey last. The door will remain open. Brad will have the empty cylinder in his hand representing the embassy prints. Going forward, this is where the timing will be important. The CIA's man in the doorway across from the van, plus Harry and I walking up the street toward Ian will be the spotters. We will be observing Ian and his associates. If Ian is true to form, he will have at least two bodyguards and a young zealot with him. Not if, but when the fanatic in his ecstasy moves forward, even five feet in front of the rest of the group, the action button will be pressed. Nick in the van, Tom on the street and all the CIA agents will receive the alert."

Phil turned toward the easel and took out his marker. He tore off the diagram and used some tape to tack it to the wall. "Here's the order of events from that point." On a fresh sheet he wrote the numbers one and two, spaced evenly down the page. "Though these numbers are far apart, they will happen simultaneously. The most important for our team will be number one.

"Nick will pull across the street between the fanatic bent on reaching paradise and the four of you." He motioned to Tom, Jack, Lindsey and Brad. "The van door will already be open, so you will all get in quickly, but orderly, and Gavin will close the door. Nick will back in a wide arc away from the site until he is at least a hundred yards away. He will execute a Y-turn, then high tail it out of there." Phil wrote out the sequence of the departure scheme by the number one, then turning to the diagram on the wall, he made a big Y where Nick would make the turn.

"Number two. While you are all staying busy, sniper number one will send a round squarely between the shoulders of the zealot. The force of the shot will make him fall forward on his face. Whether the explosive belt is activated by a pressure release button or is detonated by remote control, the power of the blast should go largely toward the street.

"That same sniper will take out the two bodyguards. The CIA spotter on the street will shoot tranquilizer darts into Ian and Rashid who will collapse immediately. If for some reason the tranquilizers miss or are not effective at once, sniper number two will wing Ian and Rashid to incapacitate them. Two CIA vans will appear from the alley. The dead bodies will be loaded into one van while Ian and Rashid will be restrained and loaded into the other van. Harry and I will, in the meantime, be hurrying down the block to our car, getting in, and driving away. We'll rendezvous with all of you here."

"From the moment the alert button is pressed, everything I've just explained will take place in under thirty seconds." Phil waited a moment for it to sink in. "Any questions?"

»Chapter Twenty-Six«

As scheduled, Brad called Rashid one hour before the scheduled meeting time. He explained that the original site had been compromised and suggested the alternate location. Strangely, Rashid agreed immediately with no objection. As the team listened to the speaker-phone conversation, Gavin was thinking that they had acquiesced too easily. Something wasn't right.

When the call ended Phil got to his feet and rubbed the back of his neck. "That was easy, in fact too easy."

They were all nodding and Jack added, "It doesn't make sense. Ian is not stupid. He has to have guessed we know who he is and how he operates. What can his motive be for being incredibly agreeable?"

Harry cut in, "Maybe he wants to be caught."

Phil shook his head. He was stroking his chin as if pondering. "Nah, I can't believe after all these years of eluding the authorities, he's all of a sudden developed a conscience, wants to turn himself in, and repent for the death and terror he's caused." Phil raised both arms in a hallelujah gesture. "Either he actually thinks Lindsey and Brad are going to turn over the goods or he just wants to kill them for making a fool of him."

Lindsey's head jerked up. "That was harsh. I'm not crazy about that second alternative. Next time give me the sugar-coated version."

"That *was* the sugar-coated version. I didn't go into the details."

Phil was visibly agitated. "I'm going to pass the recording of the conversation on to Langley and Foggy Bottom to see what the analysts at CIA and State think." Turning back to look directly at Lindsey, he said, "One thing is certain. We won't let him or any of his faction get within striking distance of our team. This operation is simply a trap at this point. We're gonna catch the son-of-a-bitch!" And he slammed his hand flat on the table startling all of them.

Phil and Harry went into the hall to confer with the higher powers on the phone. "Okay, I got it. They'll be out of the van for less than two minutes before the action starts. Whether he has a sacrificial lamb along or not." Paul paused listening. "Yes, yes, will do. Both the State agents and the Agency guys will be wired." He nodded in silent agreement. "Yes, you'll hear everything goin' down."

Gavin was wandering around the living room-kitchen area and could hear the one-sided conversation. It seemed to him the scheme was getting a little dicey, and definitely more dangerous than the original scenario. They were dealing with a real pro.

*

Phil reentered the kitchen. "Alright, listening up." The mood was tense, and a worried look was on every single one of their faces. "Hey, it's not that bad," Phil quipped. "We're just going to take a few more precautions. Not many changes. The Agency wants our team to remain in the armored vehicle until Ian arrives and is out of his car. Then the four of you will get out of the van and begin to move to the middle of the street. When you're face to face but still a half block away from them, Nick will drive the van in front of you to block any possible attempt on your lives. The rest of the mission will unfold as practiced. You'll jump in the van and follow the previous instructions."

"Won't Ian know it's a trap?" Lindsey asked.

Chuckling, Phil shrugged. "If he shows up at all, we'll be thrilled. But for the rest of it, I don't give a damn what he thinks or knows."

Phil put his hands on his hips, smiling slightly. "I've got a good feeling about this. You've all rehearsed and now it's showtime. Let's roll."

Lindsey and the others put on their vests and finished dressing. Her full-length chador restricted her leg movements. That bothered her. What if she had to run to get away? That wasn't in the plan, but who knew? Since her feet didn't show in the long skirt, she opted for her running shoes. If all else failed, she'd pull up her skirts and run like hell. God, she hoped it wouldn't come to that.

Jack came over and gathered Lindsey into a big bear hug. "I'll be right beside you, honey, and Tom's one of the best agents around. It'll only be a couple minutes of exposure and if Ian or his men make a single threatening move, they'll be dead before they hit the pavement." He clutched her even tighter. "I love you, Lindsey."

✳

In the van she sat stiffly next to Gavin. Every muscle in her body was tight with the fear and anxiety of the coming mission. She tapped one finger pensively against her lip. She'd read countless lesson plans involving just this type of action and she'd been through a pre-deployment class at Triple Shield but reading about it and executing a few exercises hadn't prepared her for this. She was in way over her head. She fidgeted in the seat. Gavin put his arm around her shoulders and gave a quick squeeze.

Loosening his hold on her and shifting his weight in the seat, he looked at her and whispered, "Lindsey, you're the smartest damn woman I've ever met." He grinned and ran his hand against her cheek. "So just follow the plan. Tom is a trained counterterrorist agent. Brad and Jack have experienced this sort of mission, too. They've been through similar training for their Special Ops units and even though it's been awhile, they're both pretty bad-ass guys. Plus, you all are in excellent shape. You can do it."

He drew her in and gave her a soft, but sensual kiss. It gave Lindsey butterflies in her belly. He pulled back looking into her eyes. "Just come back to me." And he gave her another kiss.

Lindsey's emotions were cartwheeling. She would simply need to hold on to the thought that Gavin loved her, and he thought she was an amazing capable woman. Gavin's words gave her confidence. She didn't want to let anyone down, most of all herself. As Gavin said, she could do this.

Nick rolled to a stop in the prearranged spot. Everyone sat silently. The agents were listening for the go signal to come through their ear buds. From their location in the van they couldn't see the parking place for Ian's vehicle. They were relying on Tom and Harry to be their eyes.

Nick and Tom suddenly sat up straighter. It was obvious they were receiving a message. Tom turned to the others. "A black Mercedes SUV has stopped at the other end of the street. Not quite on the X, but close enough for government work." He smiled. Tom, ever the clown, couldn't resist a joke. Lindsey sat hugging her elbows, trying to keep her shaking under control.

"Four, no five people are getting out of the SUV, all but one in the expected Arab robes."

Gavin shifted closer to the door, so he could pull it open quickly when signaled. Tom leaned forward snagging his shirt on the armrest. Lindsey noticed for the first time, he had a weapon in the back of his waistband with his shirt hanging untucked, ostensibly to conceal the bulge. She started breathing rapidly. Tom reached back and put his hand on Lindsey's arm, "It'll be okay. We've got this."

Tom signaled Gavin and the door flew open. Tom said, "Easy, easy now," and was the first one on the street. Brad followed with the cylinder under his arm, then Jack and finally Lindsey. She put one then two feet on the pavement and slipped out. Her legs were shaky, but she was able to follow without stumbling. She could see the small group of five down the street and it was just as the setup they had discussed.

There was one tall, light-skinned man in the middle, flanked by two beefy guys. A squat swarthy guy in khakis and a plain untucked white shirt was to the right and about one pace behind the dominate central figure. Then there was a wisp of a boy walking slightly ahead. The man in the middle was clearly in charge. He exuded authority by his erect stance and confident walk. Was it Ian? It had to be. The circumstances were identical to his other operations.

Brad leaned over and whispered under his breath, "It looks like Rashid behind the tall figure in the middle."

Then the man we presumed was Ian raised his hands over his head and shouted, "Miss Kelly, is that you?" With that the boy began to run forward.

Then everything happened at once.

The van rushed in front of them. Gavin was beckoning from the door. As if they were in slow motion, they all moved forward. Lindsey's feet felt like lead weights.

First, Brad got in and swung into the back seat. Jack and Tom each had one of Lindsey's shoulders propelling her toward the van. They picked her up and practically threw her into Gavin's outstretched arms.

Then they heard the explosion that rocked the van and seemed to make the whole street tremble. It was like an earthquake. Jack stumbled into the middle seat banging his shin on the door opening and, finally, Tom hopped in and closed the door, since Gavin had his hands literally full of Lindsey.

The tires squealed, and Lindsey felt the van lurch to one side then begin backing. There was the thudding sound of something drumming against the wheel well. Lindsey thought it sounded like a flat tire. They'd been hit by the bomb.

Her mind went into freefall. Are we trapped? My God, will we be blown up with another bomb blast?

Then, though the thumping was a steady beat, the van was speeding in reverse. Nick executed a perfect Y turn, even with, what they later found out, were two flat tires. Lindsey's fleeting thought before she passed out against Gavin's shoulder was, damn this guy can drive.

The six of them made it to the safe house after stopping to change the two flats with two of the four replacement tires stored behind and under the rear seats. The agents had anticipated the blast might take out a few tires, so, like Eagle Scouts, they were prepared. The tires were always the most vulnerable part of an armored car. Nick said he was happy the bullet-proof glass had held since the explosion was larger than they had predicted.

Lindsey had recovered from what must have been a sudden crash from an adrenaline high. She'd only been out for a moment but still felt like a fool for acting like a delicate girl. It wasn't like her. In fact, she couldn't remember ever fainting. Of course, she had never been in a terrorist attack before either. No one said a thing about it, so she let it go.

She and Gavin sat on the old sofa in a daze, just watching and taking in the scene in the small house. Brad sat at the table staring at his hands. Nick was the opposite. She'd never seen him so animated. He was clearly proud he'd completed his part of the mission in good form. He vibrated with excitement. She did notice, though, that Tom and Nick kept going to the window to look out.

Jack went over to Nick by the window and Tom joined them. "Have you heard anything from them?"

"Not yet." Nick said. "But Phil and Harry are good agents. They had to finish up at the site before they could start back. They'll get in touch soon."

Tom cuffed Jack on the shoulder. "I'm sure we'll hear something shortly."

They waited. They heard nothing. Everyone was edgy and totally exhausted. Of course, they were still wound up from the ordeal but now the waiting was taking a toll.

At one in the morning, Tom's cell phone rang. It was Phil. Tom put it on speaker. "I'm at the hospital." Phil's voice sounded oddly tinny over the speaker. "Sorry I haven't called sooner. I'll explain later. Is everyone there okay?

"Yeah, we're all fine. Only one skinned shin, but what about you and Harry? You're at the hospital?"

Phil sounded weary. "The plan worked well on the whole, but there were a few snafus. The blast was way bigger than we expected. Body parts and shrapnel flew everywhere. We were both hit with some of the shrapnel from the martyr's explosive belt. I got a few minor wounds on my right leg and butt, the latter location being a real pain in the ass." Lindsey was glad to hear Phil was able to joke at the situation.

Phil continued. "Harry took some to the chest and shoulder. It's been touch and go, but the good news is, he's out of surgery now. The doc says he'll be fine. The not so good news is he will need extensive rehab to get back the use of his left arm." He paused. "Happily, we're both alive. Definitely better than the alternative." He stopped again to take a huge breath. "Harry's in good hands here at the hospital so I'm headed your way."

"Are you sure you can drive? I could pick you up. Which hospital?"

"Nah, Tom, I'm fine. Be there in thirty minutes."

The mood was still tense but seemed to be easing just knowing Phil and Harry were alive. Brad was face down across the table, breathing rhythmically and presumably asleep. Lindsey was dozing against Gavin's shoulder, and Jack, Nick and Tom continued to stand close to the window watching for Phil.

»Chapter Twenty-Seven«

It was eleven the morning after the mission. Six exhausted people were gathered around the table in the conference room at the hotel—everyone from the team except Harry and Brad. Phil was standing at the head of the table. "Alright, listen up." He smiled. Gingerly patting his bum he quipped, "I think I'll remain standing." They all chuckled.

Phil, his commanding presence back in place, started the review. "I know the suspense has been killing you since last night, but due to the extreme fatigue of all parties involved, the debrief was delayed until now."

He threw his hands in the air and with a cocky grin on his face launched into it. "Congratulations! Our friends with CIA have *actually* thanked us for our help. Ian Davis and Rashid Abdul Azim have been detained on charges of terrorism. And the CIA's sanitation crew has removed all evidence of the four fatalities at the scene—the two bodyguards, the driver of their car and, of course, all the pieces of the brainwashed kid."

Phil scanned the group. "You should all be proud of the success of this operation. Your performance was stellar, and the objective was achieved. With the head of the terrorist cell under wraps, it will be some time before that particular cell can reorganize.

"Unfortunately, there are numerous religious

fanatics and simply evil people out there who will continue to spread terror across the world. Some for a cause, but most for money. They dupe the true believers into martyring themselves, and the young zealots die. Their self-appointed leaders rake in the money." Sadness seeped into his expression. "The cynic in me says that this will never change."

Breaking in Tom asked, "How's Harry this morning?"

"Good spirits. He's anxious to get back to work, though I expect it will be a few months before he sees action."

"And Brad?" Jack ventured.

"He's already on his way back to the U.S. on an Army transport plane. Joe Johnson has been rounded up, too. They'll face a lot of questions. We'll have to wait and see how the Justice Department handles their case."

Then hitting his hand on his forehead, Phil added, "I almost forgot to tell you about the money. Ian Davis actually wired the first installment of one million dollars to Brad's old account in the Caymans. The CIA snagged it immediately and will use the money to cover the expense of the operation. That means all of you just received an all-expenses paid, action adventure vacation from the government." He snorted. "If you want to call it a vacation."

The whole room burst into laughter.

Phil spread both of his hands apart palms up and mimed a stern look. "For you civilians, my best advice is to get the hell out of here. Some nut could be left who wants to retaliate against the folks who eliminated their brethren of the cause. Tom, Nick and I will stay to work with CIA on the after-action report."

Glancing at each in turn, flipping one hand up and to the side, Phil raised his eyebrows inquiringly. "Any questions?" After a couple of beats he made a shooing motion with both hands, smiled, and finished with, "Okay, people, you're outta here."

»Epilogue«

Four Months Later

Lindsey stood on the patio admiring the view. She wore a blue, silky dress with a peacock feather design around a hem that barely skimmed her knees and she carried a lighter blue pashmina to throw over her shoulders in the event the evening cooled. She looked around and noticed George Trenton pointing here and there with the ever-present Hamilton, his valet and all-round assistant, close by his side.

She thought George radiated happiness and excitement. He seemed so much younger than the sixty-seven she knew him to be. He was talking to Hamilton and directing some of the extra staff he'd hired to help with the event.

"Move these four big mums to the edge of the patio, and Hamilton, please take care of the finishing touches in the tent. The caterer probably has everything under control, but you know how I like everything to look."

Lindsey felt such joy. It was a perfect fall day in the Virginia Hunt Country. The leaves on the Blue Ridge that could be seen to the west were a patchwork quilt of color. The sun was beginning to drop toward the hill tops, but still warmed the air to a pleasant seventy-two. "I must be living right," she said to no one in particular.

George walked up behind her and ran his hand through the crook of her arm. "Yes, Lindsey, it's a glorious day."

Lindsey squeezed George's arm. "I thank the heavens for every day I wake up, throw back the covers and swing my feet to the floor, but this is an especially nice one."

George looked down at his protégé and smiled broadly. "It's not every day you have an engagement party with such a charming host." He winked at her then grabbed her hands and swung her around in a swirl. He stopped and put on a mock serious look. "Hey, I'm not sure I should be congratulating you for stealing one of my best employees. Gavin said he'd work until the end of the season, but then he'll be marrying the love of his life. His exact words, by the way."

Lindsey giggled like a schoolgirl. She was floating on air and feeling as giddy as a teenager. She'd been in this starry-eyed state for months. Ever since they'd returned from Dubai, she and Gavin had experienced a whirlwind romance. A veil of worry had been lifted and all was right with the world, or at least that was how Lindsey saw it. Gavin was the reason she was on cloud nine.

Now all their friends, family, and associates, as well as, most of the employees from Laurel Glen were scheduled to arrive in thirty minutes at George Trenton's palatial estate for a party—no a gala celebration—he was throwing in their honor. George had even invited the State Department agents from what they now referred to as the Emirates Caper. She giggled again.

Lindsey left George to the final details and wandered down by the swimming pool. The light shimmered off the surface of the dark bottomed pool, and the vista to the west was breathtaking. A Sweet Autumn Clematis draped its long tendrils across and down the pergola by the pool house. She simply stood and inhaled the scent, a feeling of complete contentment sweeping over her.

Enjoying the quiet moment, she suddenly knew she wasn't alone. She felt the warmth of his breath on the back of her neck and turned to find Gavin gazing down at her. "Hi, there, beautiful." He gathered her in, and they stood closely molded together. Gavin whispered through her hair, "Every time I'm near you I feel this heat, this need." He pulled back slightly and ran the back of his hand down her cheek. "I never get tired of simply looking at you."

Lindsey grasped his hand and looked into his deep brown eyes. "Whenever I look at you, I get an adrenaline rush. My heart beats faster and I'm a little light-headed." She tipped her head to one side and raised her eyebrows. "We've had some interesting experiences lately. But considering the larger vision, you know, I think we will be able to easily face most of life's challenges, because we will be tackling them together." She tugged him back toward the main house. "But now the festivities are about to begin. Let's go! We have a lifetime to love."

From the Author

Thank you for reading Adrenaline. I hope you enjoyed my first novel in the Laurel Glen Series. I've had the most fun writing about my alter-ego and hope you will take the time to leave an honest review with Amazon. This helps other readers decide if this book will meet their expectations.

Please visit my website blscottauthor.com for a preview of my next novel in the series, Foreign Threat. Look for the third book in the Laurel Glen Series, Tortuga Sunrise, in the Spring of 2021.

I've heard you should write what you know, so I've used my knowledge from years of being involved with a security training facility and raceway business located near Washington, DC. We conducted counter-terrorist schools Monday through Friday and hosted sportscar and motorcycle racing on the weekends. Working with both racers and government clients like the CIA, SEALs, and FBI was exciting, and I hope to express this excitement in the series based at a similar facility, fictionally christened Laurel Glen.

I live on a farm in Virginia with my very aged yellow lab, Abbey.

Until next time,

B. L.

Foreign Threat
A woman determined that no man will
orchestrate her life. A man haunted by
his past and not ready for love.
A *powerful international tale of passion, danger, and
second chances.*

Carolyn Stone knows fear, but she's vowed never to be powerless again. She must succeed in the counter-terrorist school to be eligible for her State Department deployment to a foreign posting. Everything is riding on this, and her counter-terrorist school instructor, Ben Jackson, is standing in her way. Carolyn is agitated by his high-handed, drill sergeant disposition but is also drawn to his intense, dark, good looks.

Ben feels the spark between them, but he's haunted by an incident in Afghanistan that makes any relationship problematic. He doesn't deserve a smart, sexy woman, especially one whose expressive eyes intrigue him—one moment sparkling with interest, the next filled with sorrow and trepidation.

Carolyn and Ben meet again in Jordan where the passion that has been smoldering leaps into flame. Carolyn unwittingly becomes entangled in a terrorist plot that endangers America's national security and could destroy the tenuous calm in the Middle East. Ben is running out of time to protect the woman he's falling for. After she's kidnapped and taken to the depths of the Jordanian desert, can Ben help pull off a dangerous and daring rescue to save Carolyn?

Made in the USA
Middletown, DE
16 March 2023